Break My Heart

by

Marianne Willis

Break My Heart

Cover Art by *Lisa Dawn MacDonald*

The Wild Rose Press, Inc.
PO Box 708
Adams Basin, NY 14410-0708
Visit us at www.thewildrosepress.com

Publishing History
First Edition, 2024
Trade Paperback ISBN 978-1-5092-5781-2
Digital ISBN 978-1-5092-5782-9

Published in the United States of America

Dedication

To my husband, Aaron. Thank you for always supporting me. Without you, this book wouldn't be possible.
Love you, always and forever.

Prologue

Max
Ten years ago

My feet smacked the floor, each step firing my bad foot. Evading The Top Five proved futile. Sooner or later, I'd run into them in class, the cafeteria, the dreaded bathroom, of all places where they delighted in soaking bunches of toilet paper into mushy balls and pegging my clothes. They located me no matter where I hid.

"Hey, Limp!" Alexander Braxton's annoying voice echoed from the far end of the hallway. "I'm talking to you."

And I'm avoiding you. Heat infused my face, and I wrenched my jacket collar over my nape. I suffered from Talipes Equinovarus, a foot abnormality where the ankle bends inward, but the knowledge never stopped them from calling me Limp—a quip given since freshman regarding my deformed foot. Insisting they call me Max or even Maxwell resulted in mock laughter.

Several heads shot up from their phones at the cruel remark, their cheesy grins identical to zoo monkeys. My school mimicked a center for wild animals rather than an institute of public education.

I slowed my pace past the announcement wall

decorated in uninteresting cheer posters and event bulletins, abandoning any hope of sanctuary.

Laughter confirmed the gang loomed not far behind. Here I'd hoped they'd ignore me and move on. I patted my locker handle and slanted closer. No unpleasant whiff. No foul gunk ready to prank me. Thank God.

One of them cleared their throat; the sound rose hairs on my nape. I winced, anticipating a thump to my skull from either of these jerks. Although lanky and impaired, I towered over most guys in school, but a loner without friends ticked all the right boxes as a Stonebrook High target. The odds of three versus one made my height worthless, and untrained in self-defense equaled no chance of fending them off.

One large palm whammed the locker beside mine. My larynx tightened. From my peripheral, Alex's two pals, Brent Robinson and Trevor Dallas, aligned themselves on either side of me.

I confronted Alex in all his six-foot-three-inch glory. We leveled in height, but whereas I passed for lanky and weak, Alex's unnatural muscle filled out his Stonebrook Scorpions team sweatshirt. People in town claimed he worked hard on-field to achieve his athletic figure. I restrained my scoff. Our cherished quarterback here used enhancers; I'd seen him pass the pills around to his buddies in the locker room.

Trevor and Brent shared a similar build but averaged half a foot shorter and mimicked their star player's macho persona.

Whispers rippled behind Alex. Olivia King and Roxanne Hastings.

Caged in by my bullies who fancied calling

themselves TTF aka The Top Five. Mental eye roll. Who titled their clique? How pathetic. For four years I had tolerated their vicious games, and as opposed to my freshman year when I quaked at their approach, I'd grown weary of their ritualistic torments. What I'd give for them to ignore the fact I existed, for one day of peace.

"*Limp*," Alex drawled and gave a slow shake of his head. His hand squeaked off the steel door. "How many times do I have to tell you not to ignore us?"

"I'm getting my books for next period." A while back, I opted for sarcasm as a defense mechanism, but my strategy never worked in my favor. Although my sporadic courage slipped out on occasion, the best way to address these twits involved short, sweet, and clueless responses.

" 'I'm-getting-my-books-for-next-period.' " Brent repeated my words in a whinier tone and released a lighthearted snort. "Shut up. You snubbed us on purpose."

Olivia squeezed her cheerleader's body—the kind to inspire every teen boy's fantasy—between Alex and Brent. "You guys done with dweeb here?" She puffed into her hands and scrubbed them together for warmth. "I plan to touch on my makeup sometime today."

The chill affected Little Miss Ice Queen? And makeup touch-ups, for real? Any thicker layers and she'd put a trifle cake to shame.

Another girl followed behind Olivia. "Yeah, come on, guys. I have to meet with the prom committee in ten minutes."

Roxanne. Waist-length beige hair, lush mouth twisted in distaste, and a stare capable of shooting a hole straight through your chest. The two hottest cheerleaders in school, but whereas Olivia embodied a glossy facade, Roxanne held a natural appeal, your typical "girl next door." No wonder Olivia piled on the cosmetics, no match for Roxanne's classic and graceful beauty.

Roxanne posed stiff-lipped, but a hesitant glint flickered in her eyes.

My windpipe seized. She surveyed me. No, as in *seeing me*. Her secretive gaze then skittered to the guys.

Alex's massive jaw clenched. "Not until Limp here shows us respect."

Respect? I reined in my scoff. Why respect an unworthy bunch? They ran our school, and students worshiped the ground they walked on. Their circle comprised queen bees and football players. Big whoop. They mistreated students, and their popular status carried sufficient sway to persuade anyone to dismiss their awful antics. Star-struck teachers vindicated them, an automatic privilege for our town's top players. Since I ranged at the bottom of their social chain, school staff disregarded TTF's aggressive nature, and snitching on them resulted in greater pranks and taunts.

"Come on, as if I'd ignore you guys." A lie dumb enough for these fools to believe, and yet today they avoided rising to the bait.

Alex cocked a brow. He slammed my locker shut, seized my collar, and shoved me against cold, hard metal. "Once we're done with you, you won't dare to again."

A sadistic swirl churned in Trevor's beady glare. "What do you have in mind?"

The dude thrived on people in distress. Joshua

4

McAllister broke his leg in gym class once, and Trevor ran to his side, not to assist, but to grin and cheer at Joshua's bone protruding out of his skin. The darkest parts of Trevor's soul reflected in his style from his turquoise-streaked spiky hair, half a brow adorned in a row of studs, and a labret ring he often played with using his teeth. I'd give him half a decade to turn into a full-blown serial killer.

Alex flexed and unflexed his hand. An ominous pop of joints rang in my ears, and I braved the inevitable blow. "Don't take too long. You'll develop an aneurysm." I bit inside my cheek. Sporadic sarcasm rearing its nasty head again.

Roxanne and Olivia tittered.

A comical response without me as a recipient? A first. The effect on the girls left me slow to recover. Alex's frown deepened, and he rammed my body farther into the locker. The lever handle dug into my shoulder blade, and for obvious reasons, I reconsidered reveling in the small victory. Uncomfortable, I hiked my chin, refusing to let my distress show.

"Watch yourself, Limp," Alex growled in warning. "You guys have an idea?" He flicked his bangs from his vision. "Or do I knock him out?"

Typical brainless Alex, all brawn and incapable of formulating a plan to save his life. He acted no better in class. Even amid his threats, he relied on his friends for ideas. Yeah, not the sharpest tool in the shed.

Voices muttered in the background. Another day, another audience.

Brent puffed out his chest. Oh, he meant business.

Roxanne scowled...not in a sinister way. Nervous? Strange.

Trevor bounced on his toes and rubbed his palms together. "I got one!"

Trust a psychopath to form an answer.

Roxanne surged forward, the movement awkward. She snatched Alex's elevated arm. "Guys...let's go already."

Her abrupt manner elicited a snort from Trevor and Brent. Heck, I gave an inward scoff too.

Alex shot Roxanne a savage glower. "What gives, Roxy?" His nostrils flared, bottom lip curling.

"Yeah! Are you on his side?" Trevor stomped into her personal space. A blatant leer replaced his initial sneer.

Good grief. Psycho here crushed on Cheerleader. A horror movie waiting to happen. And on my side? He insinuated Roxanne Hastings attempted to rescue me. Fat chance.

She dropped Alex's arm, her laughter diluted. "No, of course not. We're bored, okay? Let's please go?"

See, as predicted. No reason to defend me since she considered me worthless entertainment.

Alex tilted forward, and a black lock drooped in front of one eye. "Bored?" He mocked in his usual tone reserved for me.

Trevor nudged his nose close to Roxanne's ear and snaked his slimy hand around her thin waist. "I have an idea to fix your boredom."

Roxanne blanched.

My torso tensed. *Back off!* I shut my trap, terminating my shout. Why defend her when she'd not once aided me?

Roxanne yanked Trevor's arm off her middle. "I've told you over and over." Dusting his touch off her white sweater, she glared at the psycho. "Lay a hand on me again, and I'll knee you where no girl has gone."

I smothered a snicker.

"Enough, Trevor." Alex confronted the pair and warned in his usual authoritative tone.

The lunatic brazened Alex for a good minute, stretching his arms out wide and retreating.

Alex ruled the small gang. No one challenged his power. On the contrary, they followed his every command. I'd rather live as a loner if friendship entailed this level of slavishness.

A smug Alex draped one arm over my shoulder, greeting a passing teacher, and shifted his attention back to Roxanne. "Okay, Roxy. *Little Miss I'm Bored.* You choose his penalty."

What the heck, Alex!

Golden orbs widened, glancing left and right, and she tucked a loose blonde strand behind her ear.

What on earth churned behind those pretty eyes? Dunking my head in the toilet? Slashing my car tires? Whacking my lunch tray out of my hands? All had happened in the past. Either way, I'd detest whatever she doled out. *Tell him to get bent, Roxanne. Tell him to leave me alone.*

Roxanne licked her full lips; her intensity immobilized me in place.

"Kiss their feet." The obedient lackey peered toward her ringleader. "That'll teach him, yeah?" Her soft voice held a slight tremor.

The grotesque chastise shriveled my insides. *Teach me?* The one lesson learned here, Roxanne and her friends were complete and utter monsters.

Alex petted Roxanne's hair. "Genius." He turned to

me and bared his teeth. "You heard her. On the floor."

"Not mine." Palms raised, Olivia jumped back, face twisted in distaste. "Keep those loser lips away from my new flats."

"Yeah, I'm out too." Roxanne crossed her arms and joined Olivia's side. She shied from my gaze, keeping her head lowered.

"What?" Brent gaped at Roxanne. "You can't back out. You're the brains behind this idea."

"So?" Roxanne huffed, scratching at her temple with one manicured nail.

Trevor flashed his ivories. "Whatever. Get a move on, dweeb. We don't have all day."

I barged into their muscled arms, attempting escape. All three guys grabbed me. Trevor kicked the back of my knee, forcing me to kneel on the ground. Students filled the hallway. Most chortled and passed us on their way to their lockers while others dallied to whisper and observe the ruckus. I knelt there, panting. Shoe-smooch or refuse?

Alex squeezed the back of my neck, the pressure burning my skin. "We'll make this worse if you keep delaying!" His loud shout accompanied by spittle smacked my face.

Alex bragged he'd one day become a famous fighter by roaming the halls and showing off how he worked those meaty fists. I'd copped a few pummels here and there, but I'd also seen him in serious clashes and the not-so-pretty result of his opponents' busted noses and burst eye vessels.

Decline, and they'd find another way to cause me anguish, no doubt beat on me and leave evident bruises. How many lies involving my mishaps in gym class until Mom caught on?

Turf and dew assaulted my nostrils. On autopilot, I bent my stiff spine and kissed each grass-speckled shoe. My stomach somersaulted in threat of dry heaving. Never in my life had I succumbed to such humiliation. Onto the last boot. Trevor.

Blunt pressure struck my mouth, teeth dug deep into flesh, and a metallic tang confirmed blood.

Oohs and uproarious gales ensued following Trevor's kick to my mouth.

The spotted vinyl floor blurred as white noise engulfed all sounds. I flicked the lock of hair curtaining my view and made eye contact with Roxanne who made no move and kneaded her wrists.

A lump lodged in my throat. I expected no help anyway, but her attitude differed today, her usual mockery and mean-girl stance absent. Why peer at me in such a way, giving me false hope? Her cruelty astounded me.

The guys cackled and paraded away, high fiving on a job well done. Roxanne glanced back. Another first. How unusual for her to acknowledge me once done with their bullying. *I'm sorry.* Or a part of me hoped the unclear response in her eyes relayed such a message.

Chapter 1

Roxanne
Present day

Sweat coated my palms, and my stomach churned due to a nonexistent breakfast, but a lump in my throat made food impossible to swallow. Goodness, I hadn't endured this degree of nausea in years, not since pregnancy.

Horns honked in the busy street filled with the same old traffic. Typical hustle and bustle in the Windy City. However, today differed, and I wasn't simply referring to the public holiday. Aside from the increasing breeze and cigarette smoke from a man ahead—I scrunched my nose—a premonition nudged my insides. Doom lingered in the air.

Mr. Parker's assistant called earlier in the week and arranged a meeting between me and the new CEO. I sidestepped a cyclist, leather bag strap clutched in my fist. Perhaps the recent storm caused my somber mood, but an unshakable vibe warned I headed straight for disaster.

Mr. Parker had dismissed over a dozen staff members since taking over Tower Hotel. Work turned into a circus. Staff ran around in circles, reduced to sobs, while others performed their routine tasks pale and biting their nails. We all tiptoed on eggshells.

I'd racked my brain for reasons why Mr. Parker requested to see me—a random employee, an event assistant, no less. What happened to Mr. Montgomery or a manager from HR requesting an interview and discussing my employment? Then again, they most likely had the public holiday off, and only the crazy CEO dared to work and hold interviews on Memorial Day.

Not due for my one-on-one for another forty-five minutes, I stalled, hoping to pace away these jitters. No such luck.

Inside the hotel, men in pleated jackets and women in cinched, buttoned blazers passed me. New board members? Managers? I neatened my white blouse and navy pencil skirt with unsteady hands, hopeful of mimicking a similar etiquette. I smothered a snort. Yeah right. No discount store outfit compared with designer labels.

Clicking heels echoed over marble floors. Margaret Small, Tower Hotel's front-desk manager, rushed toward me. Tears streaked her wrinkled, plump face, and she blew her nose into an embroidered handkerchief. "Roxanne dear. I've terrible news."

My heart sank, and I covered my gasp. "Not you too."

Margaret let out a loud sob and blew into her handkerchief. Several passersby turned to peek at the commotion.

"Oh, Marg." I opened my arms, and she squeezed in for a hug. "I'm sorry."

Margaret sniffled above my shoulder. "I'd never forgive myself if I left without saying goodbye first." She leaned in close to my ear. "A little bluebird told me you're meeting Mr. Big Man himself."

Margaret and her bluebirds. She acquired an entire flock of them and danced on her toes whenever she gossiped. Such a trait deterred most people, but her adorable quirk melted my heart. Great-Ma, God rest her soul, used to chit-chat the same way about everyone from the postman to the pharmaceutical rep in Beaufort. And similar to my late great-grandmother, Margaret informed me first of the latest newsworthy stories, the newest employees, and the details of the secret affair between Lydia, the housekeeper, and Fred, the bellhop. Last week she'd kept herself on high alert for a sixty-something-year-old man, hoping to catch a peek at the infamous Mr. Parker and spill the tea. But she never acted out of spite. "Your bluebird's right. And I'm glad you waited to say goodbye. I'll miss you, but I have a sense they'll boot me out too."

Margaret pursed her red-painted lips, her clever makeup techniques reversing her age by a few years. "No negativity." She tapped my nose. "Lacey's kept her role. I'm sure you'll do fine."

My false bravado act failed to offer me comfort. Mr. Parker's legal team ran the show in his absence, and I hadn't performed my usual tasks since these guys appeared. One by one, employees I'd clicked with exited through the glass rotatable doors. Each lay-off splintered my heart a little further while my blood pressure skyrocketed.

"They have big plans, an entire refurbishment to suit the Parker Luxury Hotel brand." Margaret waved her hands around the space we occupied, similar to a real estate agent showing a potential buyer a brand-new home. "They intend to add shops, restaurants, a gymnasium, and extend the main event area into a grand ballroom."

A project this extreme required months, and no events amid rebuild meant no event assistant. Goodness, my queasiness returned with a vengeance.

Margaret rubbed my shoulder. "Break a leg, honey."

"Thank you." I embraced her for one last hug and blinked back a threat of tears as Margaret's short, plump figure strolled away.

Admin staff handed over a private elevator swipe card for me to head to my scheduled meeting. On the top floor, I stepped out to a mild chemical odor of fresh paint. On my left, boxes stamped with the Parker Group logo lined the wall. Buckets of paint and rollers sat atop a drop sheet in one corner, and leftover furniture once used to decorate the suite sat reposed in the parallel corner.

"Miss Hastings?" A woman rose from her neat desk, the clean space she occupied worlds apart from the opposite side of the room. "I'm Clarissa Benford, Mr. Parker's assistant."

In her last stages of pregnancy and sauntering in stilettos...impressive. I gave her my best smile. "I'm scheduled to meet Mr. Parker."

"Excuse the mess." She waved a nonchalant hand over said mess. "The painter has yet to collect his tools, and we're donating the furniture sometime this week."

"Not a problem. I'll sit and wait." I had ten minutes until my meeting.

Clarissa beamed toward the large double doors behind her. "Not necessary. He's ready for you. Please, follow me."

Heed Marg's advice. No negativity! The fact I arrived ahead of time proved my punctuality. Despite the enthusiastic PA, I fidgeted with my bag strap as if handed the death penalty while following her through the same penthouse the team and I decorated many times for private parties, but the largest room on the top floor had undergone drastic changes into a makeshift office. Works of art lined the walls, full of vivid color, beauty, and recognizable settings. Originals? They'd cost a fortune. Mr. Parker acquired the absolute best for his private workroom.

Clarissa knocked twice and poked her head inside. "Miss Hastings has arrived."

Zero response. But the personal assistant held the door open and nodded for me to enter.

I plodded inside, not at all ready to face the formidable man standing at his desk. Six-three tall, in a charcoal suit flaunting a body stacked with muscle and wide shoulders blocking the chairback he sank into.

Behind a pair of black-rimmed glasses, chocolate eyes bore into mine and stripped my soul bare, shooting a bolt from my feet to my scalp. His magnetism arrested me on the spot. *Breathe, Roxanne.*

Unlike his delightful personal assistant, his narrowed gaze proved a cold, hard, and ruthless businessman. "Mrs. Hastings?"

Certain I imitated a deer caught in high beams, I recovered and tucked a loose strand behind my ear. "*Miss*, actually." Not an old man in his sixties as Margaret presumed. Perhaps Parker Junior?

He gestured to a chair in front of his desk. "Take a seat."

I closed the space and eased into gray upholstery,

crossing my legs to keep them transfixed. My previous worry shifted from this interview to the man opposite me. A thick, corded throat strained beneath his white shirt collar, and clipped black-brown hair neatened to one side, the most stylish cut I'd seen on a man. A dark mustache and medium beard masked the entire bottom half of his face, and his woodsy amber cologne beckoned me to scoot closer. I had to be mistaken, but his gaze danced over my body as if familiar with my small curves, the possessive glare in his eyes sending a shiver down my spine.

His gaze shifted to the opened laptop on the table. No introduction, no small talk, but straight to the point. "I accessed your original resume and portfolio on the company system. You worked under Event Manager Lacey McCormac?"

His presence stirred an emotion in my chest. Unsure what, but he carried this familiar air with him. "Yes, Mr. Parker." For sure I'd seen him elsewhere. Working in the city, strangers were bound to cross paths or frequent the same coffee houses.

"Previous to working for the company, you held a PA role?" His thick finger ran across the laptop. "And I see here you also have a bachelor's in interior design."

No hint as to whether my resume intrigued him, or he found my qualifications unimpressive. A great deal lay at stake if I had to find a new job. Bills, fees, groceries, a son to support. I bit my bottom lip. Also, what about Dylan? The carers worked hard to get him settled there at the daycare center.

Mr. Parker lowered his chin, eyes assessing. "Miss Hastings?"

I straightened in my seat. "Sorry. Yes, I completed

a short course in interior decorating as well as earned my bachelor's four years ago, around the same time I started here."

A knock disturbed our meeting. His assistant ducked inside. "Excuse me, Hunter. My calendar shows tomorrow's your sister's birthday. Do you want me to send her flowers?"

He scratched the beauty spots at his temple, above his black-rimmed framed glasses. "Tabitha or Lisa?"

"Tabitha." She dabbed a capped pen over her pout.

"Yes, go ahead and arrange that. Thank you, Clarissa." He waved her away and sipped the glass by his side. Clarissa shut the door, and Mr. Parker revisited his computer screen. "Where were we?"

An ice-cold blow punched my core. No proper greeting, and no apology for the interruption? What a jerk!

"Ah yes, your academic exploits." His arrogant tone dragged out the syllables. "And yet you work here…an event assistant instead of pursuing a career in interior design. Why?"

I licked my lips, tempted to strangle him for dodging my job status. Rather than spit out my deepest fears, he questioned and teased my failed career goals. And those botched goals still carried a sharp sting. Once upon a time, I'd dreamed of making a name for myself as a top interior designer, but the dream suited a person free from parental obligation. "Life happened. I guess plans don't work out the way we intend."

His mouth curled into a slow, wicked grin. "I disagree, Miss Hastings. My plans always work out."

His personal-sounding response coiled my entire body with tension. I itched to pluck lint off my skirt but kept my hands furled in my lap. Hunter Parker proved too conceited for his own good.

He swiveled in his chair and interlaced his fingers. "And what's your verdict on Edward Daniels?"

What I uttered next affected my chances of remaining employed. Mr. Daniels vexed every Tower Hotel employee by keeping staff uninformed he'd sold his lifelong business due to massive debt. Yes, all those made redundant received a fair exit package. To be honest, a warning would have prevented unnecessary stress, but as if I'd diss my old boss to my potential new honcho. "What can I say about Mr. Daniels? What a wonderful CEO to work for."

Mr. Parker's thick arms crossed over his massive chest. "Loyalty. I figured you'd say so."

I shifted in my seat, hot and uncomfortable. What I'd give to bask in the outside breeze at this moment. "Excuse me?"

"I deliberated if I'd get blunt honesty or loyalty from you...I bet on the latter."

"Why?" A bit judgmental for someone he'd just met.

A muscle ticked in his cheek. "An impression I get from you. You seem the type to paint on a smile and go along, disregarding the conduct of others."

Oh, so Mr. Big Shot here assessed me in fifteen minutes. "I'm not lying," I defended in a stern tone.

His tightened mouth slackened. "But you're not a little disappointed in Mr. Daniels' conduct? Many employees I've interviewed have said otherwise."

Sweat broke out and spanned my nape. "A memo wouldn't have hurt."

His shoulders bounced in a half-hearted shrug.

"You're right, a memo would've saved a lot of employees stress and grief."

A loud chime erupted on his computer and gave him an opportune moment to ignore me. I bet he'd kick me out of here jobless. A single mother and unemployed, my worst nightmare. I flattened my hands on my knees. "Mr. Parker, may I?"

"Of course." He neither blinked nor flinched in my direction, his stare glued to the screen.

The action spoke volumes. I wasted his precious time. His blatant unconcern grated on my self-restraint. "Are you firing me?"

He strummed his fingers on the dark, wooden desk. Oh, yes, beyond a doubt he prolonged my torture.

"Your previous manager, Lacey McCormack, has transferred to Parker Luxury Hotel in the city's Northside. And I'm not seeking an event assistant since my current team handles such matters."

Yep, tonight I'd forage for jobs online with a full glass of Chianti. I straightened my spine in favor of the urge to hang my head. *Go on, Mr. Parker, throw me out, but I plan on keeping my dignity intact.*

He stroked his well-groomed beard. "However…"

I clenched my molars together. *Please reconsider. Please, please.* I waited to receive whatever meager role he threw.

"With my assistant due for maternity leave soon, I have weightier matters than finding a new PA. Since you're skilled and no stranger to the hotel layout, I'm offering you her job. I hope your degree in design comes in handy when we hire the remodeling company. Of course, the role includes an increased salary, plus an added annual bonus."

"Personal assistant?" The news tingled my ears. He allowed me a front-row seat in the hotel revamps, plus an increased salary. "Yes, I'll fill in for her." I controlled an urge to squeal. "I can't thank you enough, Mr. Parker."

"Call me Hunter. Since we're to work together, I'd prefer to use first names. You'll partner with Clarissa until her last shift. She'll hand you the necessary paperwork to fill out and brief you on my agenda. Wait in the foyer while I update her."

I held out my hand, and he examined my fingers longer than expected and settled in for a firm shake, sending a jolt through my palm. His hard-set jaw kicked my unease into high alert. "Thank you again." I made for the exit and turned to my new boss, who hadn't removed his gaze. "You won't regret taking me on."

His Cheshire-cat smile revealed straight, white teeth. "Oh, I'm sure I won't."

I proceeded out into the foyer, unable to shake the vibe those last words held deeper significance.

Chapter 2

Max

The pulse in my chest persisted. From the instant she entered the office, my mind flashed to our last encounter of her storming out of my life ten years ago. Her scent loitered in the room, the delicious vanilla fragrance different from the freesia and rose perfume she wore in high school. Strain coiled my muscles. I closed my laptop and buzzed for Clarissa.

Two seconds later, she ducked inside.

I waved her in. "Take a seat."

Natural light in the office brightened her copper strands. Mindful of her extra weight, she eased into the chair. "So, how'd I do?"

Determined to stay composed, I stamped an urge to cackle. "*I'm* convinced I have siblings. Well done."

Clarissa simpered, but I read the curiosity in her narrowed stare. In true corporate conduct, she'd minded her own business, but I employed her as my assistant, not my shrink...although she'd suggest one if she learned the real reason for my interest in Roxanne. "I'm sure you're eager for maternity leave."

She giggled and rubbed her round bump. "I'm eager to see my feet again." Slender fingers tucked a tawny strand behind her ear. "You told Miss Hastings to wait in the foyer. I presume you're keeping her."

I arched my brow. Keeping her? Her words impacted me deeper than expected. But yes, I planned to *keep* Miss Hastings until I achieved my goal. "She'll fill in your role while you're on maternity leave. Update her on my schedule and our computer system. You'll work together until you're finished here."

Clarissa bobbed in approval and hiked her chin. "She's an excellent choice."

My fingers twitched. Warmth spanned my nape. "What makes you say so?"

"She has an adequate resume." She shrugged. Her strong gaze followed as I rose from my desk. "And I'm a good judge of character. She seems genuine."

Wrong, Clarissa. But I reconsidered bursting her feminine instincts.

Gold metal frame armrests stood out on a detestable modern sofa. Hands clasped together, I sank against hard upholstery. The no-good furniture added style more than comfort. I wished I'd fired the decorator who designed my workspace. "I expect you to follow several rules when dealing with Miss Hastings."

"Name them." Not the slightest hesitancy.

Reliable Clarissa, ready to meet whatever challenge or request. A sufficient personal assistant indeed. "You've worked with me for three years, and you're no doubt mindful of my recent"—I waved a hand over my profile—"makeover." My physical form no doubt differed in comparison to my youth, but for Roxanne's sake, I also added drastic modifications. Realistic brown contacts concealed my pale blue-green irises. A hairdresser colored my dark blond hair, beard, and brows to a black-brown. A healthy tan coated my skin due to my recent stay in the Bahamas. In true superhero style, I'd donned a pair of faux glasses and had even visited a tattoo artist who applied a few temporary beauty spots to my temple.

"Yes…" She expressed the lone word with slow caution.

No point beating around the bush. "I expect discretion and no talk of my physical change to Miss Hastings."

She clamped her lips together and raised a finger. "May I, Hunter?"

The next words out of her mouth had better not cross the line. "Yes?"

"Although I can't fathom why you'd choose…"— she tilted forward for a closer survey—"a dark brown pair of contacts to conceal your rare and beautiful eye color or dye your hair and beard or pretend you have siblings, nevertheless, have I not done all you asked?"

"Of course." In fact, she'd recommended the hairdresser. "You're an excellent employee."

She lifted her hands. "I promise not to say a word regarding your new getup."

I drummed my knees. "Excellent. Glad I'm able to count on you."

She gripped the arms of the chair but paused midway through standing. "Anything else?"

As long as she kept quiet, I had no reason to worry. "No, Clarissa. I trust Roxanne's in your capable hands."

"Thank you, Hunter." She hefted to her feet. "Oh, also I'm about to call Sarina's on West Randolph Street. Do you want your lunch delivered, or prefer to dine in?"

Neither. In no mood to sit in a cramped restaurant,

and lunching under the same roof as Roxanne sounded no better, I needed fresh air to clear my head. "I'll collect my order and enjoy my meal in the park."

"Will do." She let herself out and shut the door.

****

Sun rays warmed my face. Leaves danced in trees, and scads swirled over the paved path and fresh-cut grass. Sugary sweet angelonias and buttery baked pretzels fused in the air. The park's wide expanse distracted from the city backdrop, and along the curb, a red and yellow umbrella sheltered a street vendor who served a line of customers.

I tucked my faux glasses inside my business shirt pocket and read Clarissa's text explaining she treated Roxanne to lunch. A good idea. I hoped Roxanne warmed to her new role, and Clarissa's friendliness won her over.

No amount of mental composure readied my soul when I interviewed Roxanne earlier. One glimpse and I lost myself. The best act of revenge involved attacking when one lowered their guard, which meant I'd need Roxanne comfortable working here. I dug into my gourmet steak sandwich and Parmesan truffle fries.

Wheels on concrete reverberated through the skate park, followed by hoots and cheers. No chance in clearing my head since children and teenagers crowded the large obstacle, taking turns doing flips, jumps, and twists, several of them showing off their stunts and enjoying the federal holiday.

"Loser!"

I blinked as the remark thrust me into the past. A small group of preteens chortled aloud and hovered over a boy perhaps a year younger than them near the ramps. The child crouched on the ground and cradled his bloodied knees.

"Told you he can't jump," blue-haired thug announced, surrounded by his crew. "Come on." He kicked the child's foot. "Get up, loser. Get up."

Onlookers hesitated, continuing to ride, and ignored the scene. Heck, no adults intervened either. I leaped to my full height, unable to mind my own business. The incident hit too close to home.

A kid in a faded red cap skated past me at full speed.

"Hey!" He skated to a halt to shield the injured boy…a boy who prolonged the survey of his bloodied knees, perhaps oblivious of the hero who emerged onto the scene in his defense.

"Get lost, you little turd." Blue-haired snickered.

Red Cap stomped the kicktail of his board. The solid wood hurled off the ground and he braced the nose-edge in his small, tight grip. "Back off." He leaned forward, posture tall and menacing.

Bully's freckled mug morphed into an ominous scowl. "Or what?" He shoved Red Cap and sent him tumbling a few inches. "What are you gonna do, huh?"

Red Cap straightened and raised his skateboard high.

My mouth dried. Good grief, he'd kill them.

"Hey!" I sprinted to the group. "Whoa, whoa, chill."

The child lowered his skateboard, nostrils flaring. "They started it!"

Freckled gang leader plonked his fists on his waist, but a flicker in his gaze gave away his uncertainty.

Funny how spineless children acted once an adult

emerged onto the scene. I clenched my jaw. "Get lost or I'll call the cops on you little punks."

They muttered among each other and skateboarded off in a hurry.

Red Cap knelt to the injured boy. "Are you okay?"

The kid's wide, unblinking gaze perceived his young hero. "Thanks. Those guys always bug me."

Red Cap offered his hand, and the injured boy took hold. "Are you fine to walk?"

On his feet, he tested his legs. "Yeah, I'm okay." His gaze met my own. "Thanks for sending them away."

"No problem." Empathy tugged at my chest. He held no idea to what degree we shared in common.

"I better go." The boy addressed Red Cap and gimped off. "See ya."

I waited until the injured boy exceeded earshot. "You're one brave dude. Do those guys go to your school?"

He assessed my eyes with fierce intensity, perhaps wary of the meddler who'd come to his aid. At least nine or ten years old, wise enough to know stranger danger.

"Nope." He dropped his skateboard on the ground, one foot arresting the deck. "I live in the suburbs. We drove out here to check out the new skate park."

I knelt to his level and balanced my elbow on my knees. "You'd done serious harm if you'd whacked him. His parents would've sued yours."

He scanned his feet, his small jaw once again rigid. "I let my anger get the best of me."

"Kid, you don't have to preach." I wished I possessed the same zeal as this boy when in school.

"Trust me, I can't stand bullies."

A fly buzzed near the boy's nose, and he shooed the insect away. "Bullies hurt my father in high school. I hate seeing anyone picked on."

No wonder he'd defended Injured Knees. Like me, the scene hit close to home for him too. "Your father's done a great job in raising a respectable young man."

"Hey champ, you all right?" A man with salt-and-pepper hair approached, two paper-wrapped pretzels encased in his hands.

"Yeah, I'm fine..." He recapped every detail at rapid speed. "...and this man here threatened to call the cops and scared them away."

I fought back a chuckle and straightened to my full height. "You should be proud of your son, sir."

The older man beamed toward the boy. "I'm beyond proud."

"He's not my dad. He's my grandpa, but I'm not allowed to call him grandpa." The kid scrunched his nose. "It makes him feel old."

"You bet. And don't forget it, little Zee." His grandfather patted his red hat.

The kid rolled his eyes. "Got it, big Zee."

Once Big Zee served the kid his pretzel, he held out his free hand for me to shake. "Thank you for getting involved. I didn't expect to run into trouble today."

I returned his handshake. "Your grandson's the real hero here. The way he defended the other boy..." I gave a low whistle. "I wish a brave person like him helped me when I attended school."

Ready to take another bite from his pretzel, the kid's jaw dropped. "You were bullied? But you're bigger than those wrestlers on TV. I bet your bullies are too scared to lay a finger on you now." He took another generous bite of his pretzel.

Kid, you have no idea. "What can I say? I wasn't a popular guy. Thank God those days are behind me now. As for my bullies, last I heard, their lives haven't turned out great." I pointed in the direction of where Freckles and his crew ran off. "So, don't worry. In the end, bullies always get what they deserve."

The kid used the back of his hand to swipe away crumbs. "Hey, you should do those anti-bullying talks for schools. I'm sure my mom can help set you up."

Pride radiated through the older man's smile. "His mother partook in a few awareness programs for several middle schools."

"She must be one of a kind." I had nothing but admiration for anyone out there playing a part to prevent the tragedy of bullying. Sad to say, detestable people roamed this world far greater than honorable ones, and I doubted talking to a bunch of school kids helped matters. Every being possessed good and bad inclinations and embraced whatever tendencies favored them.

The man took in my pristine suit and turned to his grandson. "He seems much too busy, kiddo. Besides, we've taken up enough of his time already."

A valid point. I'd dallied here long enough and better head back to the office in time for my scheduled conference call. But the little superhero deserved a perk for his bravery. I withdrew my wallet and extracted two hundred dollars.

The kid gaped at the money.

His grandpa raised a hand. "Mister, he can't

accept—"

"Please." I extended the cash. "It's the least I can do."

The man gave a slow shake of his head and stared at the cash in my hand.

"I insist. The kid deserves a hero's reward." I used my determined tone reserved for board members.

The grandfather sighed and peered at his grandson. "What do you say?"

He accepted the money, his gaze zigzagging from me to the cash in his hand. "Thank you, mister."

His high spirits lifted my own. "You're welcome, kid."

His grandfather ruffled the boy's cap and shot me a wink. "You've made his day."

"Likewise." I waved them both goodbye and meandered toward my driver, Carlo.

I slumped inside the limo and contemplated the brave youngster. On one occasion I'd assumed Roxanne acted in a similar fashion. Although not as bold, I'd believed in her own secretive way she protected me from her friends…before learning I'd fallen victim to one big lie.

Chapter 3

Roxanne

My shoes pounded the floor in tune with my quick heartbeat. I stole a peek over my shoulder at the guys chatting amongst themselves while Olivia peered into her compact mirror, glued to her image. They'd march over here soon and straight into Max if I didn't draw him away from enemy lines.

A few weeks ago, when Alex suggested I choose a penalty by the lockers, pure panic struck my core. I had to act fast, and the least harmful idea promising no blood or bruises—kiss the guys' feet. Then the moron Trevor kicked him. Similar incidents never fazed me in the past, but now a hollow ache in my chest rejected every and all excuses—horseplay, fun, and games—the more I defended our harassment, the more absurd my reasoning sounded.

I experienced an awakening. A rude one. I was a bully, and reflecting over the last four years left me desperate to shrivel into a fetal pose. The way I'd strutted these halls as though no one else mattered. The times my friends and I teased our peers, indifferent to how they'd feel...too concerned with living my best life, high on the flattery I drew from guys who begged to date me and girls who imitated me. The world revolved around me and my friends.

Instead of confronting the gang about my newfound sympathy toward our classmates, I soon learned another bitter truth. I was a coward, a frightened one.

Nose stuck in a book and clueless to my approach, I snatched Max's wrist without prelude, and he flinched. Swinging open the door beside him, I shut us inside a cramped janitor's closet.

I'd serve Max better by sticking with my clique, prepared to obliterate their schemes since I obtained direct knowledge of every planned prank.

Light seeped through a rectangular glass window on the wooden door and illuminated the dim setting.

"What're you doing?" He lurched forward, no doubt ready to leave, but I placed both palms on his chest.

Dread or surprise widened his eyes.

Trevor's boisterous laughter resounded outside.

No other choice.

I crashed against Max and pinned us both into a hard wall. Stacked brooms and mops clattered. Max's book flopped to the floor. His unsure stare centered on me, and I hushed him with a finger.

A shadow passed the small window. Max gaped from me to the view, and his rigidity melted.

"Are you sure my mascara looks fine?"

"Yes!" Alex growled.

The quarterback's attitude alone frightened me half to death. For years I deemed his protective behavior as brotherly, but make no mistake, his clear-cut demanding ways screamed narcissist.

"Ask me again, and I swear I'll lose my cool."

"Oh, I'll keep asking until Roxanne tells me otherwise." Their voices faded out of the hallway.

Brows furrowed, Max's frantic gaze searched mine. I distinguished his silent distrust, but bigger matters occupied my mind. His rough jeans secured my nylon-clad thigh. The warmth seeped into my skin and spread through my insides. Though no longer in immediate danger, my hands spanned his torso and heat oozed into my palms, the frisson too delicious to put an end to.

Soap and the splendid scent of trees in spring greeted my senses. Butterflies fluttered in my stomach at our intimate contact, and my chest ached, a duet of pain and euphoria.

I'd noticed Max in different ways. Tall and skinny but far cuter than other guys who showed off their barbell-lifting skills. A slight gap separated his front teeth and perfected his structured jawline and adorable dimples, and his mop of dark blond tousled hair framed his pale face. I'd spot him in class, nose inside a book and tongue poked out to one corner. Unlike most classmates, he took an interest and produced brilliant answers to teachers' conundrums. He outsmarted all of us.

Every time I caught sight of him, my stomach performed little flips and my lungs expanded in blissful pain. At first, I discarded the idea as hyperawareness—since I remained on constant alert to prevent a clash between him and the guys—but failed to explain the rush in my system whenever I sought him out and anticipated a single glance. The obvious stared me in the face. I harbored a secret crush on Max Fields.

One backward step broke our contact, and I aimed for the doorknob.

Max's fingers draped my hand. "Wait."

I met his wide gaze over my shoulder. His lips twitched and gave the tiniest glimpse of a smile. "Why hide me, Roxanne?"

The way he spoke my name triggered a flinch. His lenient manner equated to a slap in the face, a cruel reminder I lacked the same grace.

Max bent to my level, desperate for...the truth? Recognition? Friendship?

My heart twisted in agony. "I have to go." I rushed outside. My speed consumed the distance. I'd sound crazy confessing my secret. Protect him, keep him safe, yes, I'd try my hardest...but to give him the reason? No way! Too ashamed to confess...not of him but of myself. I'm a terrible person. I accepted the truth, but I'd crawl into a hole rather than admit said truth out loud.

"Roxanne!"

An abrupt voice penetrated my flashback. I jumped in my seat and fumbled for the intercom button. "Yes?"

"My office." Mr. Parker's voice boomed through the speaker. "Now."

Palms sweaty, I rushed into his office.

Forms and binders strewed his desk. Mr. Parker rifled through drawers, gloomy and agitated. The coffee I'd handed him fifteen minutes ago sat untouched near his laptop. A pointless hike through busy Chicago streets—because no random coffee house sufficed, but a particular joint my boss preferred—in the rain no less, all for a beverage stone cold by now.

Rooted to the spot, I entwined my hands. The large window behind him frightened me far greater than the man himself. Although the phenomenal views received great praise, high viewpoints left me lightheaded. Guaranteed I'd worsen his mood by fainting. "You called?" He stopped in his rummaging and inspected me top to toe; his perceptive stare launched a jolt straight through me.

"You ordered me the wrong coffee," he barked, revisiting the mess on his desk.

"I'm sorry." I grabbed the black foam cup. "You asked for a latte, right?"

He huffed aloud. "Correct, and yet I received a soy latte."

Darn the barista. He asked me twice to which I replied a firm and solid *No soy, thank you.* The cup almost exploded in my hand. "I'll go to the coffee house and fix your order."

He smacked both hands on the polished desk. "Roxanne, where's the proposal for Clive & Co? You left the folder on my desk, yes?"

What on earth made him assume I received those documents? We discussed the topic when I arrived earlier with his coffee. "Clive & Co has yet to send us an email."

He massaged his temples. Goodness, the pounding migraine I imagined he suffered affected me from where I stood. "Check your emails again. I need them a-sap."

"Right away, Mr. Parker." On an awkward nod, I bolted out of the room, seconds away from curtsying akin to a little peasant in his glum kingdom. I tossed the untouched coffee and the cold cup thunked into the trash.

Dashing to my desk, I rubbed my blood-red chiffon sleeves. Wrong coffee. Wrong files. Wrong agenda. The soy latte I accepted as my fault, but as for the other mishaps...any chance Mr. Parker sabotaged me on purpose? In Functions and Events, I'd grown used to a slower pace and an ability to present a perfect result. The email we'd awaited rolled in. I hit Print on the computer and rushed to the machine springing to life.

Mr. Parker's office door flew open. He supported his weight on the doorframe, all stressed and uncontrolled fury. Men in suits congested Chicago city, but Mr. Parker's black suit and tie fit him to perfection, and he executed the accomplished business style all too well.

I forced a cheerful guise and hoped my gesture abated his mood. "Printing the documents now."

He slashed a hand through his pristine hairdo, perhaps eager to tear out a few strands. *Darn machine. Work faster.* The final page ejected onto the tray. I uttered an audible sigh, tapping the papers to neaten them, and darted to Mr. Parker who stood rigid, jaw muscle ticking.

I thrust the papers at him and miscalculated, letting go too soon. Blood leached from my face. *Please God, no.*

Pages swish-swayed to the carpet. I avoided his bared teeth and irritated grumble, diving to the floor at his wide-planted legs to gather the papers. Today marked one month already since I'd worked here, and one week on my own without Clarissa, who'd left for maternity leave. I lacked in my role. How long until Mr. Parker ceased tolerating my continuous mistakes? "I'm sorry, Mr. Parker." I raised to my full height but underestimated our proximity and my chest brushed his torso.

Mr. Parker's features grew tense.

Heat spread inside my throat, and I craned my neck

at the large man towering over me. His pleasant cologne tempted me to never move again and bask in his pine and woodsy cologne.

"I told you to drop the formalities." His tender yet deep voice tingled my spine.

On several occasions, he'd prompted me to call him Hunter. "Of course...Hunter." His name left my lips in a whisper.

He leaned forward, nostrils flared, and a dark lock slipped onto his black-rimmed glasses. "Do you have a problem with my name, Roxanne?"

Neither one of us retreated a step, and his low and husky voice vibrated through my chest, triggering a ruckus in my own.

I ignored an itch to slick the lock of hair into place. "No. Hunter's a nice name." A powerful name, a name fit for a predator, and well-suited for the ruthless businessman standing before me.

Strong arms crossed over his massive chest, his biceps alone averaged the size of my head and did a fine job of blocking our current contact. "Why then continue calling me by my surname?"

I stepped back and opted for honesty. "We haven't worked together long."

"You consider an entire month not long?" He raised his chin, daring me to counteract his words.

Yes, considering for the entire month I'd interacted with Clarissa way more than Mr. Parker, and any exchange with this man resulted in an unpleasant experience. My too tense, too conceited, and too arrogant boss failed at making me feel welcome, but no, better not address his complete lack of warmth. He and Clarissa got on well enough, still professional, but at least she managed to crack a smile out of him. I, on the other hand, walked on eggshells and struggled to imagine us engaged in comfortable banter. "I'm sure I'll get the hang of it." Not true. I doubted I'd ever grow used to addressing Mr. Parker in a mere casual manner.

His brows furrowed at my words. "I suggest you *get the hang of it* sooner than later."

"Will do, Mr...Hunter." I swallowed as his dark eyes bore into me. "I'll leave to grab you the right coffee now."

"Don't bother. We have an excessive amount of work to do." He stalked for his office. "Please return to your desk and get a move on. And no calls for the next hour. As you're aware, I'm scheduled for an important phone conference." At last, he shut the door.

I sank into my desk chair, gazing at the ceiling. *God, give me strength.* Emails congested my inbox, a list of potential contractors sat piled on my desk, and mail and faxes poured in by the dozen. I straightened in my seat and rummaged through the drawer for sticky notes but skimmed a cold object. Beneath notebooks and pens, I withdrew a pair of metal handcuffs. What on earth! Had Clarissa snuck her husband in here for a little rendezvous? Or...perhaps Mr. Parker and Clarissa shared a deeper relationship.

I shoved them inside and slammed the drawer shut, letting the cuffs remain a mystery. No way I'd risk losing my job by asking Mr. Parker since I'd managed to grace his bad books enough this week.

The phone on my desk rang, startling me. "Mr. Parker's office."

"Sorry, I expected Clarissa to answer." A sophisticated voice greeted on the other end.

Phone wedged between my shoulder and ear, I snatched the computer mouse and compiled emails into their appropriate folders. Queen of multitasking here. "She's on maternity leave. I'm Roxanne Hastings, Mr. Parker's new personal assistant."

Dead air stretched the line, and I gripped the phone tighter.

"Roxanne?"

Did she recognize my voice? "Yes?"

"My name's Georgina Belmont." She cleared her throat. "I'm Hunter's friend. Any chance he's available?"

I snatched a pen and scribbled her name and the hour of her call. "He's on an important video conference, but I'll have him contact you when he's finished."

"Thank you, Roxanne." Her polite tone betrayed the strain in her voice.

What on earth rattled the strange woman? I placed the phone on the receiver, glancing at the unfamiliar name scribbled on the square, yellow note.

The phone rang again. This time Clarissa called to check in on how I managed on my own.

"I'm peachy here." I fumbled with the pen on my desk and kept spying the closed drawer as if the handcuffs inside screamed for my attention.

"Sorry to trouble you, but check the drawers to see I left—"

Oh, boy, no ignoring the elephant in the room now. "The handcuffs. You did. I saw them." Heat infused my cheeks, embarrassed for poor Clarissa. If Margaret Small worked here and stuck her nose in such a scandal, she'd have a field day. I shifted in my seat and cupped one end of the phone. "I'll pretend I haven't seen them, promise."

Clarissa broke into hysterics. "Roxanne, I called to check if I'd left you the company's backup file passwords."

Praise God no one bore witness to my scorching face. I snatched a leather-bound planner perched in the corner. "Yes, I have the diary here."

"I can explain those handcuffs. I hope you didn't assume Hunter and I hid some kinky affair?"

I curled a hand around my middle and coughed aloud.

A mock gasp echoed down the line. "You did, didn't you?"

"Oh, Clarissa. I feel terrible." I prayed for the floor to open and swallow me whole. "Talk about a preconceived idea."

She hummed, her drollery noticeable. "I don't blame you. Hunter's a hunk, but FYI, I'm a married woman. At last year's work party, I won the ridiculous handcuffs in a lucky draw. I meant to toss them ages ago but forgot, and then my desk and all its contents were moved with the takeover, so they've been sitting there this entire time."

A lucky draw? "I'm such an idiot. Please, let's forget the entire mishap?"

"Consider the incident forgotten." Laughter filled her voice. "Call me if you run into trouble."

"Thank you. Before you go, I've one question...who's Georgina? She sounded shocked when I answered the phone." Goodness, less than a month and I'd turned into Margaret. Next, I'd procure my own flock of bluebirds.

"Georgina Belmont." Her voice grew serious. "You've heard of her, right?"

I spied Hunter's closed door. "Her name doesn't ring a bell."

"She's the billionaire heiress to the world's largest cosmetic brand."

I flattened my hand on the desk. "You mean Belmont Cosmetics?" In high school, Olivia spent a fortune on the brand, whereas I deemed their makeup sponges—the least lavish item in their stores—overpriced.

"Yes. She's related to Esme Belmont." A yappy bark echoed in the background, the cry belonging to no other than Clarissa's chihuahua. "Down, Buttercup. By the way, ignore what the media says regarding Georgina. *Ladies' Weekly* is plain wrong. She's a wonderful person."

With my busy life, I had no time to indulge in magazines. I bit my inner cheek. "So, she's Hunter's girlfriend?"

"College sweetheart turned ex-girlfriend, but they're still great friends." Crunching sounded on the line. I bet Clarissa once again succumbed to her peanut butter and pickles craving. "They're one of those strange ex-couples who don't detest one another."

A person who shared no hard feelings toward their ex? In a small way, I empathized. Contrary to Georgina and Mr. Parker, my case differed. I chuckled in my head. No, my unique story comprised the makings of a hit episode on a tabloid talk show complete with an audience chanting their host's name and booing me on stage.

"A little weird, I know, but they make their

friendship work. Besides, I bet they'll rekindle their spark soon. Georgina's the sweetest person, and Hunter cares for her. They can't tiptoe around each other forever. One of them's bound to come clean, right?"

The uptight man never smiled around here, and I struggled to picture him doing the same on a date or with a girlfriend. I sagged against the desk chair, again not seeing this caring side Clarissa portrayed of our boss.

"Roxanne…you're not jealous, are you?"

Jealous? My spine straightened. "No, not at all. I'm curious because of her response on the phone."

Clarissa gasped. "Maybe she's the one who's jealous." A clatter erupted in the background. Perhaps in her startling enlightenment, she'd dropped her plate of pickles. "I mean she knows I'm married, but she has no idea who you…" Clarissa fell silent. "Oh Roxanne, I'm sorry. I'm beyond bored and I've binged too many shows. Ignore me. I'm not one to gossip. Blame hormones and TV dramas."

"For the record, you haven't started drama." I swiped the mouse across the pad to relight my computer screen. "I better go. Take my advice and get plenty of sleep. Trust me, once your little one arrives, you can say goodbye to a good night's sleep." Not to mention sleepless nights continued for years to come. Clarissa and her husband have yet to learn the toilsome challenge involved in raising a child.

"Joy." Clarissa snorted into the phone. "Cheerio, Roxanne."

I skipped lunch and poured myself into work for the rest of the day, arranging meetings and sorting both tangible and online file systems. Mr. Parker thanked me for my haste when I emailed him the latest reports, and I gave myself a mental high five. At six o'clock, I shut off my computer and tidied my desk.

Hunter pottered from his office, briefcase in his grip.

"Oh, I almost headed to your office to wish you good night." Most days I clocked off while he remained at his desk, and when I offered to stay back and help, he insisted I head home. I lacked the courage to ask the next day what time he'd clocked off the previous night, but in my short period here, I learned the man set the bar for a bona fide workaholic.

He held the elevator door and gestured me inside. "You first."

Silence stretched between us. In previous elevator rides, Clarissa's small chatter removed the awkward discomfort, and I wished for her sociable company. "Any plans for the weekend?"

His gaze stayed glued to the polished steel doors ahead. "No."

A man of few words. Perhaps he arranged to meet with Georgina. Concluding his meeting, I knocked on his door to inform him of her call and he'd brightened at the message. Now his passive demeanor made me squirm on the spot and pinch my charcoal skirt.

"You're right about what you said earlier." Though he spoke, his focus lingered on the doors.

No headset confirmed he spoke to me rather than on a call, and no one besides us occupied the elevator. "Excuse me?"

He loosened his tie. "We're strangers. I say we get better acquainted, don't you?"

I prayed my guise remained neutral. "Yeah...yes.

What do you suggest?"

Averting his gaze, at last, his dark stare landed on me. "Dinner. Sunday night. My shout. A nice way for us to break the ice."

My posture stiffened. In the past, I'd accompanied colleagues to dine with previous bosses, never on my own. Alone with Hunter? I hesitated to say his name to his face, and he expected us to sit through an entire dinner.

"It's not a date," he confirmed, his tone nonchalant.

"Of course not. Sorry, I'm wondering who I'll ask to babysit." A lie. No issues getting a sitter since my parents raised their hands on every occasion.

Oh, no. Mom. No way I'd convince her our work-related dinner for two meant nothing. I pictured Vivian Hastings clapping and cheering. No doubt she'd shake a tambourine and blow a trumpet too. The woman made finding me a good husband her life goal. At first, she insisted on matchmaking me with a young lawyer at her firm. I pictured her work desk strewn with campaign posters of my profile—*Daughter desperate for a boyfriend. Email Viv for details.* But I'd rebuffed every date my mother planned on my behalf, and as of late, she'd lowered her standards, keen to snatch anyone willing to date me. Last we spoke, she tried convincing me to go for the widowed mailman. Mental forehead smack. I expected no surrender from the headstrong woman until a gold ring encircled my finger.

"Clarissa mentioned you had kids." His voice lowered with the remark.

"One." I adjusted my handbag strap, although unnecessary. "One child. A son."

His nose twitched. "Too short notice? We can

postpone dinner for another night."

He disliked children; the clear disdain showed in his sour expression. "No, Sunday's fine." I forced a little optimism in my tone. "Name the location. I'll meet you there."

Hunter spied his wristwatch, stifling a yawn. "I'll send you a detailed text later tonight."

Neither one of us displayed excitement concerning dinner, and rather than anticipate the weekend, I dreaded this upcoming Sunday. The elevator doors drew open and I entered the underground parking garage, but Hunter remained inside and halted the door.

"I forgot my wallet upstairs. I'll see you Sunday, Roxanne." He dropped his hand and retreated into the elevator.

Waving him goodbye with a tentative smile, I then dug for my keys in my purse. Exhaust fumes intoxicated the warm enclosure, and my heels echoed on smooth concrete as I passed a few parked cars. Dinner with Mr. Big Shot. What if the entire night consisted of forced chats and awkward silence? I struggled to picture my impudent and uptight boss acting hospitable toward me, but he made a point. We'd benefit from breaking the ice. *Remember, not a date.* Clarissa confirmed he fancied Georgina…proof Hunter harbored no ulterior motive, so dwelling on the matter achieved nothing.

My feet skidded to a standstill.

A wooden cane sat propped against my car door. No random cane either. I took a step closer to observe the carved letters on the wooden stick spelling my name in a particular calligraphy I refrained from using since high school where I substituted a heart for the letter O.

R♡XANNE XOXO.

A shaky breath parted my lips.

The scratching, gritty sound of torn fibers resurfaced in vivid detail as the memory of carving out those letters, blowing away sawdust, and going over my signature with a black marker rushed to the forefront of my mind.

"Max." I spun in a slow circle, prepared to confront a tall, thin man. "Max?" I prowled past vehicles, chasing the echo of my own voice. "Are you here?"

What on earth? He'd found *me*!

The high heels supporting my shaky legs clicked faster within the eerie quiet parking lot.

A loud ding chimed, and I whipped around. Goodness, I'd neared the elevator again.

Hunter jerked at the sight of me. "Roxanne?"

Evident concern layered his tone, but in my erratic state, I failed to reassure him.

"Good grief, you're shaking." His gaze raked my body. "What happened?"

I pointed in the distance, leading him to where I'd parked. "There's…he…my car." For goodness' sake, why couldn't I catch my breath? "He left a wooden cane on my car."

"A carjacker broke into your car with a cane?" Jaw rigid, he quickened his pace.

We approached my car and my head whipped in a double take. I planted one hand on Hunter's chest, stopping him in his tracks, and took a hesitant step closer. No cane.

"Which one's yours?" Hunter's shadow loomed above me.

My shaky finger pointed to my car. Where on earth

had it gone? I staggered to the driver's door. "I saw it with my own eyes, right here."

"A walking cane?" Disbelief rang in his tone as he circled my car. "So, no one broke your window."

"No, he left a wooden cane right here against my door." I sounded insane, and from the way Mr. Parker narrowed his eyes, he no doubt came to the same conclusion. I bit my lip. My gaze roamed the perimeter. "What if he's still here?" *Please.*

"You keep saying *he*?" Hunter pinched his nose, and his gaze followed my own. "Who's he?"

Max. His name collapsed on my tongue. I refused to dive into my personal history and explain my too lengthy and troubled past to my new boss. "Whoever put the cane here in the first place."

"Look around you. No one's here." He waved his hand over the half-empty lot. "Unless…you're insinuating a staff member—?"

"Not a staff member, but someone else." How do I explain myself without sounding insane?

He smirked and dug inside his jacket for his buzzing phone. "Without a staff access card? Doubtful. Besides, the hotel's closed, and only Parker Hotel staff has access."

His words penetrated my intellect and registered. Had I hallucinated? I'd pondered my past and Max over the years but never encountered a circumstance this extreme.

"I have an idea." He unlocked his phone and jabbed away. "Let me log into the company security system and view surveillance. Give me a sec to find the correct camera."

I paced back and forth. My fingers flexed and

unflexed by my sides.

"Okay...fast forward. Here." He bent to my level and shared the screen, hitting play. A grayscale image of the parking lot revealed my car. Soon I appeared.

Bile rose, and I cupped masculine hands palming the device.

In the footage, my figure approached an empty driver's door. Empty! I squinted but discerned no cane. Heat scorched my face as the video displayed me twisting left and right, morphing into a maniac, and wandering through the underground parking lot.

I'd imagined the entire scenario. "I'm...I'm so sorry." I covered the strained sound escaping my mouth and beheld my car. A mere phantasm. But the polished oak, the dark, grainy streaks in the wood, and my signature...every detail too vivid to pass off as fantasy.

"Go home and unwind." Mr. Parker kept his head low, avoiding my eyes.

Great job leading the way to instant dismissal. No doubt he regretted hiring a lunatic for a personal assistant.

Dylan's empty car seat stole my breath...Dylan! "Oh my gosh. Dylan's daycare!" I jumped into the driver's seat and boosted the engine.

Hunter shifted aside and I lipread the words, *Your son*. The engine roared too loud to hear him. Besides, I had no time to dawdle. "I'm in a hurry. Again, I'm sorry."

I drove to the underground security door, swiped my employee key to open the garage, and drove onto the main city street. In less than five minutes, I stopped at the curb of a building decorated in pastel colors, teddy bears, and ABC block decals. Sticky humidity and adrenaline invoked a desperate need for a cold shower...and a generous glass of wine.

I rushed inside, down the hall, and opened the door to the first room on the left. Not a single toy or block lay in sight, the place neater than in the usual morning drop off. Two carers stood from the sofa beside a sleeping Dylan. "I'm sorry I'm late, Emma."

"Roxanne." She scolded in a harsh whisper and plonked the phone on the lounge. "I almost called your brother. Are you all right?"

In no mood to explain my ordeal, I waved a nonchalant hand. "I had an issue with my car."

"In the future, send us a text." Emma handed me a sleeping Dylan, and I cradled the toddler in my arms. Dark coiled hair tickled beneath my chin, and I inhaled his baby shampoo scent. "Hey, little guy. You're tuckered out."

He stirred in my arms but soon relaxed against me. Full black lashes cast shadows over chubby cheeks, and his kissable button nose twitched, a nose the spitting image of his father's.

"We struggled to drag him away from the finger painting and playdough table today." She withdrew a sheet decorated in different colored swirls from his backpack. "He made this for Jasmine and Michael."

I stroked his smooth coffee skin. Poor little guy waited too long. "I'll be sure to give it to them. Thank you, Emma. We'll see you next week." I signed Dylan out of daycare and cradled him to the car. Once buckled in, I drove to my parents'.

Although we'd all moved out and lived nearby, Mom expected us Friday nights for dinner. I rented an apartment close to Mom and Dad's, whereas my brother Michael had married his high school sweetheart Jasmine several years ago, and they purchased a house a few blocks away.

My parents adored their grandsons and bragged to their friends and co-workers, but they both counted down until their granddaughter entered the world. Jasmine confirmed we'd soon welcome a little princess into the Hastings clan. Poor Jaz left her paralegal job due to preeclampsia. Strict bed rest drove her crazy, and all of us ran around the clock to help her.

Dylan's peaceful face reflected in the rearview mirror, sound asleep. My brother and Jasmine helped me over the years—heck, Jasmine backed me in delivery during childbirth—so, I'd do anything to lend them a helping hand. Without the support of my family, I'd go crazy.

The video footage flashed in my mind. "Crazy," I whispered and tightened my grip on the wheel, losing my smile. I prayed to never endure such a fright again. A part of me dreaded tonight. No way I'd raise the little hotel parking garage scenario over dinner.

Typical, Mom slaved away in the kitchen, and I'd disappoint her if I refused to stay.

I'd put on a brave front and dwell on the bizarre event later since I had all night to reflect on what I *imagined* happened.

Chapter 4

Max

I'd last entered this restaurant when Mom and Richard celebrated their engagement, the same night my stepfather gifted me his heirloom pocket watch. No change in layout, including the tables covered in white linen, candles, and fresh roses, but a few upgrades refreshed the joint. A pianist had replaced the violinist, the ruby-red carpet appeared brighter, and the crystal chandeliers seemed larger than the last time I visited. Garlic and herbs drifted in the air; the familiar aroma kindled fond memories.

"Now…" Richard raised his hand and scooted his chair closer. *"It's not a good-luck charm, but it has instilled in me great comfort, knowing my ancestors wore it at one point in their lives, through highs and lows, good days and bad…this watch has seen far greater than both of us."*

"Richard." My trachea closed. No one ever gifted me an item this extravagant or of such sentimental value. *"I can't accept your pocket watch."*

He waved off my reluctance. "Nonsense. I planned on giving this to you at the wedding." His hands closed around mine, securing the watch in my grip. "I hope this brings you the same comfort it has me all these years."

My lungs swelled in my chest. He cared. Tears stung my vision. Not to impress my mother, or to get into my good books, but he legit cared. "How'd we get so lucky to have you in our lives?"

"Lucky?" His weak smile wavered. "I'm unable to conceive children. My first wife and I discussed adoption before her tragic car accident, God rest her soul. She adored children and desired a baby of her own." He blinked out of his daze. "What I mean to say is after I fell in love with your mother and met you, I've come to cherish you as the son I've always wanted." He tilted his head. "This has nothing to do with luck, Max. You and your mother have enriched my life beyond measure."

I bounded from my seat and hugged him; unshed tears blurred my vision. "Any child will be lucky to call you their dad...including me."

Richard hugged me in return, and a piece inside me clicked into place, a resolved puzzle. I had a father.

A waiter in a white steward jacket passed, and I waved him over.

The man greeted my table. "Yes, sir."

I raised my glass but kept my gaze on the entry. Roxanne should arrive any minute.

The waiter held an expensive champagne bottle wrapped in linen and poured the effervescent beverage.

Roxanne sidled into the foyer and queued behind an old couple. My chest tightened. A black wrap dress tied around her slim waist and flared over her slender figure in a silken caress. Compared to the spectacular frocks women wore here, her basic black number turned no heads, yet she managed to wow me. She opted for ethical poise rather than dress to impress and failed because those almond-shaped hazels alone evoked sensual allure.

I cleared my throat and shifted in my seat. Roxanne inquired of the maître d' who pointed to my table, and she stretched on her toes, her mouth curving in genuine pleasure when spotting me. Lithe legs sashayed toward the table and sucked the breath right out of my lungs. *Get a grip, Max.*

Her undivided attention centered on me. "Good evening, Hunter." Roxanne lowered herself into a chair across from me, absorbing the room's live music and patrons decked in their designer gowns and tuxedos. Her cheerful demeanor dulled as she frowned at her outfit, no doubt scolding herself for not inquiring about the dress code.

"I hope you found the place all right."

She pinched at her cap sleeves as though to transform her simple dress into a gown fit for the ball. "Yes, not difficult at all."

I bit back a mock laugh. Whereas in high school Roxanne embraced her comfortable social circles, here she stood out of place and knew it too. *You're in my world now, Roxy.* She'd benefit from a dash of color to her pale cheeks, plus alcohol might take the edge off. "Care to start with a glass of wine?"

She stowed her purse under the table and straightened. "Thank you."

I flagged the waiter again, and he poured Roxanne a glass. Her sweet display of gratitude lit his entire visage, and his grin bestowed teeth, a courtesy he withheld from other guests. From teacher's pet to people pleaser...her demeanor remained the same all these years. Taking a tentative sip, she again examined the elaborate scene.

The column of her throat triggered a distant flashback. Moist, trembling kisses sliding across her neck, the vibration of her pulse feathering my lips. I swallowed and forced my stare over my half-empty crystal flute, although the temptation to ogle her all night persisted. "How are you in the wake of Friday's incident?"

A natural blush added extra color to her cheeks. "I owe you an apology."

"Not necessary." Why apologize for a stunt executed to perfection? When my hired tech guru texted, I'd used all my strength to hold onto my façade, unbeknownst to Roxanne who'd paid no heed to my demeanor in her current state. And as I showed her the surveillance—albeit subsequent to the same tech guy who tampered with the footage—she resembled an actress straight out of a horror movie scene. "You suffered a stressful ordeal."

She cringed and took care to set her flute glass on the table. "I have to convince myself it's a mere figment of my imagination."

Fasten your belt, sweetheart. Bigger figments await. I bent my leg over my knee. "Must be awful."

Her scrunched brows and desolate expression caused an unwelcome internal flinch, and I cleared my throat in hopes of dispersing the unwanted sensation.

She flicked her hand. "Please, can we drop the subject?"

Excellent. I pinched my fingers together to mock-lock my mouth, preferring a change of topic also. "Consider the subject dropped. In fact, let's get a move on."

One soft angled brow arched.

"Select three courses." I handed her a menu. "We'll place our order and head out of here."

"What do you mean?" She sputtered and eased forward. "To go where?"

I pointed outside to a bowling alley adjacent to the restaurant.

Roxanne cocked her head, reflecting a vivacious glint. "Bowling?"

Not just bowling, Roxanne, but an opportunity for you to lower your guard and become comfortable around me. Let me in, therefore when I crush you, you'll feel every shattering piece. "As opposed to a tedious dinner, I figured a little contest might liven the night."

She slumped in her seat, her relief palpable.

I expected a dramatic sigh, but one failed to follow. "I've arranged to have our meals sent to us. If you're game, of course?"

She gave a playful wink. "Oh, I'm game."

The waiter jotted our order, and I rose from our table to escort Roxanne outside into the suffocating summer night heat. A fresh breeze tunneled through the city and blew her blonde tresses in a flurry. Most women would freak out, but she kept composed.

We crossed the street. Her shoulders slackened when we passed the threshold, and an employee directed us to our lane near an upscale cocktail bar.

"Where is everyone?" Roxanne faltered to a halt.

A citrusy scent enveloped the grand space playing radio hits and colored laser lights splashed across walls and floors, setting the mood for fun. "I booked out the entire venue."

She spun around. "Why?"

Because I'll have you to myself. One night in utter privacy. No intruders from adjacent lanes or trouble from raucous children. I punched our names into the machine and readied our game for two. Her vanilla perfume urged me to savor the pleasant scent. "Why else?" My gaze danced her entire length. Her beauty tantalized me to near insanity. "I can't let anyone see my employee best me."

Her lips smacked together. "No, I guess losing in a meager bowling game will give you a bad rap."

"Exactly." I handed her a pair of shoes.

As we bowled for the next hour, Roxanne asked questions regarding my parents, where I attended college, and how many siblings I had. Left little choice, I lied through most answers. I'd reveal my identity in due time as I'd done with the others, but not tonight.

Our dinner arrived, and we settled at a table the waiter prepared. Roxanne savored the fine cuisine; each bite she took roused a soft moan as though sampling a taste of heaven.

The night drew on and our conversation grew lighter. I shared the story of the time I gave a speech at my mother's birthday banquet. I'd run late to the party and in my rush, dressed in an old snug-fitting suit. At my parents' table in front of one hundred guests, I praised my mother, and as I bent to kiss her cheek, my pants split from thigh to crotch.

"Get out." She gasped, mouth shaped into a perfect O. "So, what'd you do?"

My ball rushed down the lane, knocking the pins and earning me another strike. "I didn't have a choice; I raised a toast to my mother and hightailed my butt home."

She clutched her chest, and her chuckle increased, the sound warming my insides.

"A night your mother will remember forever, I bet."

I grinned at the memory of Mom's initial shock, and how she fell into a fit of laughter later that same evening. "Yes, and trust me, she reminds me whenever I see her."

"Hmm, I'd do the same." She took a sip of her cocktail.

"What about you? Do you come from a big family?" My words spewed out, and I compressed my fingers into a fist. My plan to not dig into her personal life backfired. All evening our easy and natural conversation flowed, and here I expected to lower her guard, but I'd let my own vigilance slip.

Tender warmth encompassed her face. She grabbed her bright purple ball and slipped her fingers into the holes. "I have one sibling, a brother. He's a protective pain in the butt whom I adore. My father grew up an only child in the heart of Chicago. But my mother…" She tossed her ball down the lane. "Mom's from a big family in South Carolina. Four brothers and three sisters."

For sure Bruce, my private investigator, noted such details in Roxanne's file…if I'd mustered the courage to read the report. Months ago, Bruce visited my office to discuss the last and final foe on my revenge list, but when he'd mentioned Roxanne collected her toddler from a city daycare, I'd cut him off, warning him with my narrowed eyes not to spill another word. In a jealous rage, I launched out of my seat with a roar and swiped all the contents on my desk to the carpet. Since then, every endeavor to brief me on her kid incurred immediate rebuff, and he quit trying when thrown out of my office. Like with the others, he emailed me her file, but I skimmed no further than the first page showing her portrait.

An iron-clad ball slumped in my gut and seared my insides. Another man impacted her life, a man she perhaps loved enough to bear his child. Had she and her lover developed a serious romance or parted on a one-night stand? Or perhaps the jerk abandoned her, or they shared custody? Curiosity ate away. All the answers sat encased inside her file, but I refused to ascertain such knowledge, scared of confronting the life she'd lived without me, afraid to let whatever truth reopen my wounds and experience a pain worse than death.

As for her high school pals, I'd studied every aspect of them from where they lived to their favorite cuisine. Invested in my revenge plan, I acquired every detailed scrap to use against them. And my diligence paid off. Take Brent Robinson for example—moron trusted me faster than expected due to the fact I pretended we shared the same interests. He'd relocated to Iowa. On several nights he'd invited me out for beers and hosted me for dinner with his sweet wife. I crept into his life and misled him into a business contract he deemed solid and beneficial.

He'd slumped to the floor, discovering I'd conned him out of his car dealership and left him penniless while I whistled out of his permanently closed dealership to drown out his wails. Last I checked, his financial struggles persisted, and his sweet wife filed for divorce. What a shame. She made such great fettuccine. Oh well, his loss. "You have a lot of aunts and uncles."

She knocked five pins and achieved minimal for her score, which meant I held the lead. Her pale purple cocktail sat on our table, and she snatched the glass and took a sip. "Don't forget cousins. A truckload of cousins."

I lazed into the seat, chuckling at her sense of humor. "Do you keep in touch with them?"

Her shoulder bounced in a half-shrug. The action drew my attention to her chest rising and falling. "One of my aunts lives close by, so there's the odd get-together or picnic barbecue, but as for the whole family, we see them on holidays and social events. They're a good laugh."

"A shock for your dad, too, I imagine." I knew nothing of her parents or her brother. Back in high school, Roxanne always arrived at school with her friends or on her own in her little silver hatchback. "From a quiet home to marrying into one big, loud one."

She paused for a beat. "Oh, trust me, it's still a shock to him." She plunked herself in her seat and deposited her cocktail on the table. "But he gets on great with my mother's side. They adore their Zaneadu."

"Zaneadu?" I braced my elbows on my knees, eager for her to elaborate.

She snorted again, a knuckle under her nose. "My father, Zane, embraced the whole roller disco scene in his younger years. We whip out his old pictures for fun. In one photo he has true eighties-style shaggy blond hair, wearing metallic shorts and knee-high socks."

Eyes alight and features vibrant, her fast words matched her flying hands, exuding passion when discussing her dad. "So, in mimicking the eighties cult classic movie—they call him Zaneadu."

"Good grief." I grasped the chair beside me.

Her delicate hand flattened on her chest. "I'd refuse to stand for it. I mean, my brother called me Roxy-Poxy, but I tolerated the nickname." She hummed the remnants of her amusement. "What about you?"

My spine stiffened. "Hmm?"

She shook her head. "Any funny nicknames you used to go by?"

Limp. I lost my smile.

Roxanne frowned at my immediate lack of enthusiasm.

"No." I shrugged to fake indifference. "None I recall." Not allowing her a chance to prod further, I shot out of the booth and snatched my beer off the ball stand, keeping my back to her. I gulped my drink and cast my sight heavenward. Of all topics in the world, the discussion of nicknames arose!

"I hope you're happy?"

Her cold tone needled my spine. She'd caught on. A lot smarter than the others since I'd never blown my cover with them. "Pardon?" I turned and met her scowl.

She pointed to a screen above. "You won the game."

The screen displayed our scores, flashing an image of a golden cup trophy beside my name. *Won the game.* "I sure did." *And I'm not done yet, Roxy.* I flicked my wristwatch and noted the hour. "It's late, but before we leave, I have a work-related matter to discuss."

Elbows on the table, Roxanne rested her chin on

her fists, her posture a dead ringer of that night ten years ago when we played chess. Rapt by my lesson, she'd learned the pieces and their role in the game quicker than expected. She no doubt avoided playing since. I blinked out of my trance. "I expect you to accompany me to a banquet next weekend. Jean-Philippe Lemaigre is guest of honor, and I plan to hire him to remodel the hotel."

Her hands spanned the table and her jaw all but followed. "Did you say Jean-Philippe Lemaigre? He's in *Decadent Decor Magazine*'s top one hundred interior designers."

Familiar with his work. Good. I draped my arms on the padded backrest of the booth. "You've heard of him."

"Of course. He's renowned in the design world." She leaned in close to whisper, "I'll get to meet him in person?"

"And work with him too. We have our current modern and flashy lakefront hotel in Chicago, but I've new ideas for my latest venture. I purchased Tower Hotel for its grandiose space, an ideal premise for the historical Paris theme I've endeavored, and the French interior designer's perfect for the job."

She untied the laces of her bowling shoes. "I'll be happy to accompany you."

"Excellent." And for the cherry on top. "I suggest you schedule our accommodations tomorrow."

Her foot stilled halfway slipping into one high heel. "Are we spending the night?"

Head bowed, fingers holding the strap of her heel, she peered at me through lengthy lashes. Heat encircled my collar. "You don't expect us to head back from Los

Angeles the same night?"

She wobbled on the chair's edge and righted her equilibrium. "Los Angeles!"

"Do we have a problem?" I followed suit and changed into my leather shoes. "Clarissa voiced no concerns on short-notice trips."

She glanced at the polished wooden floors, lost in the strobe lights. Her steady gaze braved my intent stare.

"Uh, no." She tucked a golden strand behind her ear. "I'll make the call tomorrow."

"Perfect. Book our rooms in the same hotel as the event. I'll send you the contact details. Also, the party has a black-tie dress code. I suggest you find a gown fit for a banquet." From the hue of her cheeks, I bet I hit a nerve regarding her lack of elegance at the high-class establishment earlier tonight.

"I'll get right on it." We rose to our feet and collected our items. "I'm glad we did this. I had a lot of fun."

"Me too." I donned my suit jacket. "I'm sure tonight's the first of many business dinners together." We returned our shoes and thanked the staff on our way out. "I'll see you to your car."

Rolling noise echoed on the lamppost-lit city street.

"Don't trouble yourself on my account." She waved her hands and pointed ahead. "My car's up the far end of the street."

As if I'd let a woman wander alone at night in a big city, sworn enemies included. "I insist."

She observed me from her peripheral vision as we ambled on the sidewalk in comfortable silence. Relentless heat suffocated the night, and I removed my jacket, unable to withstand the heat a second longer.

"I don't blame you." A sardonic cadence graced her tone. "The night's far too hot for a suit jacket."

I huffed through my nose. "I left the office and drove straight here."

"On a Sunday?" She clasped my arm, utter shock widening her stare.

The warmth of her hand seeped into my skin. I dared not make any sudden protest and cease her lingering touch. "Yes."

She eyed her firm hold and returned her hand to her side. "You work a lot."

So much for her lingering touch. The small sacrifice of having a lackluster social life worked wonders for my career. Georgina and I hung out on the rare occasion, and I visited my parents whenever I found free time.

She stopped in front of her car. "Thank you for tonight. And again, sorry for arriving late. My kid forgot his favorite game and wouldn't stop whining when I dropped him off at my parents."

She'd hinted once more at her son. I avoided the subject all night, not ready to grapple with the bleak reality and risk such a conversation rattling my mood. My original intent to have a mundane dinner irked me. Deep down, the adventure, thrill, and fun we shared all those years ago left me nostalgic. For a brief moment tonight, I'd transported to the past, to the most profound day of my life. But Roxanne spent an evening with Hunter Parker, not Max Fields. A single mother too, far from the teenage girl who pranced into my life and shook my entire world.

No malice against her toddler, but the fact she

conceived another man's child irritated me, as though the father of the child tainted her. A brutal concept. Wrong even. My jealousy made no sense, and yet a raw ache in my stomach persisted. Misery clawed beneath my skin. For the last decade, she'd haunted me in a physical, mental, and emotional way. "Don't fret. I enjoyed tonight." I kept my response lighthearted, not adding to the topic of her son. "And *thank you* for losing the game."

She scoffed and crossed her arms, her defense adorable. "I didn't lose on purpose. To be honest, I tried hard to beat you."

I nodded with exaggerated ease. "Oh, I bet you did."

She narrowed mischievous eyes. "Don't drift away with your inflated head."

Her jest roused in me a low chuckle. "I can't help but boast. I get a kick out of winning." She had no idea to what degree.

She hiked her nose and planted one hand on her hip. "For your information, I'm not a sore loser, but your smug attitude gives me the urge to serve you a slice of humble pie. I request a rematch."

Roxanne's ease around me bloomed like a rose. Mission accomplished. I slipped my hands into my pockets and slanted forward. "And I cannot wait until our next replay."

An electric force ignited the atmosphere between us. Oh, she felt it too because, in the next instant, she dipped her face to hide her blush and fished for her keys inside her purse. "I'll see you tomorrow."

Tomorrow couldn't come fast enough. "Goodnight, Roxanne."

Once she drove off, I moseyed toward the restaurant. Roxanne expressed herself tonight far greater than in the last few weeks, sharing with me personal details of her life and family. Progress. Soon enough I'd have her embarking on her dream job, right before snatching the opportunity away and breaking her heart.

"I see you've enjoyed a fantastic evening, sir." The valet tipped his hat. "I'll call for your driver to come around."

No wonder he remarked on my mood. My cheeks hurt from smiling. Perhaps I relished our night more than necessary. Her smile, her laughter, and her mere presence lured me into instant addiction. I had a plan to see through, and the last time Roxanne broke my defenses nearly destroyed me. *Stay in the game, Max.*

****

"Are you out of your mind?" Georgina flounced the length of the room and shook her jittery hands. Her navy-striped skirt resembled an inverted umbrella and swished as she stomped back and forth.

Monday rolled in, and I'd allowed Roxanne the rest of the day off. Grateful, she all but sang her luck having me for a boss. Luck held little relevance, but I confessed no such truth. Georgina popping in prompted the real reason I sent Roxanne home. "You once said you'd do anything for me?"

"Yes." She froze in her tracks and pointed a finger my way. "But I didn't mean for you to involve me in your schemes." She crossed her arms over her white blouse and bristled. "I'm glad Roxanne's the last on your weird revenge list. Your whole master plan has cost you your sanity."

"Do you hear yourself?" I propped against the office printer and stroked my temples. "I'm asking for a simple favor—call a hotel and make a booking, not rob a bank."

She snatched the notepad off the desk and waved the booklet containing Roxanne's personal information in the air. "You call impersonating another person simple?"

Not impersonate her in person, but an easy matter dealt with over the phone. No big deal. Besides, I took care of the important part by giving Roxanne a fake number she assumed belonged to the hotel. My trustworthy tech guy pretended to secure her accommodation. To help finalize my little ploy, I asked Georgina to contact the real hotel and secure an actual room.

"Where are your hired helpers for such a task?" She tossed the notepad and the spiral booklet landed on the table with a thunk. "Why burden me?"

"You're a woman. You're the same age as Roxanne. You, my dear friend, are the perfect candidate. Besides, do you have any idea how tiring it is hiring people to go along with my schemes?"

"Oh, poor Max." Her monotone voice held no sympathy. "How exhausted you must feel meddling with people's lives." Georgina huffed, stamping to Roxanne's desk. She hoisted the phone, punched in the number, and shot me a scowl. "My name's Roxanne Hastings, I'm calling to secure a room for myself and my boss."

The voice on the other end sounded muffled.

Georgina grabbed a pen and paper. "A one-bedroom suite for myself and Mr. Parker." She glared, her nose scrunched in distaste. "Yes, correct. Perfect, a penthouse suite sounds great." She jotted on an adhesive note and thanked the person on the other end.

"See, how easy, right? Let's open Roxanne's online planner and change the fake booking number my guy gave her."

"You're a terrible man, Max Parker." She dropped the pen into a glass jar with markers. "Now I've done you a favor." Her grin mirrored a cat who stole the cream. "You owe me."

Quid pro quo. Fair. I perched on the desk's edge. "I'm all ears."

She echoed a sigh; the act caused her shoulders to drop. "My aunt's getting married, and I'm hoping you'll accompany me to her wedding."

"Again?" Good grief, how many aisles had her aunt prowled? "What're we up to, husband number seven?"

"Number five." She flopped into the seat and the leather squeaked. "So I take it you're not inclined to go?"

And miss out on the event of the season? "Of course, I'll go. Aunt Esme throws the best parties. Count me in."

She rolled her eyes, but humor sparkled in them. "I'm glad you're excited for her nuptials." She eased forward and encased her hand in mine. "Thank you. I mean it. Once I tell my folks I'm bringing you, they'll stop hinting at eligible bachelors since they abandoned all hope for our future long ago."

I cocked a brow. "They threw in the towel, huh."

A low hum reverberated as Roxanne's computer booted. "Not any towel, but Egyptian cotton."

Her jest rolled through my stomach and had me snorting. Mr. and Mrs. Belmont held high hopes for our relationship. On many events, we defended our friendship status, but they'd brush away our reason as a mere hilarious joke. "I'm sure the tabloids have assumed worse than your folks." I'd grown accustomed to our pictures splashed on magazine covers, pages worth of gossip, and a fabricated *friend* or *source close to the family* who detailed all aspects of our lives. For a laugh, Georgina and I read articles to one another and joked over our latest scandal.

She fiddled with an expensive diamond bracelet on her wrist. "Yes, and as opposed to those tabloids, my parents wish to see me *happy* with a person richer than them."

Her impassive tone gave her away. Raised in high-class society, Georgina grew up on a short leash, and her parents controlled every aspect of her life from her social groups to her future goals. Similar to a pet bird in a beautiful, gilded cage, she clasped the world at her fingertips but lacked freedom. "Are you looking for a wealthy man?"

She peered into nothing, trapped in a daze. "He can have a career as a schoolteacher for all I care, as long as he's the real deal. No way I'll follow Aunt Esme and march down the aisle a fifth time." Georgina logged into the company computer but froze, staring at the screen.

What on earth snagged her attention? "What's wrong?"

Her gaze never strayed from the screen. "There's a photo on her screensaver. Parents, perhaps siblings and children, even the pet dog's in the picture." I assumed she studied each exuberant detail. "She's real. I mean, she has a life, people who love her…"

I kept my spine straight and ignored the screen. No chance a photo warmed me. Bad enough logic clouded whenever I neared Roxanne. "Are you trying to guilt-trip me?"

"Don't point at me." One manicured nail poked my leg. "Let's hope your ice-cold heart's melting."

"Funny." I flashed my teeth without mirth.

"Haven't I supported you?" Her head tipped, showcasing an expression all too familiar. "Alex, Brent, Trevor, and Olivia. I never stopped you from getting your revenge. But don't lie to me or yourself. Roxanne's different; she always has been. I assumed…"

"What?" Our chat headed in an irksome route. I kept my jaw constricted.

Her shoulder raised in a hesitant gesture. "Once done exacting revenge on the others, you'd find Roxanne and pursue…"

My muscles tensed. I'd have to spit out the words for her. "What? Attempt an actual relationship?"

She blinked and stated the obvious. "Well, yes."

I nearly toppled off the table. "Have you lost your mind!"

"Me, lost my mind? You of all people have the nerve." She smirked and reared her chin in her usual stubborn way. "Whether you believe me or not, you've carried a torch for her for years."

Carried a torch? Yeah, and I planned to use the same torch to burn her dreams to the ground. "I'm manipulating her. Not the right way to attempt a relationship."

She leaped out of her seat, palms flush on the desk. "So quit playing games. You've got your revenge on the others. I wish you'd put the same drive into a real future the same way you do these schemes."

Wow, she fired shot after shot. "Every person desires revenge; it's human nature. Some people go no further than dream while others act." A lump blocked my larynx. My suffering impacted every aspect of my life—my self-esteem, my trust in people, my honesty with my mother, *everything.*

Her nostrils flared. She circled the desk and confronted me. "And you're the type to act. Feel good about yourself?"

My lips twitched. "Feels good? No, it feels *great* to turn the tables. The others culminated to this point. To her." I snared her shoulders and squeezed. "They all harassed me, but Roxanne messed with my mind, my soul...my trust. She ruined me." I released her and swallowed the prickle in my voice. "I will not find peace until they've all paid, including Roxanne."

"You're wrong. Sure, these schemes render brief triumph, but not true joy, Max." Her gentle fingers removed a strand of unnatural dark hair from my view. "I say this because I care."

My best friend. My only friend. Georgina welcomed me into her circle, not at all critical. She listened, empathized, and gave good advice.

Her bottom lip trembled. "I'd hoped we'd work all those years ago, but our relationship never stood a chance."

Our attempt at romance failed, no thanks to me, since my entire pursuit centered on the plan. After I finished Roxanne, I'd suppress her name once and for all, perhaps seek a woman to share a real future as Georgina suggested.

She cupped my bearded jaw, the seriousness in her gaze keeping me rooted to the spot. "But that was then. Just so you know, I'm over you."

One sensation struck me—relief. Nothing worse than carrying the guilt and burden of unrequited love. I'd never lied to my best friend or uplifted her spirits by having her believe I reciprocated her feelings. "You've met a man?"

"No. But I will." Determination sparkled in her eyes. "I'm ready for my prince charming."

Spots flashed in my sight. Her words struck me harder than anticipated. Not jealousy, but fear, fear I'd lose the one friendship I'd ever encountered. "Are you saying we can't be friends?"

"Of course not. Max, you're my best friend." She gripped my arms and squeezed. "How I feel has changed. Nothing else."

So, I wasn't losing my best friend, thank heavens. I held her in a hug. "You deserve the world."

"Thank you," she whispered and sniffled above my shoulder. "Same goes for you too."

Afraid to admit the words aloud, but what if I was too far gone, too damaged to find the type of life Georgina chased?

She veered back as though aware of what plagued my psyche. "Promise me you'll find love and live your life."

I raised my pinky, and she hooked mine. A juvenile tactic we'd yet to outgrow, but we'd locked fingers since our college days. "I'll try."

Chapter 5

Roxanne

Fulgurate lights and a shrill hum flipped my stomach. A giant jet taxied to an effortless stop on the apron, the familiar Parker logo on the plane's body. We'd traveled straight from our office without a spare minute to change out of my pale gray work sheath. The hot sun beat on me, tempting me to strip out of the forsaken dress. Hunter had discarded his suit jacket and tie on the drive, his top collar button undone, and shirt sleeves rolled to his elbows. Businesslike, but also relaxed.

We loitered near Hunter's limo; his flight staff already handled our luggage. Every muscle in my body coiled tightly. I'd never in my life boarded a private jet, given I observed a golden rule to abide below the earth's curvature. An unfazed Hunter—who as the wealthy son of Parker Senior had no doubt traveled by aircraft a thousand times—spoke fluent Japanese on the phone rather than behold the noise and lights around us. No clue what he discussed, but he spoke with Mr. Tsuji Katsu, the general manager based in Parker Hotel Tokyo.

My phone vibrated in my jacket pocket, and I opened Mom's text. Warmth filled my chest at the picture of my son and nephew in their pajamas, cuddled beside Dad on the sofa, popcorn in hand, and ready for their movie night. Michael planned on taking Jasmine to her ultrasound appointment in the morning, but my parents suggested they take the entire weekend to allow Jasmine proper rest. My parents already planned to babysit for Michael, but I feared they'd dread watching both little Zane and Dylan. Praise God they jumped to help when I told them of my last-minute travels to Los Angeles.

Once ushered onto the plane, I plonked into a sleek, beige leather chair and buckled myself in. Hunter chatted away on his phone, cool as a cucumber. I hooked my ankles to keep my legs stable and latched the armrests. The walls, low ceilings, and spacious seats held no effect on me. Tall lookouts or cliff edges triggered my fear of heights, but I had no idea what to expect flying thirty-five thousand feet in the sky. *Don't peer out the window. Do not peer outside!*

Hunter waved over a buxom blonde flight attendant, one hand muffling the speaker. "Scotch on the rocks, thank you."

The gorgeous woman revealed a flash of flawless teeth. "And for you, Miss Hastings?"

"Um…" A tranquilizer. I lacked the courage to voice the unusual request. "Orange juice, please."

She sauntered away. Hunter rattled off in rapid Japanese and ended the call.

His blatant scrutiny had me twisting my fingers. "What?"

"You're off the clock. I won't judge you for unwinding." He waved his hand. "There's a variety of wines and cocktails."

White noise echoed in the background and

prompted my reason to avoid alcohol. Although I fancied a nice Chianti to end the week, I'd better keep a clear head. "I'm good." I tugged the large round shade. With sunset not for a few hours, I'd prefer my view concealed.

Hunter bent forward and raised the same shade I'd lowered. "Law requires us to keep these open for takeoff and landing. Close the shade if you prefer once we're in the air."

Of course, the two flight phases I'd planned to avoid. "Why the rule?"

Head bowed, he typed away on his phone but raised his gaze to mine. "Safety reasons in case of evacuation."

Evacuation? Vertigo attacked. I yearned to inhale and exhale but refrained from hyperventilating in front of my boss. His flight attendant returned, and Hunter ordered she deliver another glass following takeoff. Takeoff? I gulped my juice in one go. Hunter arched deeper into the leather headrest and savored his beverage. Good spot. And here I occupied the chair closest to the window rather than the aisle. So foolish.

Muscles in his throat worked as he sipped his scotch and hummed in pleasure. "You're welcome to order a beverage stronger than juice."

Too tense to fake enthusiasm, I bobbed my foot. "No thanks. My stomach's full of butterflies."

He straightened in his seat. "Are you nervous?"

"A little." Out the window, dark asphalt greeted my sight. Good, still on the ground. "I've never flown."

"Never?" He leaned forward in his chair.

"Nope." Not by choice. The single-mom lifestyle made traveling hard, and no opportunity presented itself. I hadn't left my hometown, let alone visited another city or country.

He patted the expensive leather of the armrest. "We're in a safe vessel. We'll arrive in under six hours, around midnight."

Funny how words of solace worsened one's nerves. I needed a distraction, perhaps watching a movie or asking the flight attendant for a magazine or demanding Hunter swap seats right this instant! Light flashed above me, and I swallowed my scream. Goodness, I had better not jump to sounds the entire flight. No point losing my cool on account of…a seat belt sign. No problem there. I'd strapped myself in faster than my bottom hit the seat.

The pretty blonde announced takeoff.

I refused to turn toward Hunter and let him see my face mimicking a puckered, angry newborn. The engine vibrated beneath me. I directed my flinch to the window and squeezed the armrest tighter.

"Roxanne." Concern deepened Hunter's voice.

Mine, on the other hand, closed off. A loud beep sounded, and I peeked out of one eye.

Hunter unclicked his seatbelt and buckled himself in the spot beside me. "Hold my hands."

I gripped them without reservation. Heat scorched my neck. Mortified, and yet grateful for his help.

"Deep breaths, Roxanne. Breathe." His helpful command penetrated the roar of the engines.

We accelerated at an incredible speed, the momentum exceeding the race car experience my parents gifted me on my twenty-first birthday six years ago. A sinking rush dipped in my stomach. My knuckles whitened around Hunter's red ones. The aircraft steadied into a smooth glide path, the noise no longer blaring. I clenched my teeth, determined not to cry. "Oh, goodness." I released his hands and shielded my view to hide my shame. "I'm so embarrassed."

"Please, don't be." His calm voice caressed my hair.

My entire body trembled from a mix of adrenaline and mortification, and yet he sat here, reassuring me. I'd misjudged Hunter the first day we met, reducing him to some hardball boss, but he proved to be a considerate guy. After all, he ran a multinational hotel corporation. "I'm sorry. I'm such an idiot."

"Enough." He lifted my chin. "Roxanne Hastings, you're not an idiot."

We locked eyes with one another in silence. Hunter tucked a loose strand behind my ear, and his languid thumb stroke rolled a delightful shiver down my spine.

"Your drink, Mr. Parker."

I swerved away as though zapped with electricity. My gaze landed everywhere except on the flight attendant. How long had she pottered there and played audience to our staring match? Her mirth conveyed her true thoughts; she believed she disturbed an intimate moment between us.

The attendant disappeared, and Hunter turned to me and raised his scotch glass. "Here, the drink will help."

I grimaced. My introduction to scotch in high school ended with me vomiting half the night away, and I promised to never drink such a horrid beverage again. "I'm not big on scotch."

"Trust me, it'll calm your nerves." He transferred the round tumbler into my hands.

I took a tentative sip, and the strong liquid scorched my stomach, followed by an immediate flush of heat throughout my body. Granted, the brand I sampled tasted a lot better than whatever cheap bottle I drank back in high school, but the harsh liquor failed to convert me into a fan.

Hunter encouraged with a leveled stare. "A little more."

Again, taking a swig, I ignored the flame and let the contents warm my insides enough to ease into my seat and relax against the lush leather.

His brows drew upward. "Are you good?"

"Yes, thank you." I swallowed the ever-present burn. "Better."

Hunter grabbed his laptop from the seat in front.

The adrenaline rush dissipated in my system and left my limbs floppy. I retrieved my phone and opened my e-reader to continue a celebrity memoir I'd neglected a while ago.

Hunter resumed working on his laptop. My gaze veered from my book and scoped out my boss. Strong jaw, sharp cheekbones, thin sculpted lips. Butterflies returned in full swing but for different reasons. Consumed in his task and unaware of my perusal, he typed away on his laptop, tongue poked out to one side, making him seem younger, innocent, and so different from the short-tempered hardball boss I faced in the office. The familiar action of his poked tongue nudged me with déjà vu. Perhaps I'd seen him do this in the office.

Body listless from either the alcohol or the adrenaline roller coaster, my heavy eyelids kept drooping to the point I abandoned the book and snuggled deeper into the cozy seat.

"Roxanne."

I stole a peek.

Hunter's handsome face hovered above me.

"Are we here?" My goodness, I fell asleep. *Please, God, I hope I never snored.*

He packed his laptop into his suitcase. "We sure are." He nudged his head to the exit where the flight attendant stood ready to bid us farewell. "Our limo's outside."

"Right." I gathered my purse and followed Hunter off the plane, squinting at the jet lights in the pitch-dark night. A crescent moon loomed high above. Crisp air filled my lungs and woke me faster than hot coffee, scattering goose pimples on my arms.

We hopped into a limo, and I squirmed in my seat, filled with excitement over my first visit to another state. The majority of our ride consisted of highway roads and overpasses. Nighttime made absorbing the scenery difficult, but thanks to the streetlights, I distinguished many palm trees on the harbor freeway.

We arrived at a five-star hotel and set foot in the lobby. With the online planner opened on my phone, I read out the reference number to the concierge.

"Yes, we have you here in our system." The woman slid two key cards across the counter. "A one-bedroom suite for Mr. Hunter Parker and Miss Roxanne Hastings."

"Excuse me?" Hunter piped in, comparable to a deer caught in headlights. "Roxanne? What's going on?"

My heartbeat grew sluggish. I slanted closer to the woman. "Don't you mean two separate suites on the same floor? I booked two separate rooms."

The lady typed into her computer. "I'm sorry, Miss Hastings. We have you here on our system: a one-bedroom suite for two guests."

I smoothed my hands on the high desk. "You'll fix it. Right?"

She typed away. "Let me see what I can do."

Another fresh mess for my boss to add to my list of wrongdoings. "Hunter, I booked us in separate rooms."

Hunter's nostrils flared, features tense. "I'm sure they'll handle it."

"I'm afraid not, sir," the woman threw in. "Due to the fundraiser event, we're booked out."

Frown lines creased together on his forehead. "Are you certain?"

"I double-checked the system." The lady flicked her hand toward the computer and smirked my way, eyeing my boss. Her secret gaze spoke volumes—*If I worked for this man, I'd do the same, honey.* I bet her mischievous expression relayed those exact words.

Her delusions needed unveiling. "I expect you fix it, or I'll demand to speak to your manager."

"It's fine." Hunter clucked his tongue. "Please send our luggage to our room."

He'd lost his mind. "But, Hunter?"

"It's all right." He leaned his shoulder into mine and whispered, "We'll sort the mess out later. Right now, I'm exhausted." A husky sound accompanied his weary-riddled voice.

I blinked out of my daze and followed him to the elevator. To our shared room? My eyes closed against the relentless pressure building behind my lids.

We passed our bags in the foyer and entered a

grand suite. Golden sheer curtains decorated floor-to-ceiling glass windows and afforded a magnificent city view. A large bar occupied one corner, framing the scene for the sofa lounge and round coffee table opposite a grand window. No shutters. Whoever took the lounge volunteered for a horrible night's sleep. No way I'd allow my boss to suffer due to my error.

"I'll take the sofa," I called out.

Hunter stepped out of a doorway I assumed led to a bedroom and headed into the lounge area, spotting the same dilemma I happened upon. "You won't sleep well. The sun will hit in a few hours." He kneaded the nape of his neck. "Roxanne, let me take the sofa, and you can take the bedroom." He thumbed toward the doorway far behind him.

I ambled to the bedroom and stole a peek. Decorative silk pillows piled high on a large king-size mattress, a focal point among the opulent setting. "No, Hunter. This is my mistake, so I insist on taking the sofa."

What if he believed I booked our room on purpose? Goodness, I hoped not. He'd no doubt lose all respect.

"If you insist." He passed me one final glance and rolled our suitcases into the bedroom. "I'll leave our luggage in the ensuite bathroom."

The weak grin I returned in kind gesture dissolved into a pout. Beneath the coffee table sat a woolen throw blanket and I draped it over my makeshift bed for the night. Tapping my foot, I considered my choices. Shutting the sheer curtains resolved nothing. Removing the cushioned seats and rearranging them on the floor might work, but I bet my back would be cursing me come morning. If only I could reposition this lounge.

Hunter! With Hunter's help, we could transpose the lounge and block the sunrise. I hurried inside the bedroom to reveal my fantastic plan but stumbled short at a pair of biceps the size of cantaloupes and a naked torso corded with thick muscle. Black viscose pants rode low on his hips, the waistband snug against the defined V in his pelvis. Unfazed by my stare, he strolled to the bed. Sweet mercy. His taught backside put Michelangelo's statue to shame.

My pulse racketed in my throat. "Hunter. I have an idea. Let's rotate the sofa, then there's no issue." And with his enormous size and strength, we'd realign the sofa in a flash.

He flung the duvet with a sharp whoosh and ran one hand through his dark hair. "Roxanne. It's one thirty. I'm too tired to rearrange the hotel furniture. Are you sure you wouldn't rather take the bedroom and let me sleep on the sofa?"

No, how could I let this man suffer a horrible night sleep all because of my error? I bit my inner cheek.

"Unless of course you'd rather share this bed with me?" He landed on the bed, arms behind the crook of his neck, and cocked a brow. "As long as you promise not to bite."

I faked a chuckle to smother my nervousness. "Ha, ha, real funny, Hunter." I locked myself in the ensuite bathroom and extracted my toothbrush and moisturizer from my suitcase. Now was not the time for jokes, but the crazy thing was he seemed serious just now.

Oh no, no, no. Please no. I lifted my pajamas and cringed. Since I'd planned to reside in my own room, I'd packed the pair I received last year on Mother's Day—pale purple and strewn with little cartoon kitten prints. *Kill me now!*

Changed into my pj's, I flossed my teeth and assessed myself in the mirror. The once cute purple kitten on my shirt mocked me. Rolling the unstylish three-quarter pants worsened the capris, and I huffed, shaking them loose again. Hunter sprawled against the pillows out there, presenting himself as an all-you-can-eat macho buffet, and here I donned crazy cat-lover pajamas. Not that I desired to slink into a sexy piece or anything, but I bet women sashayed to his bed in skimpy lingerie or their birthday suits, as opposed to me who embodied a frumpy mess. *Wait...so I want to seduce him?* I ground my teeth and scowled at my image in the round mirror. My boss and the word *seduce*—or any s-word—equaled a big, fat no-no. What I wished for most, lay back home in my washed basket stash; my dignity attached to a plain charcoal gray sleep shirt. A pajama nightdress less inglorious than cute cats.

I switched off the light and opened the door. A pitch-black room equaled my best friend, but I stumbled upon no such luck. Bedside lamp lit, Hunter lay on the bed, one hand behind his head while holding his phone to his face. Please concentrate on the screen. *Concentrate!* He neglected to heed my silent request and lowered dark-framed glasses over his nasal bridge as his gaze roamed my entire body.

Oh, please stop looking at me! Heat burned my cheeks, and I snatched the spare pillow beside his, shielding my kittens. "Good night," I uttered and turned, close to curling into a ball and groaning. A hushed snicker erupted in the silence, a giveaway he tried his hardest not to combust. "Hunter?"

Wheezing. He wheezed with laughter.

I whirled and gave myself whiplash. "Are you serious?"

"The…" he choked out, setting aside his glasses on the nightstand. "The cat prints threw me."

I shot him a serious glare. "Will you grow up! They're pajamas." A little maturity from the multi-billionaire over here, please.

The single word, *pajamas*, triggered a new round of fits. "You're right." His voice betrayed him. "They're pajamas." He snorted and squinted. "Adorable pajamas."

Gripping my pillow, I whacked the plush object into my boss's head. Good move on his part setting down his glasses, otherwise they'd have flown straight off his face.

He gaped, taken aback.

I froze and waited for a scolding due to my unethical conduct.

His features relaxed, and his gaze narrowed into tiny slits. "Oh, yeah?" He grabbed his own pillow, took a swing, and we surged into a full-blown pillow fight.

In the short period I'd worked with Hunter, I'd never seen him carefree or spirited. His grin lit his entire countenance. His laughter boomed in the room, the sound deep and genuine, and he…enjoyed himself. My chest warmed, and my heart rate spiked. His playful demeanor and infectious laughter livened me to my core, a euphoric glow I hadn't welcomed in years. We laughed until our lungs hurt.

"Okay, okay." He collapsed onto the mattress, panting. "Surrender."

I fell onto the mattress, panting for breath.

Hunter turned in my direction. "Let's get some

rest."

Our night out at dinner and bowling differed from tonight...his smile, his cackle, and his entire persona reminded me of a time long ago. Without his glasses and from this angle, if I squinted, I swear he bore a resemblance to...*oh no you don't, Roxanne.* False hope due to my cursed nostalgia made me see a minor resemblance to the boy from my past. I dreaded when these bittersweet memories plagued me. Every flashback of Max resulted in sobs, and I refused to pay my misery any attention. No tears, no regrets...not when I still floated on cloud nine. "Goodnight, Hunter."

Taking my pillow, I made my way to the sofa. Thanks to my earlier nap on the jet, I lay wide awake, not in the least bit tired. Through the floor-to-ceiling window, the stars embellished the navy sky. I replayed the details of my and Hunter's pillow brawl, and for the first time in a long time, I smiled as I drifted asleep.

****

The next morning, I located a nearby hairdresser to preen my hair for tonight. The stylist excelled my expectations, volumizing my short hair into a twisted updo. I also visited a salon for a manicure, a treat I hadn't indulged in years. Back home, the closest pampering to a manicure occurred when washing the bathroom with warm bleach water.

I returned to our hotel by four o'clock, allowing myself a solid hour to apply makeup and change. A vibration trembled my purse, and swiping the key card on the door handle, I extracted my phone and strolled into the hotel room while reading the text from Mom. I smacked into a solid, wet wall. Gasping aloud, I stumbled backward, my phone bouncing to the carpet.

Not a wall, but a dripping wet Hunter wrapped in a towel from the hips down. I kept my gaze trained on his face, although in my peripheral vision his broad naked chest and sculpted pecs accelerated my pulse. "Sorry, I should have called first."

"Nonsense." He placed his hand on where the towel tucked into his hip, holding the white fabric in place as he lowered and retrieved my phone. "We're sharing this room. You have every right to enter."

I prayed my face produced no sweat sheen, although my body temperature increased. "Yes, which reminds me." I took the phone and slipped the device back into my purse. "I have to head downstairs and see if they've managed to fix our situation." A lie. The fact a single towel stood in the way of my boss's complete nakedness constituted my urgency to leave.

"No point." He gripped my elbow, ceasing my movements. "I spoke with them earlier and there's no availability."

I slid my arm from his grip. Bad enough the sight of his near nakedness last night sprouted butterflies in my stomach, but this plus his strong, warm grip added to the mix made my head spin. "What a shame. I better get dressed."

He nodded toward the towel. "Same here."

I refused to follow his gaze to his pelvis and concentrated on the droplets dewed in his midnight hair. Not the slightest hue blushed his cheeks. The man wore confidence like a badge of honor. "Let me collect my dress." I headed straight for the walk-in closet. "Would you be needing anything before I use the bathroom?" I called behind me as I unhooked the zipped garment bag. I found the gown online on a local classifieds site for half the original retail price—a substitute prom dress advertised brand new and tagged. Spare prom dress? Here I scoured the internet for a gown in my budget while women out there afforded secondary dresses for their events. Although my salary improved, I'd rather save extra money into saving for my boy's college fund than splurge.

Drawers opening and closing resounded behind me. "No, I'll change in here once you're in the bathroom."

Without passing him a glance, I sprinted for the immaculate ensuite and shut myself inside.

"By the way, take your time." His shadow passed over the frosted glass door as he spoke. "I'll meet you downstairs at the bar."

Good, the sooner he left, the sooner I'd come to my senses.

I hit play on a video tutorial for blush hacks since I forgot mine. A lady on the screen smeared lipstick on her cheekbones in a fancy technique, using an expensive brush tool. My makeup case contained no such tool, and if I followed her method with my fingers, I'd mirror a clown. I set my phone to one side and trusted in an old method Great-Ma taught me…pinching.

Makeup finished, I unzipped the garment bag and slipped into the deep red dress with a halter-cross front and keyhole detail over the midriff. A skin-tight bodice splayed in an elegant fit and flare design with an above-knee split revealing a hint of leg. The cut-out back epitomized both allure and demure, and the matching red heels complemented the gown.

I grabbed a champagne gold clutch and all but

sailed out of the room, determined to embrace the event since a night out seldom happened in my world.

Hunter lounged at a bar, scotch in hand.

My stomach performed little flips as guests seated near him turned first.

He too followed. His features tensed when I strode to where he perched, and his dark irises swept my attire, rousing flutters low in my belly. The stark desire I discerned in Hunter suspended my breath. He stared without a break in contact I'd deem creepy from another guy, but rather than creep me out, he stirred bravery inside me, casting aside all my doubts and fears.

His gaze rested on my own, his smile teasing. "Good to see you're not dressed in kittens."

"Don't start." Hunter Parker grew a sense of humor...about time he lightened up.

He snatched my wrist when I turned, and I met his gaze over my shoulder.

"You're stunning, Roxanne."

"Thank you." I too assessed his attire. A shiny, perfect-fit suit and black bow tie. He wore the tuxedo as if doing the garment a favor, but no way could I miss this opportunity to strike a comeback following his *kittens* remark. "As for you, I've seen worse."

Chuckling, he sidled off his seat, and a gentle hand on the small of my back led me into a grand ballroom filled with people all dressed in couture gowns and tuxedos. We bounced from person to person as Hunter introduced me to many colleagues and associates. Waiters circled the grand room, trays of beverages and hors d'oeuvres in hand, teasing our appetite for what awaited us later where they'd serve a lavish dinner and call onto the stage a famous actor who'd give a talk on cancer.

We approached Jean-Philippe Lemaigre, and in true French demeanor, he greeted me with a double-air kiss. Praise God I kept composed instead of bursting into a little teenybopper who spotted her favorite boy band. Both men conversed while I took mental notes of important details. Jean-Philippe accepted Hunter's proposal to see through his hotel design and arranged to meet in person to discuss plans, then apologized for the interruption and dashed over to another partygoer waving for his attention.

Classical music filled the room and the crowd proceeded onto the dance floor, many people brushing past Hunter and me, who stood off to the side. I racked my brain for a topic of discussion to distract us.

Hunter deposited his finished scotch glass onto an empty tray a waiter carried and leaned closer to me, one hand held out. "Care to dance?"

I placed my hand in his and followed his lead. "Go easy on me. Formal dancing's not my forte."

"A ballroom virgin?" He cocked his head, his dark irises alight with humor. "What style of dancing are you used to?"

Our close contact swooshed my gown against his tux. "Any possibility they'll play old-school hip-hop?"

He bowed his forehead, but I spotted the way he fought back a smile. "Don't fret. Mimic my moves."

Hunter made a great dance partner, and we waltzed together in seamless flow. He kept his sights on me throughout the entire song, raising a brow as a hint to change course, and squeezing my hand to signal a spin. With one final twirl into his chest, he dipped me in an elegant finish as the song ended, our noses inches apart. My heart fluttered in a relentless frenzy. Brown irises fixated on my lips. He dipped his chin, and my eyes flickered closed on their own accord.

"Hunter Parker, get outta town!" a loud southern accent intruded.

Hunter straightened us, and I weaved on my feet. We greeted an old man dressed all in white, complete with a fedora hat as though he pranced out of a Kentucky Derby time warp. What might have happened prior to Colonel here appearing? Hunter's lips had feathered my own, a whisper introduction of a kiss. Dizziness struck, and I dug my toes into my heels for composure.

Hunter, on the other hand, held a firm posture, in no way bothered while asking about his friend's health. He gave the sense he'd returned from washing his hands or a less mundane task. A kiss probably meant nothing to him. I bet he'd kissed countless women without a care. As for me, I wouldn't have escaped unscathed, but retained each detail and dwelled over every second in the late hours of the night.

"Meet Roxanne Hastings, my assistant." Hunter smiled, his demeanor no different than in the office.

I shook hands with Mr. Southern Stranger, the action robotic, not catching his name or their conversation, but thanks to this old man and his perfect timing, Hunter and I prevented dooming our work relationship.

Chapter 6

Max
Ten years ago

Gym class. My least favorite subject. Bad enough the entire school stared whenever I gimped into the hallway, however, in Phys Ed, I transformed into a circus monkey for their entertainment. Coach offered to sit me out on practicals. In fact, he insisted, but I preferred to participate and not use my foot as an excuse to quit. Besides, how boring to plunk on the bleachers alone all lesson.

Today we lined along the wall inside our school gymnasium, ready to run laps. A few guys closest to me slinked to the side, their blatant grimaces conveying their desperation. *Separate yourself from contagious Limp.* They'd heard of clubfoot, right?

Ignoring them, I stretched. Due to my deformity, the lack of calf muscle in my right leg attracted scrutiny.

Clipboard in one hand and metal whistle in the other, Coach Johnson approached, his large stomach stretched Skorpios, our Scorpion mascot, printed on his pale blue polo. "Up for a sprint, Fields?"

"Yes, coach, my leg's fine." Please don't tell me to sit out. My doctor encouraged exercise, as long as I understood my limits.

Coach squeezed my shoulder. "Okay, kid, but stay out of the way of my cross-country stars, and take a break if your leg bothers you." He briskly walked to the gym's sideline and blew his whistle.

Polished hardwood floors squeaked beneath my orthopedic sneakers when I took off in a jog. No way I'd finish an entire set, but the slow and steady pace worked unused muscle without inducing pain. Classmates passed me and ran the entire length, several onto their second lap. Focused on the basketball hoop, I accomplished one lap. A few students rushed toward me in the opposite direction and zeroed in on my foot, their wide-eyed expressions a dead giveaway, expecting me to do no more than hobble around. I bit my inner cheek to rein in my amusement.

Lithe legs in navy shorts sprinted in my path, firm breasts encased in a tight white tank top bouncing in rhythm. All previous humor evaporated. Roxanne, the one person not curious over my feet, but gazing into my eyes.

"Loser," a male voice swept past me.

Blunt force clobbered into my bad leg. The floor raced to meet me. My hands endured the brunt of the fall. My wrists throbbed from the impact. White-hot pain encased my ankle. Obnoxious guffaws echoed in the gymnasium. I cringed, and drew my knee, lifting my pant leg to assess the damage. Red and painful.

"Fields, you all right?" Coach Johnson's voice boomed.

I raised my chin to answer. A jolt shocked my body.

Roxanne. She'd not continued in her lap but hovered there the whole time.

Coach Jonson awaited my response, his gaze on my injured leg. "I'm fine, Coach. Ankle's a little sore."

He tsked, hands thwacking his knees. "Doesn't seem little to me, boy. Did you get in the way of my runners?"

No point in telling tales since nobody put a stop to their cruelty. "No, a student tripped me. I didn't see who though."

Coach straightened to his full height and observed the room, his gaze pausing on Roxanne. "Did you see?"

The shake of her head swayed her long, blonde hair. "Sorry, Coach, I didn't."

She fooled him with her genuine tone, but not me. I bet she collaborated with whoever caused my stumble, no doubt in on the little prank. No one else from her clique participated in gym class today, but their fawners spread far and wide in school, which meant the culprit could be any one of these little wannabees.

Coach waved his clipboard. "Roxanne, help Max here to the nurse's office."

A spark lit her eyes. "Yes, Coach."

Roxanne...help me? "Not necessary, Coach." She'd no doubt play a despicable prank on our way there.

He pointed to my leg. "You need ice, pronto, and I need to get back to my lesson."

"I'll make sure he sees the nurse." Again, her enthusiasm prickled my nerves. She outdid herself in her attempt to impress our school coach, but I bought none of it.

Coach Johnson winked. "Atta girl." He blew his whistle and reassembled the class. For their next activity, he ordered them to gather on the football field.

Roxanne and I remained silent as students exited the side door. Alone with the girl who contributed to my current dilemma. She held out her arm, her hand reminiscent of hot coals. Indifferent to her gesture, I planted both palms on the glossy floor and hauled myself to a stand. Wrists tender and a sharp burn lancing through my ankle, I strained my jaw and suppressed a protest.

"Careful." Roxanne curled an arm around my waist. She stood no taller than five-four, her hip lower than mine. Her breast, supple and full, mashed into my rib. My pulse thrummed. Scents of jasmine, freesia, and roses drifted to my nose. She smelled incredible. To my chagrin, her support eased the pain, and leaning onto her, I hobbled out of the room. In the hallway, I broke away to leverage my weight against the walls and lockers. Roxanne grasped the hint but kept close by my side. "You can leave. I'll manage."

Queen Bee flicked her hair and strolled in her usual dominant stride. "I promised Coach I'd take you to the nurse."

What the heck? "Sure, since you promised." My mockery triggered no response. I focused my gaze out the window, on birds swooping in the air. "First the janitor's closet, now gym class, why this sudden interest in helping me?"

Roxanne kept her gaze ahead, her throat bouncing.

I hopped along, waiting for a response, one line to decipher her motives. Since our last encounter a few weeks ago, I'd brooded over the event until bombarded with a migraine. Dead silence. Cheerleader here gave nothing away. We approached my locker, and I sank against the cold metal. "I'm not going to nurse Calvin;

she'll call my mom."

She blinked, her lush mouth opening and closing in a struggle to spit out whatever she attempted to say. "But your foot—"

"My exact point! My mom will have questions." I shook my head. "I haven't told her how you and your friends harass me. It'll break her heart." And Mom had suffered enough heartbreak in one lifetime. First, my biological father abandoned my mother the day she gave birth to me, then she'd slaved away to cover costs for several doctors and specialists, every penny earned spent on physical exams, medical therapy, casts, and foot braces. But concluding the recommended Ponseti treatment, we received further bad news when I relapsed when starting high school. Mom worked her butt off to cover the expenses of my upcoming correction surgery.

Roxanne's features paled, petite nostrils flaring. She glanced at her feet, puffed out a breath, and peered into my eyes once more. "What do I tell Coach?"

"Nothing. Not as though he'll check in." The sooner I got away from her, the better. "Go."

The flush to her profile deepened in…shame? She retreated a step, rubbing at her arms although the temperature nowhere neared cold.

"Take care." Subsequent to those two syllables, she bolted down the hallway.

Take care? Take care! *This* from a girl whose friends victimized me at every opportunity. Yes, Roxanne's mean-girl ways might have vanished, but she still hung around those guys which made her guilty by association for standing by the same people who mistreated me, and the more attention she paid me…the less safe I felt.

****

The clock ticked above the door and filled the quiet room. I situated my pen on the oak wood table and scanned students seated, noses stuck in their worksheets. My ankle ached beneath the desk. Coach Johnson's earlier suggestion regarding ice rang in my ears. Served me right for not listening.

Answers in order, and with nothing else to do, I extracted the watch Richard had gifted me last night from my pocket. The mesmeric gold ornate design flashed visuals of men in top hats and overcoats, transported in their horses and buggies. A valuable piece of history sat secured in my hands, a timepiece from Richard's lineage no less. I flipped the disc-shaped object over to observe the cursive letters. A.W.P.

Richard explained the initials represented Alistair William Parker, an ancestor. Super cool. I hesitated to place the watch in my pocket this morning when leaving for school, afraid to lose such a treasured gift, but glad I carried the comforting keepsake.

The bell rang, and people sprang for the exit, except Olivia who sat at the front desk and simpered my way. First Roxanne aided my butt, and now Olivia's interest. What were these girls up to?

I waited for everyone to clear out rather than have the impatient stampede mow me down in their rush out the door. Miss Staley minced from table to table and collected our quiz sheets, her nose scrunched in distaste when she snatched mine. Poor Miss Staley—still disgruntled because I corrected her in front of the class months ago. She'd taught on the topic of Chinese dynasties, and I pointed out she'd specified the wrong period for the Shang dynasty. The entire class jibed at her small hiccup. I never meant to humiliate her, but since I made the mistake of correcting her, she'd acted harsher than usual.

In my peripheral view, Olivia dallied in smearing her lip gloss.

Miss Staley gathered her purse behind her desk. "You'll remember to shut the door behind you, Max?"

"Yes, miss." Teachers overlooked the fact I left the room last, not bothering to wait.

Miss Staley left without a word to Olivia.

Not keen to stall, I packed away my pens into their metal tin case.

"Hey, Limp." Olivia perched herself on the edge of my desk.

"What do you want?" I unzipped my backpack and tossed my items inside.

She leered over the shiny object situated between us on the table. "Nice watch. An antique?" She gave a low whistle. "This little gem has to be eighteen-karat gold, right?" Olivia snatched my gift.

I shot from my desk. "Hey, give it back!"

She ogled the object in her hands. "What's wrong, Limp?" She retreated and put space between me and the watch. "I can't check it out?"

"I mean it. Give back my watch, Olivia."

She yanked her top and tucked my pocket watch inside her pink, lace bra. "What're you going to do, huh?"

I hopped forward. Pain shot up my leg and I controlled my facial expression, not to give away the fact I'd injured my foot in case she made a run for it.

Her shaped brow arched. "Don't you dare lay a hand on me! I won't hesitate to scream, you pervert."

My fists clenched and unclenched by my sides. "Give back my watch."

"Yeah, good luck with your poor excuse. Once I tell a teacher you shoved your hand down my top, they'll suspend you. Plus, Alex will kill you."

"Where are you going?" Ignoring the pain, I picked up my feet, but she raced ahead. "Olivia, please. Give it back!"

She threw a wink over her shoulder. "Thanks, Limp. I'm sure your little treasure here will pay for my new prom shoes."

"Olivia!" I raked my hands through my hair.

She blew me a kiss and took off in a sprint I possessed no hope of matching.

Unbelievable! I hobbled into the bathroom, turned the faucet, and splashed cold water on my face. In my reflection, a threat of tears reddened my eyes. My lungs tightened. I shut off the water and hobbled into the hallway toward the office. Inside, I found Miss Staley leaning against the tall office desk. "Please, Miss Staley, help me."

"What's the matter?" She filled out a form in her hands, avoiding eye contact.

"The watch I held in class." My voice cracked. "Olivia stole it."

Her pen stilled on the clipboard she held. "What watch?"

"I had a gold pocket watch on me in your last class." As if she missed spotting the priceless item when collecting our worksheets. "It's an antique, and Olivia plans on pawning it."

She dabbed her pen against her chin. "Olivia King, the girl walking around in designer labels, needs to pawn your pocket watch for cash?" Miss Staley stared, deadpan. "Yeah, right. If you'll excuse me, I've paperwork to finalize, and I'm in no mood for games."

"I'm not playing a game." My voice rose an octave, awarding me a hush from the secretary behind the desk. "My father gave me the watch last night."

Miss Staley clamped down as though fighting back a chuckle. "Hmm, from what I hear, you don't speak to your father, Max."

"Wh-what?" I stumbled, unsure what she rambled over.

She slammed her clipboard on the counter and sneered. "The faculty here understand the circumstances of your home life."

The secretary bounced her eyebrows in silent accord.

I tightened my fists by my sides. "Not my biological father, you idiot! It's my mother's fiancé."

She gawked in mute silence.

The secretary clucked her tongue and typed into her computer.

Great job, Max. Give her further reason to resent you. "I'm sorry, miss."

"I've heard enough." She clasped the form to her chest and flounced out of the room.

My gaze on the ceiling, I groaned aloud.

The secretary's wide forehead bobbed above the desk, and again she shushed me.

I surged from the office and barged past students, the pain in my ankle incomparable to the throbbing inside my chest. My stomach coiled into a tight knot.

Sweat coated my palms.

In less than one day I destroyed Richard's custom, a priceless item handed down for generations, gone. And for the first time, I'd referred to him as my father. The word sprung forth, natural and without forethought. Fat tears dripped off my chin. I perceived Richard as a father, but he'd be ashamed to call me his son.

Chapter 7

Roxanne
Ten years ago

"Where are we going?" Frigid air bit into my skin and spread goose pimples down my arms. Cars honked in the distance. People bypassed me on the footpath as I struggled to match Olivia's fast pace. "Olivia!"

She darted ahead, hair whipping in the wind, and when she turned, her features grew mischievous. "Hurry, Roxanne!"

Ambushed at my locker when the bell rang for lunch, Olivia demanded we skip school and leave straight away. Other than bark orders to turn left or right, she left me clueless as to our destination. I bet Alex stormed the school grounds searching for us and itched to give us an earful when we returned.

Olivia scanned several complexes aligned in the street. We'd never shopped on the mall's outskirts. So far, we'd passed an old record store, a tobacconist, a bakery, and a shoe repair shop. No way we'd find a boutique out here containing apparel Olivia credited worthy.

"Here's the place!" She peered inside a window adorned with neon lights.

The neon-lit shop name stopped me short. "A pawnshop?"

"Come on." She waved, all but bursting through the doors.

Olivia rushed to the counter and waited in line. My muscles tensed, the ice-cold temperature in here worse than outside.

Several pieces perched on display—TVs, radios, and speakers labeled with large price tags. Handcrafted wooden boats filled one entire wall, musical instruments sat showcased on several racks, and miscellaneous jewelry lay secured inside a glass cabinet. Cobwebs shrouded ceiling corners, and a sweet musk reminded me of those old books in my grandma's house.

For Olivia to pawn items for cash, the Kings' financial problems had to have taken a turn for the worse.

A boxed board game sat among a pile of children's books. The Robinson kids begged me to play their boring games whenever I babysat. My smile evaporated, and I dropped the box back into its place. No matter what good deeds I performed, a filthy revulsion prevailed deep inside. I offered to do extra house chores, volunteered at my local old folks' home, and provided free babysitting for the Robinsons and other parents who lived on my street.

What a beautiful soul.

We're so proud of you.

We need generous people like you in our world.

Parents I babysat for, and the nurse staff all applauded me. But their kind words intensified the dread in my stomach. Hypocrite. Hypocrite. *Hypocrite.* The lone word played a mantra in my ear.

Instead of getting lost in Max's eyes in gym class, I

should have watched out for him better. I had no idea who toppled him. When Max approached from the opposite path, I lost myself in his blue-green eyes. Would they sparkle if he smiled or laughed? I craved to see such an expression. Amid my zoning out, a loud thud immobilized me in my tracks. Max. On the floor. I assumed he'd fallen, if not for him informing our coach. Directed to take him to the nurse's office, I embraced the chance to help. The moment my arm encircled his waist, delicious tingles attacked my spine. The small innocent act of our joined bodies caused an instant addictive effect. As I reveled in the warmth, he detached himself in the hallway, and my lungs tightened. Max preferred to struggle without my aid and use the wall for support. Then he'd mentioned his mom.

I'm sorry. The words lodged in my constricted throat. I'd bid him farewell, and my remorse increased tenfold. *Hypocrite.*

Olivia released a pitched squeal, and I spun around.

Her hands slapped the table. "Five thousand dollars?"

The old guy winked, his toothpick jutted out between his teeth and rolled side to side. "The company brand was popular in the eighteen hundreds. The name's worth a lot. Sixteen-size, eighteen-karat gold. I have a few collectors who'd love to get their hands on this beauty."

Olivia beamed and bounced on her toes. "Did you hear him, Roxy? Five grand!"

What valuable trinket sat on offer? I approached the counter. A gold pocket watch in a beautiful swirl design rested on a velvet black cloth between my friend and the shop owner.

"Olivia," I whisper-shouted, steering her aside by the elbow. "Did you tell your dad you took his heirloom?"

"Prrfft. My dad?" She inclined close to my ear; her pungent perfume packed a punch and left a chemical taste on my tongue. "I stole it off Limp."

My stomach twisted into one giant knot. Despite the cold air, heat steamed out of my face. "Limp?"

"Yeah, he flaunted it in class. I swear he cried when I ran off." Her eyes sparkled, not at all vexed by her thievery. "Who knew the loser owned a valuable keepsake, right?"

My lip curled, and I compressed my hands by my sides. Olivia deserved a hard slap. I barged past her and snatched the pocket watch.

"Hey, hey." The shop owner protested, raising his arms. "Okay, I'll give you ten thousand. Deal?"

"Sorry, not for sale." The finality in my voice snapped the broker's yap shut.

I turned to Olivia, and she paled. Stress pinched every muscle in my face, no doubt producing a venomous scowl. Fire in my stride, I barged out of the store.

"Roxanne!" Her shouting my name drew the attention of passersby. "Roxanne, will you wait?"

I stopped in my tracks and waited for her to catch up. Arms thrown midair, she planted herself in my way. "What's your problem?"

"Me? Since when do you steal?" I gave a violent shake of my head. "I expect this from the guys, but not you!"

She gaped, speechless. Her eyes searched mine, perhaps waiting for me to cave and hand over Max's watch for her to pawn. Her lips squished into a pout. "I'm desperate for the money. Dad got tighter with our handouts, and besides, it's loser Limp. Who cares?"

"I care." I poked my chest a little harder than anticipated. "I care!" I puffed at the dark, cloud-veiled sky. "Aren't you sick of all the bullying?"

Expression still downcast, Olivia sniffled. "Why's wishing for perfect heels for prom so wrong?"

At the expense of Max's property, yes. "I'll pay for your stupid shoes, but promise me you won't steal again."

Olivia swallowed, and fat crocodile tears streaked her caked-on makeup. "I promise."

Shoving the watch into my jean pocket, I raised a pointed finger. "And I'm returning his watch."

She bit her bottom lip and examined her feet. "Okay. I'm sorry, Roxy." She shot her tear-filled facade at me again.

I hooked her arm in mine with a gentle squeeze. "Designer labels aren't the be-all and end-all. And no one will notice your shoes in your floor-length dress."

She nestled her head on my shoulder as we tottered toward my car. Materialistic objects yielded temporary satisfaction. I refused to obsess over money and trinkets in the same manner as Olivia and her sister. "Besides, I'm sure soon enough you'll spend your dad's money. Let him sort out his work troubles. Have patience. You'll see."

The small jest livened her dejected smile. "I sure hope so."

****

We arrived back at school ten minutes before the bell. Unsure where to locate Max, I grew determined to find him, even if searching took me all day. We ran into the guys by our lockers, and I stifled a groan.

Alex's arms draped our shoulders. "Where'd you girls run off to?" A sharp edge in his tone gave away his pique. Such a control freak.

Alex and Olivia maintained an on-again-off-again relationship, so keeping tabs on their current status proved pointless. Their weird liaison encouraged Alex's bodyguard front. His scary sporadic manner shifted onto us girls, over ridiculous matters such as strolling ahead of him, and if provoked…his jaw ticked, a ferocious sign he'd snap. His demeanor alone frightened me half to death. An earnest apology helped soothe his red-hot anger.

"Nowhere." I scanned the area in hopes of finding Max.

"Prom stuff." Olivia elevated on her tiptoes and pecked his cheek. The control freak would steal a minute alone with her later and either sweet-talk or outright demand the truth. I'd remind Olivia to keep her trap shut. Lie about our whereabouts, as long as no one learned Max owned an expensive pocket watch.

Trevor nudged my side. "You're quiet today." He raked his fingers through his turquoise strands and winked. "No need to daydream." His gaze pinned my pleated skirt and black nylon pantyhose, burning a hole through my outfit. "I'm right here, babe."

Remember to wear shapeless pants around Pervert. "Daydream? You're my worst nightmare." The massive sleazeball punched out his cheesy lines and sly moves. I'd lost count of how often he'd asked me on a date…while he ogled passing girls. A short while ago, he'd taped a small, square mirror to his shoe in hopes of peeking up skirts. His hideous personality negated his boyish good looks, and his creepy mania for gore movies also unsettled our group. On movie nights we banned him from choosing. The last horror film he forced us to watch left me unable to sleep and jumpy at every sound.

Brent intervened and thumbed over his shoulder. "Loser, three o'clock."

We all turned, and my heart skittered in my chest. Max climbed the top step of the staircase. He held onto the rail, features pinched as he stretched his bad leg from this morning's gym incident. My gut twisted.

The guys exchanged familiar wicked glances, the devious schemes rotating in their brains evident. I had to act fast. "So, you guys should join us for our shopping spree later. You don't have tuxedos for prom yet, right?"

My ruse failed. I followed behind as they stalked in Max's direction, heart sinking.

Olivia nudged my arm. "Now's your shot."

Yeah, right. No way I'd return his watch until the guys vamoosed, otherwise they'd steal his keepsake.

"What's wrong, Limp?" Alex blocked his way. "Your dud leg acting out again?"

The group found the dumb remark hilarious. *Not funny, Alex*, the voiceless words died on my tongue.

Max's jaw grew taut. "Back off, Roid-Muncher."

Everyone's mouth hit the floor. Nobody expected Max to possess the gall to retort. He either ignored us or surrendered.

"What'd you say, wise guy?" Brent shoved his way to the forefront of the group, close enough to nudge Max.

Max held his chin high. I half expected him to tremble in fear, but no, he'd grown a backbone.

"You heard me." His words gritted out.

I clung to Olivia's arm, all the blood draining from my head and urging me to grab hold of something.

"Don't forget who you're talking to." Cords and tendons strained Alex's neck, and a vein in his temple pulsed.

Max eyed all three guys. "Get out of my way!"

What on earth got into him? I bit my inner cheek. No doubt he was tired of our continuous taunts, and the Olivia ordeal earlier marked the last straw. But he carried a death wish. I hoped he'd read my secret plea, but Alex, Trevor, and Brent occupied his personal space.

"Can you believe this punk?" Trevor flexed his arms by his sides. "You're mouthy, aren't ya?"

Alex leaned his forehead into Max's. "Last chance, Limp."

Come on, Max. Say sorry and they'll leave you alone, my mental mantra implored to no avail.

"I'll show you, you little dweeb," Trevor grunted and thrust Max hard in the chest.

Max lost his equilibrium.

An erratic drumbeat thumped in my ears.

He tumbled down the stairs. His body whacked into each step until he slumped at the bottom.

Olivia's shrill scream pierced my ears. The force alone shook my body.

My lungs burned desperate for breath, but I elapsed into stunned silence.

People stumbled upon the scene. Gasps and shouts echoed from the bottom level. A flurry of turmoil erupted. Students ran back and forth, shouting for help. *What have we done?*

Chapter 8

Max

Seconds passed as I strummed my fingers over Roxanne's desk. Another day, another dirty trick. "Are we all set to go?"

Dressed in baggy, gray coveralls, a drastic change from his usual buttoned-to-the-collar shirt and elasticated suspenders, Julio—the hired IT guy—positioned his own laptop among the cleaning products on the cart and hacked into Roxanne's computer. "We sure are."

My phone beeped, and I opened the text from the lobby downstairs. Roxanne entered the elevator. "She's on her way."

Julio snatched a sheet and draped the thick material over the cart, concealing his device beneath. He hooked a blue bottle of window cleaner in the belt loop of his coveralls and grabbed the ostrich feather duster.

We jumped straight into action. Julio dusted priceless artwork around the room while I stood outside my office door, coffee in one hand, and newspaper in the other.

The elevator doors parted, and in waltzed Roxanne, bright and merry as usual. "Good morning, Hunter."

"Morning. I need you to download the builders' schedule for me when you can."

"Sure, I'll get right on it." She placed her handbag beside her chair and started her computer.

I sipped my coffee, unable to remove my gaze. As if I'd rob myself of the chance to witness her reaction. Her pale blonde hair mimicked the similar updo she wore at the charity event over the weekend. Roxanne in her stunning red number, secured in my arms with her sweet mouth inches away from my own, burned into my permanent memory. Thank heavens my father's old colleague, Clifford O'Neal, intruded because the temptation to kiss her senseless almost engulfed me. I should be embarrassed by my relentless flirting with her over the weekend, but I couldn't help myself. Once again, Roxanne managed to creep under my skin, causing me to forget myself. Good thing I snapped out of the trance she placed on me once we returned. Now to continue with the plan.

Julio neared her desk, duster in hand.

"Hello, you must be new to this floor. I haven't seen you here." Roxanne greeted him with the same politeness she bestowed on everyone.

Expression sheepish, Julio hesitated. "*Hola, señorita.*"

Surprised, I eyed the tech genius. Julio mentioned his Mexican ancestry but never displayed his put-on accent until now.

Roxanne's gaze centered on the lit computer screen, and her splendid expression dimmed, then vanished altogether.

Max?

Her lips mouthed my name. "You say something, Roxanne?"

Her wide gaze met mine. "What's with the desktop

wallpaper? Where'd you get this image?"

Wearing a practiced frown, I rounded her desk to view the screen. The background image portrayed a portrait of my pocket watch. I kept my features solemn. "All company computers underwent upgrades with several settings changed, but I don't see the problem." I pointed to the pocket watch. "Not happy with palm trees?"

She swiveled in her computer chair and cocked a brow. "Palm trees? Are you kidding me?" She held out her hand, indicating the image. "You don't see a watch?"

My scowl deepened as I leaned in closer. "Nope. One hundred percent palm trees."

She huffed a breath, her gaze falling on Julio. "Excuse me, sir." She stood, waving him over. "Can you please come here?"

"Who, me?" Julio pointed at himself, once again exaggerating a Mexican accent.

"Yes, please." A quiver shook her voice, and she squeezed her hands together.

Squeaking wheels of Julio's cleaning cart echoed in the silence. He parked the prop behind Roxanne's chair as we'd rehearsed.

She tucked a strand of hair behind her ear. Her outward calmness didn't meet her eyes as she gestured to the desktop. "Can you please tell us what's on the screen?"

Julio pointed at the computer. "*Veo palmeras*. I see palm trees."

She tittered, losing her charm when she peered at him. "You're certain?"

He folded his arms, holding the black feather

duster. "*Sí, senorita.*"

Shaking, Roxanne turned and faced me. Sweat dotted her forehead, her gaze distant.

I gripped her shoulders. "Hey, are you all right?"

Her face paled, eyes the size of saucers. From my peripheral, Julio lifted the large cloth on the cart and typed on the laptop. The screensaver changed to the palm trees we spoke of mere seconds ago.

Her hand waved toward the computer. Gaze once again on the screen, she froze, at last viewing the palm trees. Her previous paleness turned downright ashen.

"Roxanne?"

She didn't respond. My heart rate skyrocketed, my tongue stuck to my palate, and every limb grew tense when she froze, her body too still.

Reassure her. Calm her.

She staggered out of one heel in her rush toward the bathroom.

"Roxanne?"

"I need a minute," she called, not once looking back.

Julio raised a fist to his mouth. "Oh, dude, she looked awful."

Did I detect pity in the young man's eyes? Darkness unfurled inside me. I shot him a no-kidding look. "You can go."

The feather duster dropped to the cart, cluttering with the other products. "And the money?"

"Already sent to your account." I bent to retrieve Roxanne's high heel and tipped my chin. "Now leave."

I waited until Julio wheeled the cart inside the elevator. Once the doors closed, I slumped into Roxanne's desk chair. "I never expected this," I mumbled, referring to the pounding in my ribs. Folding my arms over my chest, my jaw muscles flexed. "We're scheduled for an online meeting in under an hour. This damsel in distress act is over the top, even for her."

Following her path, I stopped at the threshold of the bathroom. The door stood wide open, the faucet on blast. Lengthy lashes shadowed over high cheekbones, her breathing deep and labored as she splashed her face with water. A complete mess, and yet beautiful enough to make me ache. With the others, I scoffed at their tears, their shocked gasps...but with Roxanne, I suffered alongside her. My hands shook and I gripped her shoe tighter. The plan was simple—destroy her, end of story. So why did this hurt?

She snatched a few sheets of paper towel and dabbed her face. Those honey eyes met mine in the mirror. I straightened from the door jamb and took a cautious step into the room, not once breaking away from her gaze. *Why her? Why crave her? Why obsess over her?* She twirled around as I knelt at her feet, brushing my knuckles over the velvet-smooth skin of her foot before sliding her shoe into place. What a sight we must seem. Prince Charming finding his princess. Make no mistake, even if all of this plotting killed me, I planned on finishing this. So she could bat her pretty lashes and stare all she wanted because I refuse to be her knight in shining armor. *I'm her downfall.*

"Roxanne?" I swallowed and leaned back.

She cleared her throat and faced the mirror once more, gathering the sheets of towel she used moments ago and tossing them into the trash can beneath the sink.

I stood to my full height and took her hands in

mine. A lump formed and didn't dissipate no matter how hard I swallowed.

Her forehead creased. "I apologize for my behavior just now." Voice croaking, her unsteady gaze wandered around the room. She grimaced and inhaled a deep breath.

As she opened her eyes, her gaze stabbed my chest, striking deep.

"What's happening to me, Hunter?" She bit her lower lip, her chin trembling.

Her sorrow affected me greater than I cared to admit.

"I feel like I'm going crazy."

Yeah, ditto. I sucked air between my teeth and dropped her palms. "Maybe you should take the day off."

"No. I can't." She puffed out a breath. "We're meeting with Jean-Philippe soon. You'll need me."

I'll always need you. I bit my inner lip, annoyed by such a concept floating in my head.

Less than an hour later, we sat in my office on a video call. Jean-Philippe presented his designs for the hotel on the large TV screen. During Jean's talk, I kept shooting glances at Roxanne. One look at my smiling PA would leave anyone none the wiser of her earlier nervous breakdown.

"Hunter, what's your take on the layout?"

Lost staring at the woman beside me, I zapped back into the conversation. "You've done an amazing job creating the historical Paris theme I hoped for. We've had builders in here knocking down walls and clearing debris, each room a clean slate for you to work with."

"Excellent. I'm forwarding you the plans and contract as we speak. As for me, you'll see me in person real soon."

Roxanne paused from taking notes. Her computer sat open in her lap. "We can't wait."

Jean-Philippe bid us goodbye and ended the call. I set aside my coffee and pointed to her computer. "Note his arrival date."

She nodded with a proud grin. "Already added to your calendar."

I leaned over to peer at her screen as she closed off pages. An image of a glorious grand ballroom captured my interest. "Wait." I raised my palm as the cursor hovered over the X in the corner of the screen. "What's this?"

"Oh, nothing." She waved a nonchalant hand. "When you told me you planned on designing this hotel in a historical French theme, I created a little mock ballroom design on my computer for fun."

For fun? She must have devoted hours to this project. In our interview, she mentioned her failed career path in interior design, but from what lay in front of me, the woman still held a strong passion for this line of work. Dark gray, cloudy ornate walls and pillars, golden corbels and scrollwork ceilings, burgundy crystal chandeliers. Royal and navy blue floral curvilinear carpet patterned in true, historical fashion bordered a parquet-style dance floor. The entire layout screamed French chateau.

"Roxanne…" Unable to remove my gaze from her marvelous creation, I grew speechless.

"It's stupid, right?" Her giggle gave away her nerves. "A total waste of energy even."

"No, not a waste." The detail, color, and exuberance I'd expect from a designer with years' worth of experience poured off the page. "It's breathtaking."

The light in her bewildered hazels brightened her entire face. "You're not kidding?"

I found my dangling carrot. Roxanne's ambition in interior design was my ticket to breaking her heart. What a shame I couldn't use her design for real because her creative layout outdid my expectations for the grand ballroom, but my master revenge plan mattered more. "Send your design to my email." I pointed at her computer. "I'll have Jean-Philippe go over the plans."

She frowned at the screen and gazed back into my eyes. "What, why?"

I winked at her, bestowing a small grin. "To use your layout for the grand ballroom."

The laptop slipped from her legs, and she gripped the computer with both hands. "Hunter, what are you saying?"

Standing from the desk, I opened my arms in an obvious gesture. "I'm saying your design's perfect for the hotel."

She gasped, and a threat of tears surfaced. Tears of happiness. The sight struck me harder than her earlier misery. Euphoria swirled through my insides. Here I enacted each meticulous scheme to crush her and get my kicks, and her elation proved sweeter.

"This is…this is…" She placed her laptop on the table and jumped into my embrace, hugging me. "I can't believe you're interested in my design." She veered back to peer into my eyes and hugged me again. "Thank you, Hunter. What an honor. What an opportunity."

I hugged her in return, reveling in the closeness. Once again, she distracted me from my goal, and I grew determined to ignore the unwelcome tugging in my chest. What retribution existed in making her dreams come true? None. No, I'd use this as the final nail.

Roxanne gathered her notes and computer from my desk, beaming the entire time. "You've made my day. In fact, after I pick up my son, I think I'll head to my favorite steakhouse to celebrate."

A celebratory dinner with a toddler didn't sound too ideal. She told me her parents babysat for her during our trip to LA, but she'd never mentioned the kid's father or custody arrangements. "I hope I'm not overstepping here, but do you and the boy's father share custody?" The burning question sprung forth as though having a mind of its own. Strangled by my stupid curiosity, I wiggled at the knot in my tie.

Her smile dimmed. She held her closed computer to her chest. "No, he's never been involved."

"I'm sorry." No, I wasn't.

"I'm to blame." She shrugged, her voice breaking a little. "I..." She hesitated, meeting my eyes. "I made mistakes and hurt him. I tried mending our relationship, but it was too late."

A recurring habit of hers. She hadn't changed in all these years. Thank heavens this fellow escaped her clutches when he did. "Have you dated since?"

She gazed heavenward and huffed a laugh. "No, I'm far too busy raising a child on my own and working. As the saying goes, you reap what you sow."

I eased into my chair. "What do you mean?"

She surveyed the floor, her gaze far away. "Maybe

I don't deserve happiness."

"Everyone deserves happiness."

Warmth shone from those beautiful hazel eyes. Hope. She held hope.

Good, because I'd rather she deluded herself with illusions of fairytale endings, more worthwhile when I crushed her reality.

Chapter 9

Roxanne

Friday night I arrived at my parents', exhausted from another hectic working week. I made my way around the house, first embracing Zane in the biggest hug. "Congratulations on making the finals, sweety. Grandma called earlier and told me the great news. I'm so proud of you."

Those blue-green eyes remained unblinking and unsure. "The big competition's around the corner. You won't forget, right?"

I kissed the top of his hair, catching hints of his sweet-smelling shampoo. "I won't miss the tournament for the world."

Dylan whined in my brother's arms, and with one last scruff of Zane's hair, I waltzed over and took the crying toddler from Michael. Bouncing Dylan on my hip, he settled in an instant and offered his half-eaten cookie. He dabbed the cookie on my lips, and crumbs sprinkled over the front of my blouse. "No, I'm okay. It's all yours." I nudged Michael's side with my elbow. "I got a chance to visit Jasmine and baby Mia last night. Congratulations, she's beautiful."

"Thank you. And thank you for helping us out when Jaz needed bed rest." Michael brushed his fingers through Dylan's dark, coiled hair. "Once Jasmine's home from the hospital, we'll be back to our normal routine."

I slapped his arm. "Are you kidding me? It's no trouble at all. I'm happy to help for however long you guys need. By the way, how's the new car?"

A mistake to broach the topic. My brother's passion for cars never interested me, but boy, this guy talked for hours on the subject. Michael discussed the ins and outs of his latest car model and lost me during the conversation. He might as well have spoken in another language since I didn't understand *Automobilese or* come from the distant land of *Automobilia.*

Over Michael's shoulder, Dad arched his back and grimaced. I snatched the opportunity to leave the discussion.

"Hey, what's the matter with you, Zaneadu?" I wiped cookie crumbs off my blouse as I strolled toward my father with Dylan on my hip.

Dad wiped the sweat off his brow and winked. "I'm okay. My back's killing me again. I'll tell you what, I can't wait for our upcoming trip. Your mother says mountain fresh air and walking trails will do me good."

I tossed my handbag on the counter and passed Dylan his sippy cup. "You and Mom booked your tickets, right?"

"Yep, all done," my mother called from the kitchen, seasoning the mashed potatoes.

My parents planned a getaway trip every year and had been doing so since Michael and I entered high school. Souvenir fridge magnets showcasing their vacation destinations covered every inch of their fridge, and I wondered if they'd buy a bigger refrigerator all for the sake of continuing to add their little keepsakes. "I can get you guys a discount if you stay at Parker Hotel."

Dad waved his hand. "Thank you, honey, but no need. We've already arranged our accommodations. Besides, we're not keen on a fancy, city-based hotel. We've hired a beautiful cabin lodge nestled in the woods of Lake City."

The doorbell sounded, and moments later Michael strolled in with Darius. "Guess who decided to show his face?" Michael announced as he entered the kitchen.

Mom opened her arms and embraced the tall, dark, and handsome man. "Darius, so glad you can join us."

He hugged Mom's shoulders and peered at her. "I heard you were cooking your famous brisket and couldn't resist."

Mom waved a finger in front of his face. "Well, if that's what it takes to bring your smiling face around here, you can expect a home-cooked brisket every week."

Darius leaned in to kiss my cheek, and Dylan squealed in delight at the unexpected guest. "Great to see you, Roxanne." His gaze fell on Dylan. "And how's my favorite little guy?" He held out his hands.

Dylan threw himself into his strong arms, giggling, and mouth agape in wonder when Darius poked out his tongue with a cross-eyed stare.

Mom called me from the kitchen. "Can you help set the table, and grab an extra plate for Darius?"

Darius nodded for me to go ahead and resumed his funny face at Dylan. I set the table in no time, and we all dug into the delicious roast Mom prepared. Light banter filled the table, everyone sharing stories about their busy week. I sipped my wine and surveyed the room. Whatever happened, whatever troubles awaited, these people always supported me, and I'd change nothing, not even our little tradition of drawing sticks. The pile of dishes had my name written all over them since I'd drawn the unlucky short stick tonight. The Friday night dreaded ritual existed in our family forever.

Finished with dessert, I gathered the dishes in the kitchen. From the window, Michael and Zane played ball in the backyard, while my parents sipped their coffees on the patio, cheering from the sidelines.

Darius entered the kitchen, and his big frame shadowed me. He and Michael had hit the gym a lot during their teens, but Darius bulked up further during his time in the military a few years ago. Now he worked at a software company in Chicago. "Care for a helping hand?"

"Oh, you don't have to." I rinsed another dish clean and placed the porcelain on a rack. "I've got this."

He grabbed a dish towel from the drawer. "I insist." Taking from the stacked pile, he dried a dish plate. "So, tell me more about work. You didn't elaborate at the table tonight."

I rinsed a wine glass and set the crystal on a cloth to dry. "I'm keeping a little secret. On Monday, my boss stumbled upon my ballroom design. He plans on using my idea for the remodeling of his hotel. Unbelievable, right?"

Darius paused in drying the cutlery. "Roxy, congratulations, but why haven't you said anything?"

I handed over another plate. "Once the design's

complete, I'm hoping to gather everyone at the hotel for the big reveal."

"I bet you'll blow them away." He stacked the plate in the cupboard and reached for another one. "Congratulations again, Roxanne. That's awesome to hear."

We packed away all the tableware and cutlery, wiped the stone counter, and returned Mom's flower-filled vase to the center of the table. "Thanks again for helping. Shall we join the others outside?"

Large hands encased my own, and I froze on the spot.

"I hoped to speak with you in private." He nodded toward the front door. "Can we go for a chat?"

I followed him outside, my limbs shaking. Why so serious? What if this concerned Michael?

He took a seat on the porch step and examined the driveway, not saying a word.

The hot summer night caused my chiffon blouse to stick to my skin, and I craned my neck over my shoulder toward the cool, air-conditioned house. "Darius, what's going on?" I perched beside him on the porch step. "You're scaring me."

"Sorry." Darius raked a trembling hand through his short hairdo.

Since when did this super-confident guy morph into this nervous and unsure person?

He turned to me, giving me his full attention. "Roxanne, I like you."

My spine straightened at the admission. No wonder he sat here all anxious. I smacked my hands over my knees. "Since when? I mean, how long?"

He licked his bottom lip and flashed me a set of

dimples. "Since we were kids."

Impossible. We'd grown up together in this neighborhood, played hopscotch in this very driveway, engaged in water fights in the summer during our high school years, and not once did he hint at more than friendship. "But all these years...all those girlfriends I met. Heck, I got along with most of them."

He snorted a laugh. "I prayed my feelings away with every new girl I chased, but my plan never worked."

No such trait existed for me. I'd have dated again and again if rebounds cured a rejected heart. "Have you told Michael?"

He shot me a pointed stare. "He confronted me years ago. You're his baby sister, and of course, I respected his wishes when he said to stay away, but now we're older, and he sees I'm serious about you."

My shoulder bounced in a half-shrug. "And?"

Darius's throat bobbed. "And he's given his blessing."

His blessing? I massaged the skin between my eyes. Goodness, could this be the real reason Darius dropped in tonight? "I'll be honest. I see us as friends."

His Adam's apple bounced again. "So, you've never felt anything for me?"

At age thirteen, I'd noticed boys a lot more, and I used to ogle him for hours whenever he'd come over, getting high off the heart palpitations and consuming butterflies in my stomach. "Once, right at the start of high school. You were my first crush, but you're also my brother's best friend. So I got over you."

Darius cocked a brow. "Please, tell me your secret because nothing's worked."

We both snorted a laugh.

A lone cricket hopped out of the grass and onto the driveway. Darius steered my chin to face him and held my gaze. "I'll treat you right, Roxanne. Let me make you happy, the both of you."

I swallowed, touched he'd offered to care for my child and considered us both a package deal. My brow muscles ricocheted to my hairline. "You're making a pretty strong statement."

The familiar cockiness returned in full swing with his smirk. "I'm a pretty strong guy."

Either he'd never made his crush obvious, or I'd slept through the signs, but right now the transparent longing in his eyes exposed his fondness. "I'm at a loss for words here. I guess I'm in shock."

He tucked a strand of hair behind my ear. "One date, Roxanne. Go on one date with me."

My limbs trembled. One date. I never dated anyone else because I'd always envisioned a life with the father of my child, the same man who'd run off with my heart and not once returned. I mean, should I spend the rest of my days fantasizing about the past and miss out on real companionship? Darius awaited a response.

Everyone deserves happiness. Hunter's words struck my heart. Yes, perhaps I should give myself a chance. Instead of picturing a date with Darius, my non-date with my boss flashed in my mind. The way Hunter bested me in bowling, our natural conversation about our upbringing and our families. In LA we'd succumbed to breathless laughter from our pillow fight, and when we'd danced at the banquet, the heat in his eyes engulfed my stomach in flutters, as though his gaze revealed an unknown truth waiting to emerge.

Faced with my own truth, I bit my lip. A work-related relationship existed between us at best, so no point in venturing on a path destined toward a dead end.

"Okay. I'll go out with you." The words escaped before I relented.

Darius wrapped me in a hug, and I returned his embrace. *Please, God, for once in my life let me make the right choice.* Darius meant a lot to me and my loved ones, and if this failed, I'd struggle to look at him or enter the same room. After all, every childhood memory included Darius. I gazed down the street, the same street the three of us chased an ice cream truck circling our neighborhood. On the journey home, my soft serve had crashed on the sidewalk, and I'd burst into tears, but Darius handed me his double cone to cheer me up.

"Where'd you go?" He waved his hand in front of my face.

I nodded toward the road. "I'm remembering the time you gave me your ice cream." As teenagers, he'd always had my back, similar to Michael. He'd even helped Michael put together the nursery when I'd been pregnant, and he visited me at the hospital, struggling to fit a giant blue teddy through the maternity room doorway. "You've been so good to me all these years."

Darius dipped his head. "I'll always be good to you, Roxy."

At least Darius owned the guts to ask for a chance. No matter how much I dreamed, nothing would bring back my first love. As for my minor infatuation with Hunter…it was time I stopped dreaming and joined the real world.

Chapter 10

Max

The man stood from my desk, his well-groomed soul patch and mustache stretched with his smile. "Thank you, Mr. Parker. I look forward to opening night."

I walked the gentleman out of my office and shook his hand. "I'm sure you'll blow everyone away with your delicious cuisine." In my peripheral vision, Roxanne sat at her desk finishing a phone call and placing the handset down. Heat swept the collar of my neck at the show of smooth legs peeking from under the table, taking my breath away. I indicated my assistant with a held-out hand. "Roxanne, say hello to Parker De Luxe's new head chef, Jacques Durant."

She beamed at the Frenchman. "Congratulations, Mr. Durant."

His gaze danced over her longer than I preferred. "Thank you, Roxanne."

All week long I'd endured men admiring this woman. Interviewees devoured her with their eyes while others dared to flirt. Roxanne never encouraged their behavior, but every occurrence irked me. "If you'll excuse us—" I tipped my chin to the elevator, giving the Frenchman a clear hint to skedaddle. "—we have plenty of work to do."

"Of course." He shook my hand one last time. "We'll be in touch, Mr. Parker."

I waved as he entered the elevator, my equitable mannerism forced. Wiggling the knot in my silk tie, I ambled toward Roxanne's desk. "Any messages come through?"

"Yes." She stopped typing and snatched the yellow adhesive notes on the table. "One from Jake. He said the new furniture arrived."

Great to see my general manager kept me in the loop. "Excellent."

Scrunching the yellow paper, she read the next note. "Also, a reminder you're meeting with the board of directors tomorrow. Ten a.m. at Parker Hotel."

"Noted."

Reading the last message, Roxanne grinned. "And one from Clarissa. She said thank you for the adorable outfits but enough with the gifts because baby Chelsea's outgrowing her clothes faster than she can wear them."

I chuffed, leaning into the desk. "Nice to see motherhood hasn't changed her attitude."

Roxanne nodded toward the elevator. "So I gather everyone's impressed with Mr. Durant."

Contrary to what I told our new head chef, I perched at the edge of Roxanne's desk, no part of me in a hurry to return to my office. "Yes, the management team and I chose from three excellent chefs, but Mr. Durant's dishes transported me back to Paris. He's the perfect candidate for our French-themed hotel."

She rested her chin on her cupped hands and sighed. "Hmmm, Paris, how wonderful."

"An amazing place. One of my favorite

destinations." I flicked my wrist to view my watch. "One hour to go until you finish for the day and collect Dylan."

She glanced at the computer screen. "Oh, wow. Look at the time. I better finish this paperwork." She typed on her computer. "My brother's collecting Dylan. I have a date tonight."

"Date?" I froze from sliding off her desk. "You said you didn't have time for dating."

She shrugged, taking a stack of papers and stapling them together. "Darius asked me out, and he's a great guy too. Besides, what's one date? I'm not getting married or anything. I mean, he might change his mind about us later tonight, right?"

"Roxanne?" I pointed at the papers.

She held the stapler. "What?"

Since working together, I detected whenever Roxanne grew nervous because she rattled on, but her actions screamed borderline neurotic. "You stapled those at least seven times." A clear indication she held doubts regarding this date.

She glanced at the cluster of loose staples and messy holes in the corner of the piled stack. "Oh goodness, sorry."

"So, this Darius? Where'd you meet him?" I hoped I sounded apathetic, in spite of the fact my right eye verged on the brink of twitching.

She collected the mess and tossed the staples into the trash can beside her. "Let's see. Twenty-two years ago, he knocked on our door because he moved into the area and asked to play."

"What?" I unfolded my arms, unable to sit still.

She dusted her hands and grinned. "He's my

brother's best friend."

"Oh." Great, a guy she'd bonded with since childhood. Perfect. "I'm sure you'll have a blast." I shot off her desk. "I have to return an important call."

I strolled back into my office, shutting the door behind me. Grabbing my cell, I called the man needed for this situation. "Tom. Drop what you're doing. It's urgent." I strummed my fingers against my desk, my leg shaking with impatience.

"Hunter. Haven't heard from you in a while. What can I help you with?"

I lowered my voice. "I need to disable a car."

Car hoods slammed in the background accompanied by drilling. "I'm all yours...for the right price, of course."

Tom lived an hour away. No way he'd make it in time to disable her car, but I needed him here for the aftermath. All my hard work would explode in my face if Roxanne called her own mechanic. Left with no other choice, I rattled off the address and waited for him to jot the details. "Now listen, I need you to leave this instant. In an hour, I'm going to call you to request your service. Pretend you're meeting me for the first time when you arrive, and make yourself crystal-clear to the owner that her vehicle's undrivable. In the meantime, you're going to have to walk me through what I must do."

The flick of metal followed by a drawn-out exhale confirmed Tom hadn't quit smoking like he said he would. "Sweet."

Of course, the news thrilled him. To do none of the work and get paid, I'd cheer too.

Another outward breath sounded down the line. "I

hope a prissy rich guy such as yourself can follow instructions."

My gaze narrowed on the phone in my hand. "Tom, before becoming a prissy rich guy I counted on myself to fix both my and my mother's cars. I know my way around an engine. Therefore, don't patronize me."

"Okay, fine." He grew silent, no doubt realizing his mistake in ticking me off. "So how shall we do this?"

The analog clock on the wall ticked away, the irritable sound louder than usual. "Once I'm downstairs, I'll call you back and we'll get started."

"Reminds me of the last time with Trevor or whatever his name. I'm dropping everything and on my way."

"Excellent." Tom assisted me in the past when I'd marked Trevor Dallas off my revenge list. The psycho who'd shoved me down a flight of stairs turned into a colossal gambler with a sky-high criminal record. No surprise there. I instructed Bruce to keep a tight leash on him and all his illicit activities. One night in a shabby Las Vegas nightclub, I cleaned him out in a poker game and sicced an undercover cop on his tail, surrendering proof of all his recent offenses. Tom had worked fast in the parking lot to disable the junkie's car since Trevor frequented his backseat multiple times throughout the night to mainline whatever drugs he stashed inside. I'd never forget Trevor's aggressive yet failed escape attempt when the cops surrounded him, nor the pure fury shaking him when I revealed lanky Limp, aka Maxwell Fields destroyed his life.

I ambled out of my office and over to Roxanne's desk. "I need to duck out for a bit, but can you file Mr. Durant's resume? I've left the paperwork on my desk."

She glanced away from the computer screen. "Sure, no problem. I'll do so right now."

I waited until she entered my office, then rummaged through her handbag beside her desk. Car keys in my grip, I stuffed them into my pocket and hastened over to the elevator.

****

Half an hour later, I rode the elevator to the lobby to wash dirt and grease from my hands. To avoid staining the expensive suit and shirt, I'd removed them ahead of starting, and buttoned myself while traveling back to the top floor.

Roxanne spoke on the phone. Distracted. Perfect. Sitting on the edge of her desk, I fake coughed, loud enough to override the tinkling of keys sliding down my leg and dropping into her open bag.

"No, I'll call again if there's anything else. Thank you." She placed the phone down, her hand flattened on the table. "Are you okay?"

"Yeah." I rubbed my fingers over my throat. "A tickle."

She stood from her seat; a concentrated frown etched on her face as she checked my temperature with the back of her hand. "You disappeared for a long while." Her gentle hand remained on my forehead, checking for a fever. "I hope you're not coming down with a cold."

I clamped my lips together. "Yes, a small errand, but all taken care of."

Those honey-colored eyes widened. She dropped her hand by her side. "Sorry, I didn't mean to play nurse. There's a nasty flu going around and I..." Her words faltered when I placed my hand over hers.

"Thank you for checking on me." Warmth filled me. She cared. Roxanne Hastings cared.

She tilted her nose and glanced around the room. "Do you smell engine oil?"

I swallowed, dropping her hands. "No." A handy bottle of cologne sat in my drawer, and I made a mental note to mask my smell. I hopped off her desk and stepped back. "Why don't you finish for the night?"

"Oh, you sure?" She pointed at her computer. "I don't clock off until six."

"Positive. Go home and get ready for your date."

She stacked a pile of documents on her desk into a neat pile. "Okay, thanks."

I strolled to my office and situated myself behind my desk.

Roxanne sauntered in with her bag over her shoulder. "I'll see you in the morning. Goodnight, Hunter."

I raised a finger. "I'll head out with you."

Her slender body leaned against the frame. "What?" she joked. "No burning the midnight oil?"

No, I suffered my fair share of oil for one day. "Not tonight." I grabbed my backpack and shut off my computer.

We departed the elevator into the underground parking lot and waved one another goodbye and departed to our vehicles. I'd given Carlo the day off and rode my motorcycle this morning. Once on my bike, I dawdled in putting on my helmet. A cranking sound echoed in the parking lot. Removing my helmet, I faked a startled expression, hopped off my bike, and stalked over. "Everything all right?"

She tried the ignition once more. "My car won't

start."

I stuck my head inside the window, pretending to be interested in the flashing lights on the dashboard. "Has your car given you trouble in the last day or so?"

"No, not at all." She slumped back against her seat. "I had no problem starting it this morning."

I snatched my phone from my pocket. "I'll call a mechanic."

Tom snorted on the other line while I requested his service. "Yeah, sure, buddy. I'm fifteen minutes away. And to confirm, I'm to drag out inspecting her car?"

"Correct, take your time." I ended the call and waved the device at Roxanne. "One's on the way."

She sighed, running her fingers through her hair. "Amazing, and you found one at this hour too."

While we waited, I escorted her back inside the building and showed her the renovated downstairs bar. Roxanne circled the plastic-covered furnishing, the smallest detail captivating her widened gaze. Her gasp echoed in the room when she took in the bronze antique textured ceiling and provincial pendant lights. She ran her hand over the brown leather baroque booths and blue velvet stools, all the while voicing her compliments of Mr. Lemaigre and his team.

We strode to the parking lot to meet with Tom. He played his part, checking the engine over and testing the car. An hour and a half later, he fabricated a mechanical problem and told her the car needed towing to the repair shop.

"Sorry, sweetheart." Tom sucked air between his teeth. "Nothing I can fix tonight. You're lucky I came out here now."

"It's fine." I interrupted their conversation. "Come

back tomorrow and tow her car for repairs."

Roxanne swung in my direction. "But Hunter..."

I raised my hand, silencing her. "I'll give you a ride home. Let me grab the spare helmet from my office."

"Hunter, I can't expect you to drive me home. Tonight's the first night I've seen you finish on time, and I've already ruined your evening."

Tom snickered, packing away his small bag of tools.

Roxanne and I both snapped our heads in Tom's direction. Returning our attention to each other, she shot me a funny grimace regarding the conspicuous mechanic, her brows wobbling. "I can take a cab."

"Nonsense." Her stubbornness irritated me to no end, and a strong urge to either kiss or shake her into silence persisted. "I'm not going to abandon you here in the parking lot. Besides, we're wasting the evening by arguing."

She rummaged through her handbag and grabbed her phone. "Okay, fine. I better call my date and cancel. He's no doubt on his way to my place." She studied me, her shoulders sagging. "I'm in no mood to go anywhere but into a nice hot bath with a glass of wine."

Mission accomplished. "Go make your call. I'll be back in a sec."

Tom announced he'd return tomorrow and waved goodbye. I made for the elevator, texting him on a job well done. As planned, he'd loiter around the parking lot out of sight, and once we left, he'd reverse my earlier tampering.

Jealousy burned my gut. Exhaling a drawn-out breath, I forced myself to relax. I managed to sabotage this Darius guy's date plans with Roxanne. No point in getting agitated, but the idea this guy set his sights on her didn't sit well with me at all.

Collecting the helmet, I shoved my business jacket into my bag on exiting the elevator ride, swapping the blazer for my leather one.

Roxanne paced with her phone to her ear. "I'll call you when I'm home." She gave me a small wave. "Oh great, he's on a sugar high. Tell Zane not another piece of chocolate cake, okay." Her gaze rolled heavenward, and she chuckled. "I gotta go. I'll call you soon, Mom." She slipped her phone into her handbag and met my stare.

I placed her handbag in my backpack, dumping it into the storage compartment on the back of my bike. "Here, put this on." I handed her the helmet, and she made a gloomy face at the protective headgear. "What's wrong?"

She tilted her head to one side, her smile apologetic. "I've never ridden on a motorcycle."

On our jet trip to Los Angeles, she'd freaked out and needed coaching through her panic attack, but her composure then differed from now. "Confidence in the rider means confidence in the bike. The real question is, do you trust me?"

She sucked in a sharp breath, then clipped on the helmet.

Roxanne's silent admission tingled my spine. I mounted first. Taking hold of my hand, she climbed on, settling behind me. "Wrap your arms around me. Hold on tight."

Firm hands slid beneath my arms, latching to my midriff, and my eyes closed on their own accord.

Unprepared for our contact, in spite of the fact I'd waited ten years, I swallowed hard at the warmth of her body against my back.

Donning my helmet, I started the bike and revved the powerful engine to life. Not to spook her, I eased out of the parking lot. Though the bike ran smoother than butter, Roxanne clutched me tighter, her body right up against mine. Adrenaline pumped in my veins, and I revved the bike again. The machine vibrated beneath us as I increased speed.

She yelled directions into my ear the entire ride, and in twenty minutes, I entered her street. Fat raindrops splashed my helmet, running down my view. Stopped in front of her apartment building, we both removed our helmets, and I helped her off the bike and returned her handbag.

"I can't thank you enough." She wrapped her arms around herself against the sprinkle of rain. "Well, I guess I'll—"

She slipped, tilting back, and I caught her, hauling her into my chest, the contact better than on the ride over here. Cold droplets splashed the nape of my neck. Instinct told me to hold her close, to prolong the moment. Common sense, however, screamed to back off. Her beautiful hazels hooded in desire and locked on mine. I tucked a wet strand of hair behind her ear, wishing to caress lower than the smooth curve of her cheekbone. Those plump lips parted, the delicate curves of flesh urging me to kiss her.

"Care to come upstairs for coffee?"

Yes. A thousand times, yes. "No. I should go home." From the way she trembled against me, I suspected the last idea on her mind involved making coffee.

Her gaze snapped from my mouth to my eyes. "Of course, no problem."

If I entered her apartment tonight, I'd make sure not to leave until morning. Unwanted emotions messed with my head, and I'd come too far to risk botching my goal. My simple plan involved hiring her and dangling her dream career in her face right before firing her. As for the cherry on top, I also planned on driving her a little mad with my mind games. One problem. I still very much desired the blonde bombshell. I straightened Roxanne to her feet. "I'll see you tomorrow."

"Goodnight, Hunter." Beneath the streetlight, a red hue added to her blush, and she stormed into the building.

I'd be foolish to allow one night to erase years of anguish. In spite of her betrayal, I wanted her, dreamed of her, and craved her beyond belief. But I wanted to hurt her too, to stand aside and gloat as she crumbled. No less than she'd done to me, and I planned to ignite her ambitions with a single flare and let the flames burn until a full-blown inferno blazed. Afterward, I'd trample over the ashes and inhale the smoke of this burning ritual for the final time.

Chapter 11

Roxanne
Ten years ago

I rapped on the door with a shaky fist and flexed my fingers by my sides, urging away the jitters surging through my body.

"Come in." Max's faint voice sounded.

I gripped the steel handle and pushed the heavy door open. Sunflowers bloomed from a white vase perched on a polished oak side table, and an accent armchair sat near a draped bay window with golden rope-edged throw cushions. Next to the exit, an open door hinted at a private restroom and shower. I'd assume Max stayed in a luxury hotel if not for the hospital bed, hints of disinfectant, and beeping machines.

I'd called every hospital in the vicinity earlier and got hours' worth of run-around. At last, one pleasant nurse informed me he'd been transferred to this private hospital. I viewed the dotted pattern floor, my heart breaking at the idea of peering at the boy in bed. He didn't greet me, and who could blame him? To be honest, I expected him to reach for the nurse call button and have me thrown out. "I'm the last person you want to see." Swallowing my cowardice, I locked eyes with him.

Max lay strapped to machines. A lump the size of a golf ball protruded from his head, and a blue-black bruise marred his cheek. My knees buckled as my aching heart begged to sink to the floor and cry, but I'd be strong because Max deserved to hear what I had to say. "Trevor never should've pushed you."

He straightened in bed, flinching as he did so. "Pushed?" He snickered, the sound shooting me straight in the heart. "Oh, you didn't hear? They said I had a bad fall." He bared his teeth and puffed out a breath, forceful enough to dribble spittle over his lip. "A fall!"

Sweat dotted my brow and I remained still. My ears rang from his shout. He told the truth. My so-called friends fed the school principal and staff some bull story and the teachers devoured every word, convinced by the not-too-far-fetched lie the kid with a limp had a fall. The first sting of tears blurred my view. Crying solved nothing.

I rushed to his side, wishing I could wrap him in a hug and remove his pain but didn't dare touch him. "I'm so sorry."

Max shrugged. "For what? Me ending up in a hospital, or for the last four years? Because every taunt, every shove, every time you and your posse targeted me culminated to this point."

"Everything." I threw my hands in the air. "Today they took things too far."

The pulse at his neck thrummed. "Did they send you to pacify me, keep me from revealing what happened?"

My brow muscles pinched together. "What? No, they don't even know I'm here."

His red puffy eyes narrowed. "Why are you here?"

The tears I held back dribbled out of my nose, and I rubbed the wetness away with my shirt sleeve. "Because you're not the only one disgusted by what happened. And you deserve an apology."

"How heroic of you," he gritted through his teeth. "You and your friends harassed me for four years; four years I haven't experienced one day as a normal teenager. You, on the other hand, get to enjoy high school. Hanging out with your buddies, partying, living your best life." He scoffed every time I sniffled. "Now I'm meant to believe you've developed a conscience? Prove it. Why don't you confess? Tell the principal what happened."

I choked on a sob, shaking my head, releasing the floodgates. "Max...you don't understand." I *did* tell Principal Carmichael the truth regarding the incident, and he urged me not to repeat the news to anyone. He preferred the fabled story of Max's accident, worried about ruining the reputations of his precious football star students with such a scandal and how he didn't have the heart to ban them from the upcoming graduation and prom ceremony. Our school principal snubbed Max altogether. My heart squeezed tight in my chest at the idea of telling Max. No way could I break his heart by telling him our principal cared little about him.

"Oh, but of course I do. The idea of losing the respect of your peers means more than confessing. Perhaps afraid the truth will obliterate your chances of becoming prom queen?"

I couldn't care less about becoming prom queen, or my social status. Popularity depended on status alone, and high school resembled a den of wolves on the hunt for a little lamb. One turned on you, and the rest followed. Before today, I feared what backlash I'd receive by ending my current friendships, afraid I'd be their new target. *Such a darn coward.* But now, I planned on cutting everyone off and never setting foot in their social circle again. "I don't expect your forgiveness, but I'm still sorry, and I'll make it up to you." A notepad and pen sat beside the floral arrangement on the side table. I took the pen and scribbled my phone number. "We stole your teen years, and I promise I'll be the one to give it back to you, Max. I'll give you a day you'll never forget."

Those puffy eyes widened, and he gave a slow shake of his head. "The best way for you to repay me is by leaving me the heck alone."

I placed my hand over his arm. Soft skin and a dusting of hair tickled my palm. A muscle jerked under my hold, and his gaze bounced to my unflinching face. "Please, Max. Give me a chance." I dug into my pocket, placed the pocket watch in his lap, and turned to leave. I clutched the door handle and craned my neck over my shoulder. His gaze fell on the pocket watch, his mouth agape. *You can trust me, Max.* And with those mental parting words, I left the hospital.

****

My heart pounded hard against my chest with every quivering inhale I drew. I sat in my car and as I steered onto the road, I replayed our encounter, hoping he'd give me a shot to seek his forgiveness and perhaps form a friendship.

My phone buzzed beside me in the passenger seat. I ignored the call at first, but the device kept ringing. Olivia's name lit my screen. Stopping at a red light, I answered the call and placed her on speaker. "What do you want?"

Muffled sobs reverberated in the small space.

"Olivia?" My voice rose an octave. "What's wrong? Are you okay?"

"Where are you?"

"Almost home." I didn't dare tell her I'd visited Max in the hospital. No way I'd risk them learning of Max's location. Gaze fixed on the red light, I waited for the signal to turn. "Why, what's going on?"

"Trevor…" She sobbed his name. "Alex and Brent left Trevor's house, and I got stuck hanging out with him alone. I told him how I stole the pocket watch and what the pawnbroker offered."

My fingers squeezed around the steering wheel until the knuckles turned white. "You told him!"

She sniffled. "I didn't mean to. The topic came up. Trevor needs money for pot." Her voice echoed in the small space of my car, irritating me with every word. "And I told him we planned on returning the watch but haven't seen it since the staircase accident." Her voice rose with her next words. "He yanked out a chunk of my hair. He kept asking, *who's we?* I didn't say your name, but he figured I meant you."

"Where is he?" I demanded, peering out the window, expecting one of these passing cars to belong to Trevor.

"He mentioned heading to your house. I'm sorry, Roxy."

Lights flashed in my rearview mirror. Bile rose. In the dark, I made out the metallic green car belonging to one person. "Olivia, I'll call you back." Hitting the end-call button, I turned into the next street. Trevor followed. The front end of his car lingered far too close to my rear, and if I slammed my brakes he'd crash straight into my tail. A row of factories lined the street, and I bit my lip. Not the safest place to stop with a pissed-off Trevor ready to confront me.

Trevor's horn blared behind me.

I veered to the curb and turned off my car. My limbs resembled cement, and I gripped the steering wheel as though my life depended on it.

The rap at my window made me jolt in my seat. I gaped out at a pair of flaring nostrils and a hard-set mouth.

"Open the door, Roxy." He didn't perceive me with his usual leer. No, his body tensed, the veins in his arms protruding. Trevor acted unlike I'd ever seen him.

Gaze locked on him, I refused to blink or reveal my trepidation. I stepped out of the car, leaving behind the warmth and solitude by shutting the door. To keep his crude gaze from ogling my body, I wrapped the jacket over my chest and tilted my chin high. "What's your problem, Trevor?"

He ran his tongue over his teeth. "Olivia told me she stole Limp's watch. Do you have it?"

I cringed at the horrible nickname for Max. A name I used in the past without flinching but now regretted ever uttering. "No, I don't." I shrugged, trying to regain my composure while deep down my stomach knotted into a ball.

A brief grin accompanied his vicious groan and morphed into a full-blown scowl. "Are you saying you gave it back?"

I flattened my spine against my car. A strong breeze swirled through the air, blowing tresses of my hair over my face and tumbling rubbish and leaves across the road. "I...I lost it."

Trevor snickered. His closed fist landed beside me against the roof of my car. "I don't believe you. You returned his watch, didn't you?"

"I swear I don't have any watch." Desperation filled my voice with conviction. "I lost the thing when you shoved Max down the stairs!"

His hand gripped my throat, ceasing my breath.

"Stop," I mouthed.

Trevor eased his grip but didn't let go. "Max? Since when do you call him Max? What's up with you, Roxy? You've developed this weird protectiveness to the limping loser. I brushed the idea off at first, but every desperate attempt you made trying to distract us gave you away." The tip of his nose rubbed over my own. His body strained against mine, preventing me from budging an inch. I grimaced when he arched into me. The sicko derived pleasure from my fear. "Consider yourself lucky I haven't told the guys my suspicions. And you better not tell the school what happened."

Oh goodness, would he check to see if I'd spoken to Principal Carmichael?

Trevor's nostrils flared, and those beady eyes narrowed and searched mine. "Have you?"

"No." I rasped the lie, my limbs shaking. Every bone in my body begged for him to get off me. His unwelcome warmth invaded me, and my insides coiled. With enough force to hurt me, he shoved me hard against the car and at last freed my neck. I wrapped my hands around my throat, barricading myself from his forceful grip in case he grabbed me again. Hot tears itched my skin, and I swallowed back painful sobs.

He waved a pointed finger. "You better be telling the truth."

I didn't answer but turned to open my car door.

"Baby, wait." His voice softened.

Ignoring him, I jumped into my car and locked the door.

"C'mon, Roxy." He tapped my window, the action gentle enough to coax a frightened rabbit. "Come out of there. I'm sorry. I'm super stressed, okay."

With shaky hands, I turned the key in the ignition. The car roared to life, and I slammed my foot on the accelerator and sped out of there. Peering into the rearview mirror, I saw as Trevor threw his arms in the air.

I raced all the way home and charged into my house. Shutting the front door behind me, a sob I'd held back echoed in the hallway. Through the blur of tears, a figure approached. Darius, my brother's best friend, stood in the foyer, his dark fingers squeezing the beer can in his hand. His intense gaze stilled over me, on my neck in particular where my skin throbbed from the pressure of Trevor's thumbs moments ago.

"Who did this to you?" he demanded, closing the space between us. "Hey, hey."

I sobbed harder when he tilted my chin, the sting marks on my neck ever present.

"Roxy, what happened?" Darius studied me, nostrils flared. Those dark, wide eyes appeared ready to kill.

"Mikey, get in here," he called out over his shoulder.

The back door screeched open, and jogging

resounded in the short distance. My brother entered the foyer, a dirty rag thrown over his shoulder. Grease stained the old, white shirt he wore. His somber expression paled. "Roxanne?"

He threw the rag on the floor, taking one step closer, and I leaped into his arms and cried with all the pain emanating from my chest. Both guys demanded the reason for my tears. Once I caught my breath, I told them everything. How Olivia stole the pocket watch, how Trevor rammed Max down the stairs, Olivia calling me followed by Trevor confronting me. The guys listened the entire time without interruption. Each explanation flashed another glint of fury in their eyes. "Don't worry." My brother hushed and hugged me. "We'll fix him, right, Darius?"

Darius squeezed my shoulder. "He'll never lay a hand on you again."

Chapter 12

Max
Ten years ago

What sane person agreed to hang out with the girl who'd bullied them for years? Insanity. Temptation itched in my veins like a drug whenever I weighed the pros and cons. Pros won. Five drawn-out weeks of boring recovery made me cave, and I texted Roxanne.

I'd picked her up from her place this morning and she mentioned making a list of activities for us to do. First, we headed to an arcade where we challenged one another to several games, playing everything from Whack-A-Mole to Sports Shooting USA. As we played our last game, Speed of Light, a kid called us out for cheating since we helped one another hit as many lit buttons as possible. We paid no heed to the child, too breathless from fits of laughter to play by the rules.

Speaking of laughter, hers sent a rush of warmth through my insides. I'd never seen her this jubilant in school. My jokes caused her to clutch her tummy, in tears with hysteria, the reaction dosing me with dopamine.

The theme park happened to be next on Roxanne's list, and not until we ascended the peak of the rollercoaster and she panicked, did I discover her fear of heights. On instinct, I grabbed her hand and helped her through the thrill ride. We queued in lines all day, not stopping for lunch because Roxanne worried if she ate, her meal might reappear on the rides.

Roxanne took over driving when we left the theme park since our all-day walking cramped my leg. The essence of her floral perfume seeped into the upholstery, and I bet I'd detect the fragrance tomorrow. "I'm okay to drive home once we arrive at your place."

"No need." She checked the rearview mirror and concentrated back on the road. "We're not going to my place."

My muscles tensed at her declaration. "We're not?"

"Nope." She dropped the sun visor and increased the radio volume. "Hope you're ready for the finest fried chicken in Chicago."

I flopped back in my seat, pleased our day didn't have to end. "Tonight's prom night. Don't you need to get ready?"

She spared me a glance. "I'm not going to prom."

My gaze darted to her, waiting for the joke. "Why not? Aren't you part of the prom committee?"

"Yes." Her chin hiked a notch. "The gym looks great, by the way. We finished decorating last night."

I bet. Stonebrook High loved an opportunity to go all out, and prom marked the event of the year. "I'm sure everyone's expecting you."

"Oh, I bet they are." Her shoulder bounced in a shrug. "But I'm where I want to be."

Out the window, the sun beamed on the road, and Roxanne's hip-hop playlist filled the space again. Why ditch prom for me? She kept her promise and showed me an awesome day. Why not leave when she had a chance?

We arrived at Navy Pier and purchased two fried chicken burgers with fries and strolled along the pier to kill time waiting for our order. The giant Ferris wheel loomed above us, and I nudged Roxanne with my elbow. "Let's go on one last ride."

Her wide eyes took in the humongous size of the Ferris wheel. "Pretty high, don't you think?"

"Oh, come on. You did great on the roller coaster." I'd joked that our harnesses loosened, and she screamed and begged to hop off. She'd composed herself when I took her hand and reassured her, and once the ride finished, she'd beamed with self-pride.

Roxanne glanced at her feet. "Yeah, but..."

"To overcome your fears, you have to face them. How else can we move on?" Using myself and this day as an example sat on the tip of my tongue. All week I stressed over hanging out with Roxanne, but this day turned out better than expected, all thanks to her. "And...I'll be with you."

She cocked a brow. "Oh right, because you were so helpful on the roller coaster."

I raised my hands in surrender. "Okay, okay, no pranks. Trust me on this."

"All right." She grabbed my hand. "Let's do this."

The sun hung low on the horizon in the pink and purple sky. Roxanne sat in silence beside me, hand squeezing mine as we were hoisted off the ground. I didn't dare let go either.

I tilted closer to her ear. "You good?"

An older man with a boombox strolled the ground beneath us, selling single-stemmed roses to people passing by. A classic eighties rock ballad played through his crackling speakers, and couples in other seats snuggled together during the song.

"Max?" Her tone carried a hesitant note.

"Hmm?" The way she gazed at me...intense, electric. I lost myself while the sappy music and lyrics—stating the inability to fight certain feelings anymore—echoed around us. She released my hand, her trembling fingers inched toward my face, and her warm palm cupped my cheek as she arched in her seat and planted her mouth on mine.

I froze as her lips worked mine to life. With no idea what to do with my hands, I kept them at my sides and kissed her in return. Roxanne's fingers trailed from my jaw to my chest, easing from the kiss. Long lashes fluttered open, and again those eyes captured my full interest.

She bit her bottom lip. "Thank you for agreeing to come with me today."

"S-sure." Great, I stuttered now.

She turned to the open space while I fixated ahead. What the heck? She kissed me. Roxanne Hastings kissed me. She needed a distraction from her fear of heights. No way I'd read into what happened since she either expressed her gratitude as she'd mentioned, or the kiss diverted her current fear. End of story. I thrust the matter aside, not allowing Roxanne a chance to discern my strange behavior. What if she pointed and mocked me for drawing the wrong conclusion?

The Ferris wheel ride ended, and we collected our order, headed to the car, and ate the crispiest chicken burgers Chicago had to offer.

"So, for our next activity." She spoke above the music as we drove out of the city. "We have to leave the car and go on foot."

All day she'd read from this scrunched-up paper in her back pocket. I should insist on seeing this list. "We can drop the car off at my place. My mom and her fiancé are in New York and not due back until tomorrow."

She shot me a wicked grin. "Your parents aren't home? Nothing screams teenage experience than throwing a house party."

Yeah, and an unchaperoned party would be the last stunt I ever did alive. "Roxanne, no way!"

Her lips scrunched, and she snorted a laugh. "Max, I'm kidding."

I inhaled a steady breath. Thank God.

Darkness blanketed the sky as we drove through Willowbrook. I gave her directions to my house, and parking in my empty driveway, Roxanne rounded the trunk to retrieve the duffel she placed inside this morning. "What's with the bag?"

She puffed her hair out of her view. "Let's go inside and I'll show you."

We entered my house, and I removed my shoes, leaving them by the door. Roxanne followed my lead, doing the same. Using my cane, I hobbled into the kitchen and turned on the light. She placed the duffel on the counter and unzipped the bag, nodding for me to take a peek. I set the walking stick against the countertop and stepped closer. White rolls sat on top of clothing, shoes, and a makeup bag. I rubbed the base of my nape. "Toilet paper?"

"Yes." She grabbed a roll. "Stupid, I know, but I've never TP'd a house."

I scratched the side of my temple. My stomach

jumped into my chest, a mix of excitement and nerves.

"We'll need a target. Anyone on your street you don't like?" Her brows puckered, perhaps reading my uncertainty. "Or we don't have to. Dumb idea—"

"Mrs. Donovan." The name shot from my mouth without regret. A chance to get back at the hag who demanded I clean her dog's poop in my yard. What a load of crock! "She's this middle-aged snoop who lives at the end of my street. She's lived there forever and gossips behind my mom's back to other neighbors, and she lets her dog dump on our front lawn. Mom ignores her of course, but she irritates the heck out of me."

Roxanne tossed the roll and caught the tissue paper with ease. "Mrs. Donovan's going to get what's coming." She eyed my walking cane and placed the roll on the table. "I have an idea." Grabbing a marker out of the tin pen holder my mom kept beside the shopping notepad and the box cutter in our kitchen drawer, she wrapped her hand around my cane. "May I?"

I shrugged, unsure what she had in mind. She placed the walking stick on the counter and carved away at the wood. I hovered over her as she worked, recognizing the same calligraphy etched into desks at school. She leaned forward and blew away the sawdust, little fragments scattering over the table. Using the marker, she repeated her carved signature in black ink.

I forgot to breathe.

She turned to me, handing over the stick. "Here, now you'll have me walking with you whenever you use this."

I took the staff from her hands and observed her carved name in large capital letters.

"What's over there?" Roxanne ambled over to the

small, round dining table, the chess board and pieces set out from last night's game with Richard.

My face flamed. As if the most popular girl in school found this cool. "Um…it's chess."

She tucked a silky strand of hair behind her ear. "Do you play?"

I should've guessed her next question. "Yes, with my mom's fiancé."

She picked up the queen and sank into the chair. "Can you teach me?"

A joke? But her face gave nothing away. I dared not move. "I doubt a game of chess made your list."

"We can make a small amendment. Let's do an activity you consider fun."

Never in my wildest dreams had I imagined Roxanne Hastings showing an interest in my hobbies. First, I acquainted her with the files and ranks on the board, introducing her to each piece and demonstrating their full range of motion. She asked a hundred questions and doubted herself, but as we played, she got the hang of the game. An hour later, we sat engaged in a heated match of chess.

"Ha, checkmate!" she declared with a hoot.

I studied the board. My lungs expanded with pride.

Her cheerful expression softened, and she studied the king in her hand. "It's checkmate, right?"

I leaned back in my seat, taking a sip of water. "You're a fast learner."

"Well, you're a good teacher." She rested her chin in her palm as she placed the piece on the table. "This was a lot of fun." Her gaze veered to the clock on the wall above my head, and she hopped from her seat. "Are you ready to toilet-paper Mrs. Donovan's? Come on, let's go."

We dashed out of the house with her duffel bag. The waxing gibbous moon and the streetlights shone above our heads. I left my cane behind in case Mrs. Donovan peeked out her window and recognized who destroyed her precious yard.

The night pulsed with energy, and my heart raced louder than beating drums, fearful of a neighbor catching us and yet pumped to see our plan through. Roxanne suggested we both wear hoodies in case anyone detected us. The statement made me snicker. I'd be the first to go down if busted since my limp gave me away. "There's her house." I pointed to the double story at the end of the street.

Beneath the streetlight, the old hag's immaculate garden resembled Eden. Aside from Benji, her Pomeranian from hell, the rose bushes received her undivided attention, and Mrs. Donovan never missed a chance to work in her garden, even pruning throughout winter.

Roxanne grabbed my hand, and we ducked behind a parked car at the curb closest to the house. Unzipping her duffel, she handed me a roll of toilet paper and took one for herself.

"On three," she whispered, raising her fingers and counting. "One. Two. Three."

I sprinted onto the lawn, throwing toilet paper at the tallest tree in Mrs. Donovan's front yard. The tissue paper sailed and looped around branches. Roxanne prowled ahead, looping her roll over my nosy neighbor's rose bushes and front porch. Our panting resounded in the night as we worked hard at disarranging the front lawn. Roxanne's giggles grew contagious. I too joined, not caring if one of my neighbors caught us. Her carefree attitude hooked me. We cheered and hooted, dashing through the yard and designing the beloved garden into a toilet paper wonderland.

The balcony light flickered on. Roxanne squealed as we gaped at one another. Discarding the roll, she dashed to my side and snatched my hand. "Run!"

We sprinted down the darkened street, Roxanne snatching the duffel on the way. Our quick breaths echoed in the night. My foot ached, but adrenaline masked the discomfort.

Sprinting across my lawn, Roxanne slipped and grabbed my arm, taking me down with her. She fell flat on her back with me tumbling on top. I heeded for signs of pain, but her chortle confirmed otherwise. I chuckled too. Nothing but the streetlight illuminated her face. Our laughter faded and we gazed at each other, both gasping from exertion. She caressed my face again, her gentle touch the same as on the Ferris wheel. "You have the most beautiful eyes I've ever seen."

The way she gazed at me, the way my heart leaped in my chest, every ounce of me screamed to kiss her. Giving in, my mouth crashed against her velvet lips.

I was kissing Roxanne Hastings!

Ending the most perfect sensation of my life near killed me, but I leaned my forehead into hers. "Sorry." How I hungered to keep going. "Earlier when you kissed me, I get you were saying thank you."

Her nose scrunched and she leaned farther into the plush grass. "You assumed I thanked you on the Ferris wheel?"

I shrugged, hovering over her. "Yes. Unless you

added kissing to the to-do list?"

Her tentative fingertips trailed my lips. "Kiss me, Max. Not because of gratitude or the list, but because I want you to."

I blinked. Roxanne Hastings asked me to kiss her. *Me*, Max Fields.

Kiss her, Max! A voice shouted in my subconscious. I mashed our lips once more, slow and gentle, and when the tip of her tongue swept mine, I fought back a groan. Her warm hands ran over my shoulders and circled my neck.

"Don't stop," she whispered against me. "I want this, Max. I want my first time to be with you."

I swallowed hard. "I don't have…protection." As if the loneliest person in school needed some.

"It's fine. I'm on birth control."

Birth control? "But you said…"

A blush flushed her cheeks. "It is my first time…but I'm on the pill to regulate my cycle."

"Oh…" Screw a response. Taking her mouth, she returned my kiss with a white-hot ferocity, morphing my lungs into a mythical winged creature ready to soar away. We struggled to find the door in between kisses but made our way to my room and shared a night neither of us experienced.

We epitomized two starved souls, created for one another, devouring each other. Would intimacy always be this powerful, unlike anything I ever imagined? Riveting. Poetic. Our encounter imprinted into my core, into my bones as though we exchanged more than carnal pleasure, but an entwining beyond the physical. My body was hers, and hers mine. The idea of sharing this with anyone else repulsed me. Always Roxanne.

Only Roxanne.

****

"I later learned the song relates to a prostitute." She scooped another spoonful of scrambled eggs off her plate. "The discovery mortified me, but my mother insisted she fell in love with the name *Roxanne* rather than the song."

"At least your name doesn't sound like an old man." I leaned over the dining table and served her another helping of eggs before scraping the remainder onto my own plate. "On my mother's side, it's tradition to name the firstborn son by her father's name."

Roxanne took a swig of her juice. "Why the mother's side?"

"Since the child took their fathers' surname, it's a nice way for the mother's lineage to continue."

She tilted her head, a sparkle twinkling in her eyes. "I like that sentiment."

I shrugged. "My surname, Fields, my mother's maiden name, didn't stop her from pursuing her tradition."

She paused with her fork halfway to her mouth. "So, you have your grandfather's full name."

"Maxwell Fields." I stopped to ponder that for a moment. "I can't believe I didn't realize, but yeah."

Roxanne glanced at the clock above my head. "What time's your mom due home?"

"Late this afternoon so there's no need to rush breakfast."

Roxanne stood from the table. The clean shirt I let her borrow fell past her knees. "My mom thinks I'm sleeping over at Olivia's. I better go get dressed and head home before she calls."

I cleared our plates and deposited them in the sink. "Give me five to freshen up, and I'll drive you."

"Thanks, Max." She gathered her hair, tying it into a messy bun atop her head. "Let me take care of the dishes while you freshen up."

"Oh, you don't have to do that."

"Please." She waved a playful hand. "It's the least I can do since you cooked us breakfast."

"I won't be long." I entered the bathroom to wash my face and brush my teeth, shaking my head at my reflection. Last night legit happened! Roxanne and I were, in a sense, official. I paused, toothbrush hanging from my mouth. *I'm dating a cheerleader!* Nerves spiked as I perceived my lanky form, uncomprehending what she saw in me. Finger-combing my hair, I rinsed my mouth, then sniffed my armpits. No bad odor, but I had a hot blonde out there to impress. Spraying two pumps of deodorant, I donned a clean shirt and track pants and made my way down the hallway toward the kitchen but stopped short at Roxanne's voice.

"So what, I missed prom. Like I said, our plan will work."

Plan? I froze, keeping myself hidden behind the hallway wall.

"Yeah, and look how he acted toward Olivia, all over a pocket watch." Cupboards squeaked open and closed. "He's a freak and will get what he deserves."

All the blood drained from my head. She spoke of me and my pocket watch. To whom? Alex, Brent, Trevor? They planned something, something big. Flashes of yesterday invaded the memorable events taunting me.

"Do you need to ask? You saw for yourself last

night, the guy's putty in my hands. I'm surprised you restrained yourself from punching him then and there…"

One of those jerks spied on us last night? Where, at the burger joint? On the Ferris wheel? When we'd trashed Mrs. Donovan's?

"I know, I know, keep his guard down, timing's important. I can't wait for you guys to handle him, so he'll regret laying his filthy hands on me." Her soft sneer echoed in my house. "Oh, I'll get him to the diner, don't you worry." The squeak of the faucet drifted into the hallway followed by the click of glass hitting the counter. "I'll tell you everything once I text Trevor later. Okay, bye."

My stomach churned. We shared nothing but lies last night. She softened me worse than butter, and I'd fallen for her tricks. I inched my way back down the hallway and into my bedroom. Slumping onto my bed, I raked my hands through my hair. Every word of her conversation repeated in my brain, and I compartmentalized yesterday's events—the way she ogled me, the kiss on the Ferris wheel, the way she jumped my bones in this room… *The guy's putty in my hands.* My fists clenched by my sides, and the strain of my jaw hurt. Well, this putty swallowed a hefty dose of cement.

"Hey?" Roxanne stood in the doorway, dressed in the same clothes as yesterday. She must have changed when I was in the bathroom. Her gaze roamed over me, but the warmth I found in them coiled my insides. "Are you okay? You seem in a daze."

"A little tired." I snatched the car keys off the dresser, the jingling ringing in my ears. "You ready?"

She collected the duffel and slung the bag over her shoulder. "Yeah. Oh, I placed your shirt in the laundry hamper."

I didn't respond, my mind racing a mile a minute. We slipped into our shoes, with me taking a little longer with my bad foot. At this point, I harbored no embarrassment nor cared what Roxanne thought regarding my deformity.

I locked the house and jogged to my car in the rain, not bothering to help Roxanne with her duffel. She sat in the passenger seat with her bag over her knees. Silence stretched between us. Too ticked off to fill the void, I remained silent.

A gray haze encased the road, the bitterness in the atmosphere matching my mood. We passed Mrs. Donovan's house and Roxanne gasped. The snooty crone stood in her front yard, an umbrella in one hand, a broomstick in the other, and a garbage bag at her feet as she struggled to clear the toilet paper out of the tall tree. The rain turned the toilet paper into mush, making the task of cleaning impossible.

"Did you see Mrs. Donovan?" She glanced back over her shoulder, her face animated. "She'll waste the day clearing the mess we made."

A sensation erupted in my limbs at the hag grunting and stomping all over her yard. Priceless. The served justice erased none of my current anger but helped boost my mood.

"You're quiet." Roxanne leaned forward in her seat.

Rounding the corner, closer to dumping this trash from my life once and for all, I stopped at the curb in front of her house.

Roxanne unclicked her seatbelt and turned in her seat. "I can call you tonight. We can go see a movie or grab a bite to eat?"

Oh, I'll get him to the diner, don't you worry.

"Not going to happen, Roxanne." The tension in the air crackled.

"Why not?"

I inhaled a deep breath and regarded her. "Let's not pretend we're friends."

Stark fear shone in her eyes. "What're you saying?"

The wind picked up outside, howling against the car door. "I'm saying yesterday changed nothing. I don't wish to hang out with you or for you to call or come over to my house. In fact, I hope to never see you again."

She visibly swallowed. "But…last night—"

"What about last night!" The bite in my tone made her jump.

She blinked.

I tilted my head at her stunned silence. "You want a rating score, how's this? The arcade, the theme park, and the prank on my horrible neighbor…an eight. But the exchange of v-cards…" I gave a low whistle. "The *literal* cherry on top. I mean, you outdid yourself. In total, ten out of ten." The harshest words I'd ever uttered to another person spewed from my mouth.

Roxanne paled at the statement, her gaze narrowing.

Who's putty now, sweetheart?

She seethed, her face morphing into a scowl, but I didn't care. Jumping out of the car with her duffel, she slammed the passenger door shut and stormed toward her house.

Go ahead, Roxanne, sulk over how you didn't trap me into coming with you to whatever sick plan you and your buddies organized. Had they hoped to do permanent damage this go-around?

Without peering into the rearview mirror to see if she entered her house, I slammed my foot against the pedal and sped the heck out of there. Adrenaline pumped through my veins, and no matter how deeply I inhaled, I struggled to calm down. An outraged roar belted from my lungs, and I punched the steering wheel.

On my street, I wound my window and flipped off Mrs. Donovan in her front yard. Her jowls hit the ground. My mother raised me to respect everyone regardless of how they treated me, but not one despicable person in this town deserved anything other than my contempt.

Back at home, I tidied the mess in the kitchen, tossed my bedsheets into the wash, and flopped onto the lounge in the living room. No chance of catching up on sleep, not with my emotions all haywire.

She threw herself at me to lower my guard. My throat closed. I shouldn't let them get away with this. Done with ignoring the abuse, I allowed their actions to fester, to eat away. I'd permit this fury to boil over to the point I poured out my wrath.

Chapter 13

Roxanne

I avoided Hunter's stare the entire time during our quick chat in the hotel lobby earlier this morning. He shot off to his big meeting and left me in the hands of the hotel's manager, Alberto Giordano. The charming Italian gave me a small tour of the hotel, showing me to an empty conference room to conduct my work without disturbance. Without disturbance? A lie. Reflecting on my embarrassing encounter with Hunter last night disrupted my work.

Hunter expected an email of the most recent financial reports by the end of the day, and also the last four weeks' worth of correspondence organized in our online file storage. I'd rather do all this at my desk back at the office, but he asked me to stay close by in case he needed me. So far not a peep. I'd assisted Hunter in our last few meetings, but not today. Today, he avoided me.

And who'd blame him? What a horrible idea inviting him up. The words spilled from my mouth without consent from my brain. The way he peered at my lips, holding me in his arms and brushing a strand of wet hair behind my ear, I melted and prayed he'd kiss me. Yet instant rejection resulted from asking him to join me in my apartment.

I puffed out a breath, turning my chair to the floor-to-ceiling window. The height sent a chill down my spine. I'd seen this hotel featured in advertisements but never visited until now. Located on South Lakeshore Drive in the heart of Chicago, the building bestowed a splendid view of Lake Michigan.

No point in stewing over what happened. I'd use this separation to recover from mortification and work up the courage to face him by evening.

For lunch, I hailed a cab and drove to a place I'd avoided for ten years, Navy Pier. I passed a restaurant where the burger joint once resided, the warm weather replicating the long-ago day. My appetite fled, replaced by an empty void. I strolled over to the large Ferris wheel, peering at the ride's intimidating size. Unlike long ago, no man waltzed around with a portable stereo playing classics from the eighties. I removed my light cardigan, comfortable warmth chasing away the chill from the air-conditioned cab. Inhaling a deep breath, I shut my eyes.

To overcome your fears, you have to face them. How else can we move on? Beautiful moments merged into bittersweet memories as words from the past seeped into the depths of my soul. I'd forgotten his actual voice and certain details of his appearance. If he had freckles or birthmarks, I couldn't recall. The more years passed, the vaguer he grew. However, the sound of his heartbeat beneath my ear, the warmth of his flesh against mine, his laughter and the way his words coursed through me remained. Crazy how details and clear pictures fade from the mind, and yet the heart never forgets. The cherished moments forever tattooed inside me which I would carry until my heart stops beating. Goodness, my love for him hadn't abated in the slightest but heightened and intensified to the point of pain.

"Miss, are you purchasing a ticket?"

I blinked at the man in front of me. "Excuse me?"

"You're holding up the line." He pointed from behind his desk. "Are you purchasing a ticket?"

One peek over my shoulder confirmed I indeed delayed the line. To save myself from further embarrassment, I bought a ticket and sat in an empty chair on the Ferris Wheel. No dizzy spells, no queasiness, the usual onslaught of sensations caused by my phobia nonexistent. I'd grown numb. The chair lifted off the ground and into the expanse of Chicago. I lowered my wrist to the empty seat beside me and imagined Max holding my hand.

"He's my boss, the last person I expected to develop feelings for." I spoke as though he sat right here beside me. "I've searched for you. I've waited. I don't know if you're dead or alive." Those final words croaked. "Maybe you're married with children of your own." I swallowed the lump in my throat. "You've moved on, and I'm stuck in the past." I puffed out a breath. "To top it off, you're haunting me because there's someone else, and perhaps my conscience insists on reminding me of you. So, what do I do, wait or say goodbye?"

I wished he sat beside me to give me closure. The breeze whistled past my ears, and the Ferris wheel circled round and round. With nothing but loneliness for company, I sat in silence.

****

Once back at the hotel, I dove into my work for the rest of the day.

Alberto entered the conference room in the evening. "Mr. Parker asked me to pass on a message. Your car's ready to collect from the valet out front. He also said you're free to finish and he'll see you tomorrow."

I straightened in my seat. "Oh, they're still in the meeting?"

"The meeting ended. Mr. Parker and the rest of the board mentioned going out to dinner." Alberto held out his hand, and the gold cufflink on his suit jacket sparkled beneath the downlights. "I hope this isn't our last meeting."

I strung my handbag over my shoulder, slid my laptop under my arm, and gave him a firm shake. "I'm sure Mr. Parker and I will visit again soon. Thank you." I slid past him and took the elevator to the lobby. Clearing the air with Hunter failed since he sent Alberto to pass on a message rather than see me himself.

My brother finished work early and said he'd collect Dylan, which left me with free time, and I had an urgent matter to tend to.

I hoped for a quick and smooth exit out of the city, but greeted the typical traffic nightmare and spent the next hour flipping stations and traveling at a snail's pace.

As I entered Darius's street, my heart palpitated in my chest, and I forced myself to shut off the car and stroll to his porch. My knocks resounded in the air.

Darius greeted me, beaming at the welcome surprise. "Roxy? Did I get my days mixed?" Dressed in sweatpants and a towel draped around his nape, he dumped the fluffy cloth aside. "Our rescheduled date isn't until tomorrow night."

"Sorry for showing up unannounced." Perhaps I should have called first.

He took one step forward. "Roxanne, what's wrong?"

Don't do this, don't hurt him. "I'm sorry, Darius. I can't go on a date with you. You deserve a woman who's going to adore you for the wonderful man you are—"

He lifted his hand, cutting me off. "Roxy, please…" The timbre of his voice sounded heavy.

Complimenting him on his worthiness while rejecting him? Great going, Roxanne. Why not rub salt in his wounds, too! Desperation clawed at my insides. "I'm not the girl for you," I whispered. "I wish I was, but I'm not."

Here I stood trying to soften the blow but failed. "It's not my intention to hurt you."

He grimaced, but when he opened his eyes, his hard stare met mine. "I'll see you around, Roxanne." Darius retreated inside and shut the door.

My gaze remained on the solid wood longer than necessary. I slogged back to my car and berated myself the entire drive to my parents'. I told the truth. But I hadn't always made the best life choices. What if I ruined an opportunity at happiness? All for what, a man off-limits? What if I repeated history here? I scoffed in the small space of my car and chastised myself. "Always chasing the guy who gets away. Right, Roxy?"

Arriving at my parents', I lingered in the driveway, in no mood to face anyone, not even my little boy. Light shone out from the two-story house, and everyone's car sat parked in the driveway. At this point, my stomach twisted at the idea of food. Checking my reflection in the rearview mirror, I scoffed at my wide eyes and pale complexion. No way I'd waltz in there without twenty-one questions thrown my way. Reversing out of the driveway, I drove around the block and stopped on the side of the road, regaining my composure.

Not long until Michael learned what happened today. I hoped instead of scolding me, he'd appreciate my honesty, grateful I didn't mislead his best friend. Heck, he might be relieved. Who cared if I sacrificed a real chance at happiness, as long as I didn't set Darius up for bigger heartbreak. If I lived to regret this choice, fine, an additional regret added to the long line of others. Right now, my heart battled in a tug of war between the boy of my past and the man I mused over more than I should. No room for a third.

Chapter 14

Max

Three hours to go until my next prank on Roxanne played on the radio. Driving to her place, I set the car radio to the correct station and kept the volume at a medium level. Today we headed to a French-themed art gallery to view canvases Jean-Phillipe chose to decorate the guest rooms and restaurants.

Roxanne stood waiting on the curb. Navy business pants and a white blouse shaped her slender figure and robbed me of breath. Perhaps I should have called her on the weekend since I'd not spoken to her since Friday morning. I parked beside her, and she strolled over to the passenger door and hopped in. The warm breeze gushed into the car, carrying a hint of Roxanne's vanilla perfume.

"Hi," she greeted with her usual polite charm. "Ready to check out the gallery?"

I turned in my seat. "I apologize for Friday. My father insisted I join him and the rest of the board for dinner, and we rushed out of the meeting room and straight to the restaurant."

"No need to apologize." She placed her purse over her lap and buckled her seatbelt.

"Let's stop for lunch on the way back." I veered onto the road, in the direction of the gallery. "To make up for deserting you."

"You don't owe me anything." She avoided my eyes, keeping her gaze out the window. "But lunch does sound great."

****

A variety of artwork and paintings filled the large gallery. Each unique canvas embodied a French flare. Roxanne found her piece of heaven, her face animated in pure bliss. She drifted to each painting, her wide stare mesmerized as she oohed and aahed. "Oh, look at the use of color. Gorgeous."

My gaze refused to stray from her. "Sure is."

We ambled around for another hour, admiring the chosen paintings to use for our prestigious suites. Mindful of the time, I kept spying my watch. I spoke with the owner and made the necessary arrangements regarding the artwork, and we left the gallery.

"We'll arrive back in the city around two thirty. I hope a late lunch suits you. Do you have any suggestions?"

She smacked her lips together. "Hmm…Oh, Moretti's down the road from the hotel. It's my favorite place to go during lunch hour."

We exited the highway. My gaze bounced from the clock on the dash to the road. The radio host announced a quick traffic report, then the long-awaited moment arrived. The intro to the song played, its melody filling the space of the car. From my peripheral vision, Roxanne stilled in her seat, her hand hovering over the volume dial.

I held my breath. *Don't you dare turn it off!*

She increased the volume and slipped into her own little world, wrapping her arms around herself as she peered out the window. The sun shone on her and reflected her faraway gaze on the glass.

My hands clenched the steering wheel, and I anticipated snapping the part clean off. Had she listened to this song over the years, and if yes, then why? Why listen to a song from our first kiss? She didn't utter a sound either but remained in complete silence. Shock zapped through my body. I aimed for her to react to the announcement after this, not become affected by the song itself.

I stopped at a gas station. No fuel light lit my dashboard, but I needed a safe stop for what might happen next. The song ended, and the radio host announced himself back on the air.

"That song dedication goes to Roxy from her high school sweetheart, Max. Call TCQ Radio for all your requests."

Roxanne straightened in her seat, the purse in her lap slipping between her knees. "What station's this?"

I pointed to the dashboard. "TCQ."

"I need to use the restroom." She jumped out of the car, and the dark and overcast sky loomed overhead. The bleak setting harmonized with her determined strut as she stormed inside.

I loitered in my seat for several minutes longer and followed her inside. No sign of her at the counter or in the aisles. I darted toward the back, to a door labeled toilets. Inside stood another two doors and I stepped closer, leaning my ear against the door with the female symbol.

"What do you mean I've either misheard or contacted the wrong station?" Her voice sounded frantic. "A few minutes ago on your radio station, you said his name."

Although the radio host couldn't be heard, I trusted he'd deliver the right message.

"So, you're saying Matt as in short for Matthew, dedicated the song to his girlfriend Rosie."

Mission accomplished. I dashed for the car in case she burst out of the restroom. Outside, I hopped into the driver's seat and retrieved my phone.

The owner of the radio station answered on the second ring. "Mr. Parker, I expected your call. So, how'd we do?"

"Job well done." I stroked a finger down the leather steering wheel. "I'll hold up my end of the bargain."

"Nice doing business with you."

I ended the call and transferred the promised money.

Roxanne returned a few minutes later and sank into the seat beside me without saying a word.

I started the engine and drove onto the main road, and this time she turned off the station, ending another song playing. She stared into nothing, unblinking at the road.

I cleared my throat. "Roxanne?"

Again nothing.

Leaning a little closer, I tapped her shoulder. "Roxanne?"

Her entire body jolted in the seat. "Sorry, you say something?" She blinked at me, her usual charm dimmed.

My gut tightened. "Are you all right?"

Her throat bobbed.

"We can stop at the nearest restaurant." I pointed to

the next exit. "It's not Italian, but we have a bit of a drive until we reach the city."

"Do you mind taking me home? I'm sorry, Hunter, but I'm not feeling well."

"Oh." My shoulders slumped and a tightness squeezed at my chest, disappointed I wouldn't be sharing another meal with her. "Sure, I'll drive you home."

She turned to the window, but not in time for me to miss the tears pooling. Changing lanes, I drove in the direction of her apartment building, and we sat in silence for the remainder of the drive. The successful plan left me defeated. Whatever sensation coursed inside me yielded no delight.

A billboard sign on the street corner flashed STRIPCLUB. The title enough to jolt my memory of a low-lit room, cheap perfume mixed with cigarettes, and Olivia King attempting to grind against me on a faded, navy lounge. When her turn arose to mark her off my list, I hadn't lifted a finger, she'd destroyed her own life, from popular cheerleader to junkie out for her next fix in an Oregon strip club. An easy lure too. One wave of a big wad of cash and her face radiated. She snagged my wrist, led me into a private backroom, and admitted to having no memory of me. No surprise there. With those bloodshot eyes, I doubted she recalled her own name, let alone her life as one of the Queen Bees who bullied me in school.

Regardless of her poor memory, she straddled me on the velvet lounge and offered a free lap dance to atone for the past. I'd shoved her off, reminding her how pitiful her life turned out, and advised her to get her act together. *Advised?* What a polite way to express my behavior since I'd flushed her entire night's stash down the toilet while she screamed and clawed my back, desperate for me to relinquish her precious pills and powder bags. I'd blown her a kiss, the same way she did me when taking off with my pocket watch, and swaggered out of the club.

Clad in skimpy lingerie, she'd run out in pursuit of me, screaming expletives for all of Powell Boulevard to hear. The glorious event once again evoked in me a euphoric response. I yanked the brake at the curb, leaving the engine running.

Roxanne unclicked her seatbelt and gathered her purse.

Her hand brushed the door handle, and I placed my palm over her wrist. "Thanks for coming out with me today. I hope you feel better soon."

Her mouth sloped downward, but she didn't gaze at me. "No need to thank me, Hunter. What do you pay me for, right?"

I freed her wrist to place my hand back on the steering wheel. "See you tomorrow."

She shut the door and the distance between us grew. I veered back onto the road when she disappeared around the corner.

Each maneuver against Roxanne made me less thrilled. What on earth was I doing wrong? The last Queen Bee in my pursuit of justice remained trapped in my clutches, and yet revenge on the blonde bombshell troubled me.

Chapter 15

Roxanne

The elevator doors parted, and I trudged out with Dylan on my hip, struggling with both my large handbag and his diaper bag on my shoulders.

Hunter stepped out of his office, his gaze widening, the awkwardness between us a living entity. First with the embarrassment of last week when he dropped me home, and I humiliated myself by inviting him to my apartment, then bailing on him yesterday. An apology danced on my lips, but if I apologized, I'd have to explain I hallucinated in his car when the radio played.

"Hey, what's going on?" He rushed over and placed his empty coffee cup on my desk.

"The daycare center closed due to a small electrical fire in their kitchen, and they aren't letting parents drop off their kids this morning. I had no choice but to bring Dylan here with me."

"Do you need help?" He ambled over.

"Yes, please." I eased Dylan into his arms and relieved my shoulders from the heavy bags, searching through both, unsure where I placed my phone. "I'll call my family to collect Dylan."

Hunter held Dylan at a distance as if the kid would explode at any second. The humor rising in my throat erased my previous discomfort. "You've never held a child, have you?"

He glanced from me to Dylan. "You can tell?"

I found my phone in the side pocket of my handbag and stood. "Here, hand him over."

Hunter deposited the little toddler into my arms with gentle care. "He's not a bomb ready to detonate."

He rubbed the back of his neck. "I'm not used to kids."

Dylan laid his head in the crook of my neck as I bounced him on my hip. "Most guys aren't until they have children of their own."

He scratched the side of his temple, his gaze dancing over me. "I've never contemplated having kids. My life revolves around work." He tilted his head, nodding toward Dylan. "I see a lot of you in him. He has your nose and your smile."

I ran my fingers through Dylan's coiled black hair and leaned in close to his small ear. "Did you hear, little guy, you're graced with my good looks."

Hunter chuckled at the remark. Perhaps my weird demeanor the other day didn't faze him. "Can he sit at my desk until someone comes? He shouldn't cause trouble. There's an app game on my phone to keep him occupied."

"Of course, Roxanne." He thumbed behind him. "I need to head back to my office."

Dylan, the little angel, sat at my feet with my phone, playing his puzzle game. I attempted calling everyone. My parents, Michael, Jasmine, and Jasmine's mother, but with no luck. Since Dylan behaved himself, I proceeded with work while I waited for my family to return my call.

The elevator doors slid open. A beautiful, tall

brunette entered the foyer and approached my desk. "You must be Roxanne."

I took her offered hand for a shake. "Yes, and you are?"

"I'm Georgina." She placed her delicate, manicured fingers on her chest. "We met on the phone."

Hunter's ex, the one Clarissa mentioned. "Right, you called several weeks ago. Nice to put a face to the voice."

"Same." Her gaze did a double take at the floor. "I see you have another assistant with you."

"Oh, I'm waiting for a relative to collect him." Perhaps she considered this unprofessional? The need to explain rushed through me. "The daycare closed due to a small emergency."

She knelt to his level and gave him a small wave. Dylan returned her wave with a big, goofy grin. "He's gorgeous."

The kindness in her voice slinked me into my chair. "Thank you."

"Do you need anything?" She straightened to her full height. "It won't be easy heading out on your break with a toddler. I can bring you both lunch if you'd like?"

Talk about kicking me in the chest with her wonderfulness. Goodness, this woman epitomized an angel, an angel who had her heart set on my boss. Hot coals consumed my stomach. "Thank you for the offer, but I promise we're fine." I cleared my throat. "I'm sure you're here to see Hunter. I'll check if he's available."

"I thought I heard your voice." Hunter stood at the entrance to his office, his warm gaze locked on

Georgina. The burning in my stomach intensified.

"Sorry I didn't call first." She gripped the crystal-embellished handle of her silk purse. "I'm meeting my father for brunch and decided to drop in."

He held out his hand to his open door. "Come on in."

What Clarissa said weeks ago made sense—chemistry lingered between the two of them.

"Hold my calls." Hunter addressed me and shut the door.

The solid wood closed, and I sank into my seat, my teeth clenched tight, the spreadsheet on the screen a blur. God help me, I recognized this foreign emotion. Jealousy. I rubbed my fingers over my temples. *Pull yourself together, Roxanne.* I huffed at my computer. My brain refused to work, too busy trying to catch a sound from the couple on the other side of the door. And if I did happen to hear anything, my stupid heart would convince me they watched a televised tennis match.

Dylan whined, tossing my phone onto the carpet.

"Hey, kiddo." I cradled him in my arms. "You're sick of the puzzle game, aren't you."

"Mamma, dada." He whined, fidgeting in my arms.

Puffing out a breath, I eyed my computer. "There's no point in continuing with work here, right?"

Dylan lay against my chest and let out a loud yawn. He'd be due for his nap soon. Retrieving my phone and the dreaded heavy bags, I carried Dylan over to Hunter's office and knocked on the door. Exhaling a quivering breath, I waited.

"Come in."

I opened the door to find my boss seated at his desk

and his ex on the opposite side. Praise God I didn't interrupt them in a compromising position. "I'm sorry to disturb you."

Hunter raised a quizzical brow. "Everything okay?"

"I can't get ahold of anyone. I can get most of my work done on my laptop at home and use my phone to make calls and confirm meetings."

Hunter blinked and glanced around his desk, a clear sign he contemplated how he would manage the day without me.

Great, I disappointed him. Not professional, Roxanne.

"Of course. Not a problem." One dark brow arched, questioning. "I'll see you tomorrow?"

"I promise you will." The weighty bags killed my shoulders, and I readjusted them while struggling to hold Dylan, ready to dash for the elevator. "Nice to meet you, Georgina."

She returned my smile, the sparkle in her eyes sincere. "You too, Roxanne. Would you like help to your car?"

I swallowed a lump, and keeping my gaze downcast, I stepped out of the room. "No, no, I'm fine. Thank you." Act rude or shoot me a death glare...anything to relieve my shame for disliking the woman, but no, nice-as-pie Georgina burdened my conscience.

Entering the elevator, I hit the button for the underground parking lot, desperate to run far away from Hunter and sulk alone with my one-sided fondness. I snickered at history repeating itself. How typical of me to fall for a guy who didn't reciprocate my feelings. Why did I stink at reading people?

I huffed and puffed to my car. Dropping the bags to the ground, I buckled Dylan into his seat and draped his blanket over him. He'd managed to fall asleep during the time I approached my boss and hopped into the elevator. Popping the trunk, I ambled over and dumped the bags inside.

"Roxanne."

I gasped and turned around. "Hunter? What're you doing here, where's Georgina?"

"She left." He closed the remaining distance with two steps. "I'm glad I caught you."

I flattened my hands against the sides of my skirt. "Why?"

He hesitated, his gaze darting around the parking lot and meeting mine. "You seemed upset in my office."

God kill me now; he'd read my envy like an open book. "I'm fine. The day's thrown me off a little."

Gaze unflinching, he shrugged. "It's not your fault there's a problem at the daycare."

Not what I meant. Seeing him with the gorgeous brunette threw me more than the small fire at the daycare center. "I'm sorry I interrupted you with your girlfriend."

Dark brows drew together. "Georgina's not my girlfriend. We're friends."

"Oh." I hoped for neutral but feared relief showed. "Sorry, I assumed…"

"You assumed wrong." Hunter dug his hands into his pockets. "Aside from Georgina, all the women in my life are either married or dating."

False. I'd top the charts as the number one longest-running single woman. "Not all of them…I'm not."

"Yes, you are." He lowered his head, gaze strong and sure. "Last week, you said you had a date."

Darius's stooped posture and glossy eyes flashed in my memory, splintering my heart once again. "I, um…canceled."

He leaned back on his heels. "Why?"

"Because I didn't feel the same way he did. And I won't mislead him into believing there's a chance for us." I bit my lip as his tensed features eased into…relief? No, impossible. If this news pleased him… "Why didn't you come up for coffee when I invited you?"

"Roxanne." His Adam's apple bobbed, eyes unblinking. "You're sure you want to know?"

I'd have to handle hearing his rejection sooner or later, might as well rip off the bandage now. "Yes."

"Because I didn't care for coffee." He stepped into my personal space, his large hands cupping my face and hauling me close. "I wanted this."

Firm lips landed on mine, and I let out a soft moan at the feel of his thick beard tickling my chin. I kissed him back with everything in me, embracing every nanosecond of this moment. "Um," I muttered between kisses. "The exact brew I hoped for."

He broke the connection, gazing down. "You don't say." The pad of his thumb caressed my cheek. "Roxanne?"

"Yes?" My voice remained low, breathless.

"Dinner, next Saturday night." He tilted his head, his eyes intent on mine. "Will you go with me?"

I squished my lips together and tapped my chin. "Depends, are we talking business or personal?"

A low groan escaped, and he rubbed my nose with the tip of his own. "Personal. One hundred percent personal."

Don't stand there, gawking. Answer him! "Yes, I'd love to have dinner with you."

He leaned in for another brief kiss. Stepping back, he pointed at my car. "I'll let you get home."

On shaky limbs, I shut the passenger door, going over to the driver's side, but staggered with no chance of salvaging myself.

He wore a smug grin as he waved me goodbye, aware of his effect on me. I drove out of the parking lot, and not until I turned the next street did I burst out a cheer, waking poor Dylan in the process.

Chapter 16

Max

Representing a cliche, I stood, bouquet in hand, and knocked on Roxanne's apartment door Saturday night. The door swung open, and my gaze roamed black ankle boots up smooth legs to a face capable of twisting my chest in unbearable yet addictive pain. Her floral dress wrapped her thin waist, flowing out and stopping above her delicate knees.

Her face brightened at the sight of me. "Hello, Hunter."

I'd stressed over the dress code for our pub date, glad I'd gone with my designer jeans and leather jacket. "You're stunning." During the week—between meetings and calls where I'd sneak in a few kisses—I'd prompted her on where she'd like to go, and she'd suggested a pub where we'd play a game of pool. None of the few women I'd taken to dinner ever proposed such a place for a first date, expecting to be treated to haute cuisine and luxurious casinos. Women who circled in high society bored me to tears. Even Georgina—the most down-to-earth person—scrunched her nose whenever we passed a downtown pub. Roxanne differed from the likes of those upper-class women. Her fun and buoyant demeanor gave me the same rush as the time I cliff-camped in Australia, exciting and yet dangerous, the complete harmony of adrenaline and absolute ecstasy.

A blush accommodated her soft grin. "Thank you. Are those for me?"

I handed her the roses, and she hugged the bouquet to her chest, inhaling the sweet aroma.

"They're gorgeous." She waved me inside. "Come on in while I put these in water."

I stepped toward the threshold, and my phone buzzed in my pocket. Retrieving the device, Alberto Giordano's name flashed on display. I showed Roxanne the screen. "Sorry, I should take this."

She puckered her lip. "I hope it's the last work call you receive this evening."

Me too. I stepped out into the hallway and answered the phone. Mr. Giordano apologized for the accident, meaning to contact another person, and briefed me on an earlier resolved incident. As I bade him goodnight, I turned to find Roxanne locking her apartment.

"Sorry for the interruption. False alarm." I placed my hand on the small of her back, leading her to the elevator. "I forgot to ask what time the babysitter expects you back home tonight?"

She hit the ground floor button. "No babysitter. My son's staying with my parents."

Perfect, at least no curfew restricted our night. We drove through the city and located the pub with ease, parking in a dark street behind the building. I kept my face neutral, although not too comfortable with the idea of unsecured parking. Years of valet service conditioned my appreciation of such luxuries. I ran around to the passenger side to open her door. Roxanne shot me a grateful smile, grabbed her purse, and stepped out into the crisp night.

She hooked our arms, the act shooting warmth through my body as we walked along the street-lit path. A nostalgic memory of our day at the theme park flashed in my mind, of a teenage Roxanne linking our arms in the same manner as we raced from ride to ride.

"Have you played pool?" She tilted her head.

Over the years, my social activities ranged from golf, polo, yachting, to jet skiing. Most of the time such recreation included business associates or friends of my parents. In college, when Georgina introduced me to her crowd, I enjoyed a few rounds of billiards and brandy with the affluent guys in her social group. "Yes, when I—"

A man in a dark hoodie stepped out from behind a wall, blocking our path. "Wallets and jewelry. Now!"

My heart shot to my throat at the glinting blade he held in his tight grip.

Roxanne squeezed my arm, inching closer to my side. Adrenaline pumped through my system and my heart pounded hard to the point of collapsing. The fact Roxanne stood a foot away from the knife-wielding crook sent a cold sweat across my nape.

I raised my hands in surrender and inched forward to block Roxanne from view. "Calm down. Don't do anything stupid."

The mugger's frantic gaze zigzagged between the two of us. He tilted his scruffy chin and raised the blade higher. Over the last few months, I'd orchestrated several crazy games with Roxanne, my ploys calculated and meticulous in detail. Right here, right now, no sham took place. Might this be payback for all my recent schemes? Roxanne's shivers seeped into my back, and her palpable fear coiled my muscles. I gritted my teeth at the man who ruined our night.

"Now!" The man shouted.

"Okay, okay," Roxanne uttered, handing over her purse.

He gave a slight thrust of his blade. "Earrings too."

I'd never forgive myself if the mugger hurt Roxanne. As long as we played by the rules and let this scum take off with our belongings, we'd be fine. She'd be fine.

"They're not real pearls, but okay." She sniffled, unclasping her earrings, and handed them over next.

The mugger spotted the gold watch on my wrist. "Your turn." He pointed at me with the knife. "Come on."

Although not Olivia, this man sure stirred the same bitterness from all those years ago. How the hell had I come full circle to a place of vulnerability? I promised to never again let anyone make me powerless in the way Olivia had when she'd taken off with my pocket watch. "You want this?" I unhooked Roxanne's grip from my arm and shook my wrist, showing him the flashy watch.

Dark eyes brightened, no doubt spotting the valuable brand. He nodded, the motion short and jerky. "Your wallet too."

"Sure." My voice remained low and calm, perhaps even a little snide. "My wallet too." I took my sweet time unclipping the Swiss watch, then secured the eighteen-carat gold timepiece in my held-out fist. "Here."

He held out his palm for me to drop the jewelry

into.

I decked him right in the nose.

Roxanne screamed.

I thrust her far behind me.

The mugger straightened, and I clutched the hand gripping the knife, arm-wrestling him for the weapon.

Instant pain rocketed through my scalp. Son of a gun. The crook head-butted me. My grip loosened. He swung the knife, and the metal blade flashed in the dim light. I ducked. A swoosh of air rushed past my ears. Wrapping my arms around his waist, I hauled him to the ground. We struggled on the dirty concrete, both taking and delivering punches. Adrenaline pumped through me as I gained the upper hand and my knuckles numbed, connecting with his face. Blood splattered across his cheek, my sole confirmation I made an impact. Kicked in the chest, I staggered backward. The guy used the opportunity to hop to his feet. A guttural moan escaped him as he covered his dripping nose and took off with his weapon, leaving behind our belongings.

"Hunter!" Roxanne rushed to my side. "Are you all right?"

"Piece of scum." The rush eased from my system. A sharp sting pulsated in my forearm, and warm stickiness trickled down my wrist.

Roxanne gripped my hand, crimson covering her fingers. "Hunter, you're bleeding!"

I slipped out of the jacket, rolling the sleeve for better inspection of the nice long laceration on my forearm. When did the knife cut me during the scuffle?

Roxanne stripped off her cardigan and wrapped the knitwear around the wound.

"It's a scratch." With the mugger gone, I focused on continuing where we'd left off, not allowing the attack to ruin our date. "Let's head inside."

Roxanne collected our belongings with trembling hands. "Are you insane? I'm taking you to the hospital."

And cancel our date? No chance in hell. "Roxanne, you're stressing over nothing."

"Hunter." She straightened, and her hazel eyes gleamed beneath the streetlight. "You might need stitches, or a tetanus shot."

We headed to the car, all the while she compressed my wound, and once we got there, she withdrew my keys from inside my jacket pocket. "I'll drive. Sit tight and keep pressure on the wound."

A woman on a mission. She started the engine and sped onto the main road within seconds, heading to the hospital. I pursed my lips to hide my smile, a part of me soaking up the attention. We arrived at the city hospital, and Roxanne took me straight to the emergency room and explained our situation to the nurse behind the desk. Told to sit and wait while the nurse alerted the ER doctors, Roxanne fussed over me for the next hour, keeping the garment firm over my wound, unfazed by the blood soaking her cream-colored cardigan.

She squeezed the material into my arm. "I'm so sorry, Hunter."

Sorry? I swallowed hard and placed my palm over her small hand. "Why apologize? You didn't attack me with a knife." At least not a literal one, but a figurative knife in my back a decade ago.

The doctor called my name, and Roxanne stopped her ministrations and locked eyes with mine. "I'll be waiting right here. Go on."

I followed the talkative doctor down the bright hallway and into a room with a privacy curtain bordering a bed and a metal table stacked with all sorts of medical equipment. No TV, no real furniture other than a few stackable chairs in one corner. Taking a seat on the bed, I interrupted the doctor's ramblings. "Will this take long? My date's waiting out there."

The older man raised his head from his chart and chuckled. "No date night for you, pal."

He dragged a metal table closer to the bed and unwrapped Roxanne's cardigan from my arm and cleaned the wound. I flinched. Perhaps he asked what happened as a simple distraction or to fill dead air, either way, I told him what occurred in the back street.

He prepared the stitching thread and scooted closer to the bed. "You're going to need several stitches, and I'll have a nurse administer your TD shot. You might be left with a nice battle scar to impress your lady outside."

No wonder people waited hours in emergency departments. I might have a chance at salvaging my date if Dr. Wise Guy stopped joking and got to work. Too late to take Roxanne out to dinner or for a game of pool, but with any luck, I might be able to at least take her out for a hot cup of coffee. The doctor took his sweet time cleaning and stitching the wound. A clock above the door ticked away, each second announcing how long Roxanne waited out there alone. I bit the inside of my cheek.

The doctor changed his rubber gloves, spending another ten minutes, pausing between wrapping my arm in gauze, all to share a joke he deemed hilarious. "I'll arrange for the nurse to return with pain meds to see you through the night. No driving or alcohol. In two days, visit your GP to change the dressing. There's no tendon damage. You're lucky to walk away with minimal injury."

"Thank you, Doctor. Any chance my date can enter the room? She's waited out there for a while."

"What's her name?" His sheepish grin traveled my way. "I'll send her in for you."

I leaned back against the pillows. "Roxanne Hastings."

He strolled from the room, leaving me alone. Thirty minutes later the nurse delivering my shot arrived but still no Roxanne. Panic tightened my throat.

What if she left? My anxiety escaped a second later when Roxanne entered, and déjà vu struck of the time when she visited me in hospital a decade ago. Concern drained from her pale face, and a few short steps carried her to my bedside, her shoulders hunched from either exhaustion or stress.

She attempted a smile but soon lost the gesture. "Are you in pain?"

"I'm fine." What a disastrous night. Roxanne should be bent over a pool table, cue in hand, teasing me with hints of her sexy legs and jesting about how she planned on beating me in the game. "Sorry you spent our first date sitting in an emergency waiting room."

"Don't be ridiculous." She snatched a chair and took a seat by my bed, her gaze dancing over my bandaged arm. "I spoke to a police officer and reported the incident. I hope you don't mind, but I gave them your details since they might need to contact you."

I cocked a brow. In all retrospect, she'd done right by contacting the police but wasted her time. "I have a feeling they won't find the perp."

"Hunter, what happened tonight?" She cleared her throat and slid her hand over my good arm. "Why didn't you hand over your watch and wallet?"

A flashback of Olivia snatching my pocket watch filled me with pure rage. "I promised myself a long time ago I'd never let anyone steal from me again." Stupid of me. My actions toward the mugger put Roxanne's safety in jeopardy.

Roxanne narrowed her honey-colored eyes and fell into a dead silence. She blinked out of the strange trance she'd fallen into. "I'm guessing you're no stranger to muggers, considering how well you fought."

The nurse waltzing in interrupted me from answering and handed me a cup of water and two pills. "Take these," she instructed, waiting for me to swallow the medicine. "No driving or alcohol consumption. I've left your discharge papers at the front desk." She delivered her swift message and exited the room.

"Come on." Roxanne stood from her seat. "I'll drive you home."

We dealt with the discharge papers, left the ER, and headed back to my car.

Roxanne leaned over to help with the seat belt. "Are you still at the Parker Hotel penthouse on the city's Northside?"

"Yeah." I lifted my knee to better rest my arm.

She laughed at my response. The first time she'd laughed all night. "How do you live in your hotel? Are you planning on moving into Parker De Luxe upon completion too?"

I shrugged. My dwelling situation matched my lifestyle. "Those buildings become home when you travel a lot."

"So...what?" She eyed me from her peripheral vision. "You don't have roots set anywhere?"

"I mean, there's my parents' mansion in New York. I guess owning my own home never suited my lifestyle." I loved living with Richard, but the servants and groundsmen took a long time for Mom and me to get used to. I'd helped in the house my whole life, and not a day passed when I hadn't seen Mom cleaning. My mother struggled to accept her new status in Richard's mansion, and staff urged her multiple times not to concern herself with the mess. "Yeah, no hotel gives a sense of home."

"Neither does a house." She gave me a wink. "A family can provide such a feeling."

Roxanne joined me in the hotel's private elevator to the penthouse. She stepped inside and at a safe distance peered out at the cityscape views in awe.

When she helped me over to the lounge, she propped several cushions beneath my arm. "Are you comfortable?" She straightened, gazing over me. "Can I get you anything?"

"A scotch on ice sounds nice." I shot her a mischievous grin.

She met my gaze with a stern one. "I'm pretty sure the nurse said no alcohol."

I groaned, leaning my head against the comforter. "You're right. There's bottled water in the fridge. Feel free to help yourself."

She nodded and returned with two drinks, twisting one open and handing over the plastic bottle. I accepted the water with my good arm and took a long swig.

Roxanne drank a tentative sip, placed the bottle on the marble coffee table, and lowered into the seat beside me. "A date to go down in the history books."

I snorted a laugh. "I apologize."

"It's not like you planned for a mugger to be there." Her light tone hinted at humor.

She'd make no such comment if she discovered all of my recent schemes. "I hoped for an enjoyable night with you. Raincheck?"

She nodded, biting into her bottom lip. "Of course. You owe me a proper date."

I owed her more than she realized. Next date night I planned on organizing the entire event. Roxanne had her heart set on beers and a game of pool, but I'd treat her to a night at a fancy establishment with no chance of running into anyone shady.

Clearing her throat, she stood from her seat. "I better call a cab."

I grabbed her wrist on instinct, and sharp pain lanced through my tender arm. Regretting the action, I cringed and groaned aloud.

"What are you doing?" she all but shouted, sitting beside me and propping my arm over the cushions once again. "Are you trying to hurt yourself?"

I cupped her shoulder, this time using my good arm. "Don't go."

"What?" she whispered. Her eyes locked with mine and she licked her lips.

"Please. I've spent no time with you. Don't end the evening yet. Besides, I kind of like having you nurse me."

She smirked, her nose scrunching. "You're

welcome…I guess."

I tucked a strand of hair behind her ear. "In all seriousness though, you've amazed me tonight. What would I do without you, Roxanne?" Her name faded on my lips as my words sank in, and to be honest, what would I do without Roxanne? She swarmed my dreams and thoughts for years.

She nodded, her gaze glued to my own as we grew lost in each other's stare. My finger lingered behind her ear, and I glided the lone digit along the softness of her slim jaw, tilting her chin. "Tonight petrified me."

She shook her head, the action brushing her soft skin over my fingers. "Petrified? You appeared in control, especially when you whipped out all those tough guy moves."

Not what I meant. "Not scared for me…if anything happened to you—"

She cupped the hand holding her face. "I'm fine."

"Thank God…" A gruffness overtook my tone. "I'd lose my mind if anything happened to you, Roxanne." I tilted forward, and her eyes drifted closed when I sealed our lips. Deepening the kiss, I snaked my good arm around her waist and dragged her close against me. Warmth from her body seeped into my flesh, awakening buried desires.

Wound tight for years and at last finding relief in the familiar embrace, every part of me cherished the sensation. "Stay the night," I whispered, kissing her again. "Stay with me, Roxanne."

Her soft hands circled my neck. All the encouragement needed to take her mouth deeper. Ten years, ten years I'd waited to feel again, to breathe again, to live once again. With each breath, caress, and kiss, Roxanne rescued me back from the place of the damned. I cursed my injury for preventing me from carrying her into the bedroom and ending the night the way I imagined since asking her on this date.

Her breath grew shallow, and she tensed, breaking from the kiss and leaning her forehead against mine.

I confronted the horror on her face. What the heck happened? She'd burned hot and heavy mere seconds ago and now turned downright frigid. "I can't." She hopped off the lounge faster than a speeding bullet.

I sprung to my feet, and shooting pain pulsated through my arm, but I controlled my aggrieved features. "My arm's fine if you're worried."

"No, you don't understand." Head bowed and fingers trembling, she struggled to meet my gaze. "I can't do this."

My chest twisted in excruciating pain, worse than the stab wound. "Roxanne?"

She ran to the bathroom, and I followed.

Her slender hands gripped the basin, and she inhaled deep gulps of air. I stood at her back but feared laying a comforting hand in case the action frightened her. "Roxanne, what's wrong?"

She raised her head, her pretty face greeting me in the reflection. "I'm sorry."

"You don't owe me an apology." Disappointment echoed in my gruff voice and the one big question shouted in my head. "Please tell me what's wrong?"

She sniffled and rubbed a hand over her trembling mouth. "It's me."

How original. I'd rather her spit out what line I crossed. "Roxanne, you're going to have to elaborate."

Her gaze met mine in the mirror. "I...I haven't

slept with anyone since…since…"

"Since the father of your child." My guess sounded like a statement.

She laughed without humor. "I feel like I'm betraying him. We're not together, we've never been together. At least not officially…so why?"

Her words sucker-punched me straight into my stomach. I nodded, and the reality of my situation sank in. "You're in love with him."

"No…yes." Her gaze danced over the faucet. "I don't know." She winced and made a move for the door. "I should go."

I grabbed her waist, preventing her from taking another step. "Please stay. I'm not expecting anything, but don't go. Not when you're this upset."

She snorted a laugh, wiping beneath her eyes with her fingers. "I'm surprised you're not kicking me out."

Good grief, I hoped the sleaze father of her kid never treated her as such. Yeah, okay, intimacy tonight no longer sat on the table, but no way I'd give her the boot. "You've stood by me tonight, in more ways than one. Let me be here for you. No expectations." I tilted her trembling chin, stroking her wet cheek with my thumb. "I want to hold you. Let me be here for you…please."

Her arms wrapped around my waist, and she hugged me. Relief flooded my system, and closing my eyes, I held her head against my chest. My fingers played with the strands of her silky hair. Jealousy engulfed me like poison, jealous of a man I'd never met, of a man who possessed her heart regardless of my efforts.

Three hours later, I tiptoed out of my room and

carefully closed the door behind me. Once seated at the glass dining table, I opened my laptop and located Roxanne's folder containing the list of schemes.

When I first set out to destroy Roxanne, creating a list seemed almost poetic. After all, she had written out a list ten years ago, plotting her friendship mind games for our fun day out, and fooling me so good that for many months after our day together I'd replay the events in my mind and struggled to find fault in her flawless act. I believed she'd had a great time with me. I believed she'd harbored real feelings and wanted to be with me.

The whole point of the list and the mind games was to mess with her the same way she did me. I wanted to convince her just as she had me convinced. The closest she'd come to what I experienced was by making her believe she witnessed things that weren't true.

With the first three already completed, I tapped backspace and deleted the three remaining detailed plots, including the grand finale which involved revealing my identity when presenting her with Jean-Philippe's ballroom and crushing her hopes of her own design. Not one part of me desired to see her dreams crushed. I glanced toward the closed bedroom door, and even though she lay safe and sound now, the image of her inches away from the knifeman shook me to the core, the powerful response crystal clear. No one hurts Roxanne, not some creep mugger, and not even me. Done with the lies and schemes, I released a long sigh, having no idea what this meant for us.

Chapter 17

Roxanne
Ten years ago

Five months and still no word from Max, not since he'd dropped me off at home and sped out of my street. He never returned my voicemails, and perhaps blocked my number. I'd stopped by his house twice but received a clear message when my knocks passed unanswered. My desperation should've embarrassed me, but I didn't care. Then I stopped. Stopped the calls, the texts, knocking on his door. I stopped scouring the stores and streets whenever I left my home in hopes I'd spot him. I never quit checking outside my bedroom window though, waiting for his car to enter my driveway, and each day my chest twisted in unimaginable pain. My mind accepted the fact he had no intention of arriving at my doorstep, even though my heart refused to.

How had we shared an awesome day to an even better night, all for our little paradise to come crashing by morning? My heart refused to admit we were over. The intensity of our relationship freaked me out too, but not enough to drive me away, unlike him. If he worried about my friends intervening, they no longer mattered. I'd shunned them since the incident, well, except for Trevor, but I'd never speak to the moron again after our meet-up today. Olivia got the hint I avoided her and quit calling, leaving a final text saying goodbye since she and Alex planned on leaving town soon.

I'd even quit going to school. Walking those halls without Max by my side and seeing all of those faces irked me to no end. The shy boy I kissed, whose embrace I melted in, the boy who crawled out of his shell disappeared overnight. I'd seen a side to him he'd hidden from everyone, a person who enjoyed pranking people when they verged on hysteria, a person who challenged me to take a risk despite my fears, and a person who showered my body with gentle yet passionate care.

And here I sat freezing my butt off, five months later, and once again parked across the street from Max's house. My reason for driving here didn't involve confronting him or demanding answers, nor seeking closure. I strummed my fingernails over the steering wheel. The clock on the dash confirmed I had twenty minutes until I headed to the diner. I blew out a winded breath and opened my car door before changing my mind.

A black car pulled into the driveway. Breath ceased in my lungs. Did Max get a new car or perhaps his mother arrived home from work? A man in a business suit exited the vehicle. Dark brown hair and a goatee. No resemblance to Max.

The young man jogged around to the open trunk and retrieved a massive board and wooden stand. He hammered the stand into the lawn, nailing the cardboard over the top.

On autopilot, I crossed the street and headed toward him.

For Sale.

I froze. My heart sank. "Are the owners no longer at this address?"

The man jumped and spun around to face me. "Whoa." He clutched his chest. "You startled me."

I repeated my question, and he blinked, brows pinched together. "The premises have remained vacant for a couple of months. The owners contacted our agency a few days ago to put the house on the market."

My chin trembled. *He's Gone. Max is gone!*

"Are you okay, miss?"

"A couple of months ago." My mind raced with his words. "Did they mention where they moved?"

He wrinkled his nose. "Sorry, I can't help you. My job's to pitch these signs."

"Right." I sniffled, tilting my chin high without one ounce of confidence. "Um, thanks." Vision a blur, I raced to my car and sped down the street. Every muscle in my body grew stiff. I gritted my teeth until my jaw ached, pent-up frustration and pain screaming for release. My foot hit the accelerator harder than usual. I raced by sidewalks, houses, and trees. Uncaring, I sped like an uncontrolled maniac.

I headed into town, in no mood to show my face in public and at Danny's Diner no less, but I made a promise. The sooner I got this over with, the sooner I'd head home, crawl back beneath the covers of my bed, and hide from the world.

Once parked in the dirt lot, I applied a generous amount of concealer, and stormed inside. I slumped into an old-fashioned maroon booth. Trevor's name lit my screen. The message mentioned he'd arrived and parked his car out front. Good. We aimed to deal with Trevor months ago, but I'd spiraled into a mess since parting with Max. Despite my life crashing around me, I planned on putting Trevor in his rightful place once and for all.

A couple with two small children occupied the booth in front, and across from me sat a party of nine singing happy birthday. With this many witnesses around, I doubted Trevor would risk a stunt like at our last encounter. I punched a few keys into my phone, informing Michael that Trevor had arrived. My brother and a small group of his friends waited around the side of the diner, ready to dish out what Trevor had coming. No guilt or remorse.

Trevor walked in with his cheesy demeanor and glittering gray eyes. I grew eager to stomp on his high spirits.

"Hey, babe." He leaned in and kissed my cheek. I forced myself not to recoil. I'd told him in the past not to call me babe. Persistent jerk. Over the years, I made my indifference crystal clear, but the fact never stopped him from sending me gifts and flowers whenever Valentine's Day or my birthday arose. Mom declared Trevor lovesick. *Wrong, try plain sick.* The creep believed a heart-shaped box of chocolates paved the way to my pants.

"Thanks for meeting me."

"Of course." He tugged at his light jacket. "Hungry? Can I order you a burger?"

Greasy fries and sizzled steak fragranced the room. Other than crackers and water, I'd eaten nothing in days and the idea of ordering from the deep-fried menu options churned my stomach. "No, I'm fine."

Trevor leaned into his chair and framed his big yap with his hands. "Yo, can I get a soda over here!"

I stopped myself from gazing heavenward. The back of my neck prickled. Several people glared his way, including the waitress who slapped her hands on her hips.

He puffed out his chest in a pompous manner, spinning his attention my way. At first, he stared, and whatever his gaze hid made me squirm in my seat.

"I'm happy you asked me out here. I haven't seen you since that night." He leaned in closer over the table. "I'm sorry for chasing you down in my car."

I fiddled with the cardboard coaster in my hand, bending the corners. "You already said sorry."

He scoffed. "I sent you a hundred messages, but I meant in person."

"And here we are." To outsiders, I appeared delighted in his presence, the smile on my face an utter fake, but my revulsion showed in the way I twisted the coaster, tearing the cardboard a tad. "I shouldn't have driven off." Yeah, right. Praise God I escaped when given the chance.

He shrugged, perhaps recalling the horrible event. "Everything turned out. I managed to get my hands on some pot." He fist-pumped the air. "Besides, water over the bridge, right?"

Under the bridge, moron. I inhaled a quick breath through my nose. "Right."

"Things are going to change for us, Roxy." He placed his elbows on the table and leaned in closer.

I scrunched my nose. "What changes?"

Mirth switched his features into a wicked mask. "We're going to be perfect together. I've waited forever to call you my girlfriend."

I further tore the cardboard in my hand. "Trevor,

I'm not dating you."

"Oh, but you will because I have this on you." He leaned back and dug into his jacket pocket.

My pulse thrummed as he placed a red card on the table and slid the shiny pasteboard beneath my nose. The title, Monster-Coaster, stamped across the cover. My breath hitched. The ride Max and I rode. Trevor opened the card. Inside sat a photograph of Max and me, animated in a blend of delight and terror. The camera snapped the exact moment we descended from the top of the roller coaster.

"You and Limp, huh? I had no idea you're into losers." He flexed his jaw. "No idea."

Ignoring the fresh pain in my chest, I managed to speak. "How'd you get this?"

He clutched his chest in mock pain. "Oh, you don't pay attention to me? Ouch, Roxy." A mock pout livened his mug. "Did you forget my brother works at the theme park?"

All the blood drained from my face.

"Yeah, he ran the photo booth on this particular ride. And you can imagine my surprise when he waved this little beauty in my face. He recognized you straight away, said you and this guy looked chummy."

In the picture, Max faced me, lips stretched into a smile. During the entire outing, he'd smiled, and I'd absorbed his sweet exuberance all day, up until the moment we'd awoken the next morning. What the heck changed? I blinked out of my stupor. I should have never stopped calling, stopped visiting his house. I should have fought harder. Lesson learned. No matter how long I had to wait, I'd fight for Max because—a hot tear escaped—I loved him.

Trevor closed the card and dragged the precious photo back to him with the tip of his finger. My limbs trembled. Max's image sat in the hands of this despicable slimeball. I lurched for the card, but he held the picture out of reach.

"Nah-ah-ah." He snatched my wrist.

"Give me back the photo!"

He leaned in, close enough for our noses to touch. "Tell me, did you screw him?"

I yanked my arm away, the action futile. "Jerk."

He threw back his head and chortled. "Oh man, Alex's leaving town soon, but wait until I tell him and Brent. I'm sure he can't wait to visit Limp. I sure can't."

"Don't you dare lay a finger on him," I gritted through my teeth. Max and I had gone on the rollercoaster months ago. What if Trevor had already visited Max? What if the reason for Max moving involved Trevor? "I swear if you and the guys did something to him, I'll hunt you down myself. Give me the photo."

"Oh, babe, this little gem's my ammo." He used the image as a hand fan. "We haven't touched your disabled boy-toy, but I promise to leave him alone, under one condition…"

"He's not disabled, moron. And what condition?" I yanked my wrist out of his tight grasp, to no avail.

His eyes widened and his mouth thinned. "Be my girlfriend, and I promise to not tell the guys, or lay a finger on your loser boyfriend. But if you refuse, I'll show this picture and reveal your dirty little secret to all of our friends."

No wonder he held onto the picture for so long. As

if I cared about their judgement. Perhaps before, but not anymore. Screw hanging out here and playing nice. Time to lure Trevor outside to where my brother and his friends planned on jumping him. I shot from my seat. "Let me go, Trevor."

He glanced around at the other customers staring at us and let go of my wrist. "We're not done here."

"Yes, we are." I snatched my handbag and stormed for the exit.

Powerful steps pounded behind me. "You'll have no one, Roxy. You wanna roam town the same way loser Limp roamed around school, a loner?"

Outside, I passed the wooden bench adorning the front of the restaurant. The cool night chased away the warmth from inside the heated eatery. A few smokers stood in the parking lot, invested in their conversation, oblivious to the commotion going on at the front of Danny's. "I'd rather be a loner than have you for a boyfriend."

I charged down the pathway, passing the diner window displays of specials and hiring signs. Pebbles crunched beneath my shoes as I rounded the side of the building where the guys waited at the far end near the dumpsters.

"Bull!" He snatched my arm and swung me around. "You're mine, Roxy!"

"I suggest you take your hands off my sister." Michael's voice called out from the darkness beyond.

Trevor's gaze narrowed over my shoulder in the dark, no doubt at the silhouette of my brother and his friends.

Trevor's gaze shot to me. "You set this up?"

"He said, let her go." Darius's tone held no

patience.

Trevor released me, and I skittered over to my brother and his four buddies.

Michael and Darius circled Trevor. "What's this I hear you wrapping your filthy hands around my sister's neck?"

Trevor raised his hands in the air. "Dude, no. Roxy and I talked inside. We're cool. Tell him, babe."

"She's not your babe!" Darius's shout pierced the night.

My brother threw his jacket to the ground while his other friends circled Trevor. "Enough, Trevor. No calls, texts, no following her. Do you hear me?"

My brother's friends snatched Trevor's arms behind his back, holding him still.

Trevor's desperate gaze trained on me. "Roxy, tell him!"

"Darius." My brother's leveled stare met his best friend's. "Get her out of here."

Darius put his arm around my shoulder. "Come on. You don't need to see this."

"Wait." I placed my hand on Darius's chest, stopping him.

Trevor's shoulders sagged when I approached. He deluded himself if he believed I'd stop them. Another mistake he made concerning me. With his hands trapped behind his back and unable to stop me, I shoved my hand into his jacket and took the card containing the picture. Throwing him one last death glare, I turned and left.

"Roxy, wait!" His shouts morphed into grunts behind me, confirming my brother and his friends pummeled him.

Darius opened the passenger door to his convertible. "You okay?"

We sat in the parking lot in silence, my fingers brushing the photo card in my lap. Out the window, an array of stars ladened the night sky. I turned to face my brother's best friend. "He's gone." The words grated out in a bare whisper. "He moved. I'll never see him again."

Darius rubbed my back in a soothing motion, but nothing helped. "Who?"

The last person I expected to break my heart. "Max."

Silence lingered between us. "Is he your boyfriend?" Darius cleared his throat. "Roxy, is this why you're cooped in your room? I feel like we see so little of you these days." His gentle laughter and reassuring smile failed to cheer me. "Hey, it's okay. You'll forget him. You're seventeen; you'll fall in love again."

The statement almost made me laugh. Of course, he'd seen little of me, I'd hidden for months. The entire summer I'd dressed in flowy dresses or peplum tops. Even now, I got away with the puffy jacket I wore because of the cold front in the middle of October. "No, I won't." I gave Max a part of me I'd never given anyone, and in return, he'd left a part of himself.

Darius's dark eyes widened. "Roxanne, what aren't you telling me? I won't judge. Promise."

No point in hiding the truth any longer. Yes, I'd waited to share the news with Max first, but he disappeared from town, and I couldn't hide forever. Besides, my parents and those close to me deserved the truth. "I...I'm pregnant," I managed to choke out.

Darius veered back in his seat, unblinking. A nanosecond later he composed himself and dragged me in for a hug.

Chapter 18

Max
Six years ago

The chilled glass in my hand numbed my fingers. Shooting back the golden liquid, I welcomed the heat burning my throat. Loud music pumped throughout the building, and strobe lights lanced across the walls and floor of the popular New York City nightclub.

"Another," I called to the bartender.

The guy in a black vest strolled over, tapping the bar with a pointed finger. "Dude, you're onto your fifth scotch."

My neck and jaw stiffened. How dare he berate me. "I'll tell you when I've had enough."

He rolled his eyes and poured me another whisky over ice.

"Add this to my tab." I snatched the glass and ignored the upturned lip of the bartender who played therapist. Inside my jacket, I extracted a newspaper and laid the page on the sticky counter.

CAREER OVER. UFC Fighter Suffers Serious Injuries In Car Crash Following Secret Underground Match.

Doctors told a distraught Alexander Braxton he'd never again step inside a ring. The article detailed how the young man threw away his future over his poor decision to enter a secret underground fight with no physicians on hand, no media attention, and no money involved. Quotes from Alex admitting his loss contributed to his drunk driving, and how he wished he'd never insisted on a rematch in the first place. The entire article made an example out of Alex, encouraging other fighters not to partake in such dangerous escapades if they aimed to evolve their careers in the MMA world.

Right after moving to New York almost four years ago, I hired the best bodybuilding dietitians and MMA coaches money could buy. They placed me on a strict diet and exercise regime. All of my hard work paid off when I met my eventual goal—heavyweight. Alex made a living as a fighter, hoping to succeed in the major leagues. My moment arrived when I faced him in the ring and defeated him for all to witness on live sports television. After my win, I crouched over him and revealed my identity. His mouth had floundered similar to a fish out of water. Before I could storm off, he grabbed my leg and begged for a rematch. I didn't hesitate. We kept it low key in some underground basement with a few witnesses. My foot always stiffened a little right after a fight, and because of the dull pain, I'd been close to defeat. But then my high school years flashed before my eyes. The bullying, the humiliation, the painful trip to the hospital filled me with so much rage, I'd forgotten the slight discomfort and finished him on the spot.

I shot back the drink and hooted. Four years since I'd left high school and waited to get back at this jerk, and my attempt at evening the score paid off in spades. Nothing killed my buzz.

"Hey there." A sultry voice from behind called out. "You're in a good mood."

Over my shoulder stood a gorgeous blonde showering me with attention. She stepped closer to the bar, her tight white dress hugging her curves and leaving no room for the imagination.

"Sure am." I slurred the words, tilting my glass in a salute.

She sat on the stool beside mine. "Are you celebrating alone or waiting for a friend?"

Vision hazed, I gripped the leg of the stool and dragged her closer to my side. "Not alone anymore."

Her eyes gleamed with heated surprise, and her bee-venom lips stretched into a grin.

I waved my hand over to the bartender. "Take the lady's order."

An hour and many drinks later, Catherine or Katrina slinked from her stool and into my lap. The music pumped around us, not once relenting. Half the time I missed what she said, and I'm pretty sure the same applied to her since she'd laugh at my questions as if I cracked a joke. Her arms draped over my neck, her body tucked into mine, filling me with her sweet and summery perfume. My eyes dipped to half-mast, and I deliberated how long until I crashed.

"Let's go back to your place." Catherine-Katrina's hot breath tickled my ear.

My place? Mmm, yes. Comfy mattress, a pillow to lay my head, the perfect place for me to rest away from this spinning room. Her wet tongue licked at my earlobe, nibbling the flesh. The action rattled my brain and sobered me a tad. Here I dreamed of crashing to sleep, but this woman divulged other intentions. Unsure if the alcohol or the high from my victory possessed me, I squeezed her closer, cupping her face with one palm, and kissed her fake, stiff lips. The longer I kissed the more I compared her to Roxanne's soft luscious mouth. She couldn't hold a candle to the woman who crushed my heart in the palm of her hands.

"Max!" a female voice hollered over the music.

Kat and I inched our heads in the direction of the person shouting my name. Georgina eyed first the blonde in my arms and trailed those narrowed green eyes on me.

"Georgina, what's up?" I held out my fist for her to bump, but she left me hanging. I'd never used the phrase *"What's up"* nor fist-bumped my longtime friend. No wonder her gaze widened.

She turned to the group of girlfriends standing behind her. Each one scowled at the woman in my lap.

"Georgina, don't bother." Her friend sneered, her face twisting in distaste.

"It's fine," she called over the loud beat. "Go, I've got this."

The girls sauntered away, scoffing at my good-natured wave.

Georgina returned her accusing gaze. "What's gotten into you?"

"What?" I blinked several times, forcing away the fogginess in my head.

"Hold on," Kat interrupted, her arms loosening their grip around my neck. "This woman's your girlfriend?"

"No," I proclaimed at the same time Georgina announced, "Yes."

Kat scoffed, hopping off my lap and snatching her

purse off the counter. "Jerk!" She stomped away in her tall stilettos.

My brows drew together. "We're not together."

"Yes, but better she believes otherwise." She clutched my arm and encouraged me to stand. "Come on. Let's get you home."

I threw my arm around Georgina's shoulder, and she led the way to the exit. My ears rang as techno-beats followed me out of the building, and the floors and walls shrank and expanded.

"Max, walk straight." She puffed out a breath. Her forceful steps in those high heels echoed along the sidewalk. "You're no featherweight."

"S-s-sorry." I forced my feet to walk in a horizontal line. "Two hundred and thirty-eight pounds if you're wondering," I mumbled.

The fresh air outside hit, and each breath I inhaled spun my head faster. Wait a minute, where'd my drink go, and what happened to Fake Lips? The streetlight glowed over the top of Georgina's silky brown hair like a halo. My very own killjoy angel. "Hey, you spoiled my fun."

She raised her head, those brown brows squishing together. "What fun? You would've led her on to turn her away."

Brutal yet honest. "Ouch."

Georgina snickered, tugging my slipping wrist high over her shoulder. "It's true."

A group of partygoers cleared the sidewalk as we passed, and I ignored their snickers. "She could have broken the spell."

"Ah, you forgot I used to be your girlfriend." A hint of sarcasm graced her tone. "I've seen you drunk, and, trust me, nothing's breaking your curse."

"Double ouch!" I stopped in my tracks and glared at those blinking green eyes. "You're spiteful tonight."

She dropped my arm, letting me stumble back a step without her support. Opening the door to her flashy sports car, she nodded for me to get in. "No, Max, I'm honest. And I care about you."

Heading home with the blonde would've wasted her and my time. For this exact reason, I avoided relationships. I stepped toward the car and Georgina cupped my jaw, her soft thumb rubbing the short beard. "Since when did you grow a beard?"

Georgina showed immediate interest in me when we met. She approached me at the gym during our first week of college and asked for help with lifting weights. Prior to starting at New York's top university, I gained a bit of weight and muscle with the training program I'd been placed on preceding my successful foot correction surgery and calf implant. All thanks to my stepfather and the world-renowned orthopedic surgeon, six months after the procedure I'd walked out of the private hospital a new man, and for the first time experienced a normal school life in college.

"What?" I gave her a hesitant smile. "You don't like beards?"

Georgina narrowed her gaze. One shoulder bounced in a shrug. "You look different. The beard sure does suit you."

I wagged my eyebrows. "I'm a bigger chick magnet than usual since growing it."

Georgina rolled her eyes. "Get in the car, Max."

I chuckled, slumping into the passenger seat. The expensive cream leather squeaked beneath my body.

She ran around to the other side and snatched the seatbelt from me when I struggled to buckle up.

We drove in silence, passing tall city buildings and closed boutique shops. The streetlights made me wince every time we drove past one. I kept my gaze out the window. Aside from Richard, the only other person privy to my plans included Georgina. I'd never called someone a friend until I met the uptown woman. Confiding in her relieved the weight off my shoulders, and although she disagreed with my plan, she supported me.

"So you're back from California." She broke the silence and lowered the radio volume. Her mouth curved into a wicked grin. "You sure knocked out Alex Braxton."

"You watched the fight?"

She removed her eyes from the road to spare me a glance. "You fought on live television. Of course, I watched. How do you feel?"

I closed my eyes and inhaled a deep breath. "On cloud nine."

To my coach's dismay, I quit right after my match with Alex. He'd hoped to lead me to bigger and better competitions. Regardless of my growing reputation as a fighter, I stuck to the plan. That was my motto. And with Alex defeated, and the world of martial arts behind me, I planned on targeting the next person on my list of foes.

The bright mega screen lit the car as we passed through the heart of Times Square. "Georgina, if every single victory instills this intense feeling, then I can't wait until the next one. All of them will get what they deserve."

She cleared her throat. "Why go to a club tonight? Back in college, you'd use every excuse to leave the scene when my friends and I partied."

My head flopped in her direction again. "Your lifestyle rubbed off on me."

Georgina got me out of my little isolated bubble. She introduced me to her friends and always took me to their hangouts. One night, her friend spilled her secret and confessed to Georgina's interest in me. No one coerced me to date her. In fact, I'd liked her too, but several weeks into the relationship, my feelings never bloomed beyond friendship, and I made a big mistake dragging out the relationship longer than necessary.

Her lips twitched into a smile at the mention of our time in college. "Come on, Max. You complained at every frat party and club I dragged you to. Why hang out at this sleazy joint, philandering with girls you have no interest in?"

"What? I'm celebrating. They have great music and top-of-the-line scotch. As for women, I don't ask them to flock to me."

She scoffed, the sound echoing in the car. "Celebrate or drown your sorrows?"

"I stand corrected the first time." What sorrows of mine needed drowning? Regardless of what she assumed, my drinking and flirting with Blondie wasn't a cry for help.

Her fingers stretched and gripped the steering wheel. "So there's no purpose in life without revenge?"

Sudden heat invaded my neck and I tugged at the collar of my shirt. "Nope."

We stopped at a red light, and she shot me a serious glare. "Don't you have dreams, ambitions?"

All these questions hurt my dizzy head. "Such as?"

Her brow cocked. "For one, a woman you desire, marriage, children?"

I snorted a laugh. "We're fresh out of college. Who the heck plans for marriage and kids?"

Georgina rolled her eyes in her usual dramatic way. "We graduated months ago, and trust me, countless people consider their future. Everyone has a five-year plan."

I leaned closer, lowering my head. "What plan?"

She swallowed, keeping her eyes on the road, but flicking her gaze my way. "To enjoy life, travel, chase your career dreams, and settle down."

How original. "Is this your plan?"

Her mouth fell open. "Yes. And I'm scared you don't have a similar goal." She huffed out a breath. "You're so invested in this vendetta, it's going to take over your life."

She missed the point. I'd go to my grave with one of my enemies kicking and screaming rather than concede. "I won't quit, Georgina. Ever. I plan to ruin their hopes and dreams. I won't—" I hooked my fingers into quotation marks. "—*settle* until I've destroyed them."

Her lips pouted, and those green eyes glossed over. "Then I feel sorry for you."

Feel sorry for me? The words left a bitter taste in my mouth. I crossed my arms over my chest. What if she spoke true, and this attempt at retribution turned out all in vain? People couldn't treat others like absolute garbage and suffer no consequences. My stomach churned. "Stop the car."

"Oh, come on." She gaped at me in pure outrage.

"You can't get offended because…"

I clutched the sleek interior of the door, the churning in my stomach rising to my throat. "I'll be offending your upholstery in a minute if you don't let me out." Bile rose, and I smacked a hand over my mouth.

She slammed on the brakes. The car stopped, and I jumped out, landing on my knees on the cold, wet grass. A nanosecond later, I hunched over and hurled my guts out.

Chapter 19

Roxanne

I followed the rumble of gentle snoring and found my boss splayed out, deep in peaceful slumber, on his dark sofa. The blood stain on his shirt sleeve invoked the events of last night and the incredible way he defended us against the mugger.

When Hunter complained about our failed date and asked me to stay, at first every part of me said yes, but as we kissed on the sofa, each brush of his lips triggered familiar emotions of the boy who stole my heart at seventeen. In my mind, I kissed and held Max, the one guy I experienced the deepest levels of intimacy with, and as Hunter awakened my senses, an onslaught of guilt ushered in. I'd raced into the bathroom, clutching the basin for dear life, fearing I'd encounter another delusional episode...like the ones suffered in the past few weeks.

Maybe my subconscious fed me all those hallucinations, playing mental tricks to prevent a shot at happiness. In reality, Max and I never declared our status officially...though at the time he'd left an infinite stamp on my heart. A part of me would always love him. I mean, he gave me the greatest gift in the world. And if we ever crossed paths one day, I still planned on revealing the truth, but focusing on my life mattered too. What if taking a chance with Hunter led to love, marriage, and children?

"What's the time?" Hunter stretched his good arm over his head, his voice gruff from sleep as he rubbed at his tired eyes. He leaned over and snatched his phone from the coffee table. "It's nine o'clock." Placing the phone back on the table, he eased into a sitting position, cringing and gripping his arm.

Out of touch with the dating scene led to my frantic internet search for the top ten first date ideas. The dumb suggestion of a downtown bar resulted in me rushing my date to the hospital. "How are you feeling?"

He stretched out his bandaged arm. "A little sore, but nothing I can't handle. And you?"

I placed a hand on my chest. "I'm fine. You're the one who got hurt."

He paused from rubbing his bandaged arm and shot me a stare. "No, I mean…after last night?"

Oh, he referred to my embarrassing breakdown during our heated make-out session. He'd been incredible last night. The fact he held me in his arms, letting my tears soak his shirt while he stroked my hair until I fell asleep, shocked me to my core. Not once did he try initiating more between us. He told the truth when he said he simply wanted to be there for me.

He encouraged me to spill with a firm nod of his head.

No avoiding the question. So instead, I avoided his gaze and pinched the hem of my sleeve. "Like a fool."

Silence stretched between us for several moments, his features growing solemn.

My heart plummeted into my stomach. "What?"

A pink hue stained his cheeks, and he sighed with a

sad smile. "I can't force you to like me, Roxanne."

Force me to like him? No force necessary when I'd fallen hard. My admission regarding my past love opened up a can of worms. "I do have feelings for you, Hunter. Every day I'm eager to see you. The way you look at me makes me giddy with excitement...like I'm the center of your world. You helped me through my meltdown on our flight to LA, and you noticed my talent and gave me a chance to pursue a dream I never believed would come true...you're amazing, and I'd be a fool to ignore what's between us. I want to explore this and see if we can be great together." With Hunter, it was like I stood at the edge of a cliff, my heart hammering but not from duress, my mind screaming but not from fear. Yet the most baffling part about the whole experience was embracing the rush and eagerness to relive such a daring act.

He glanced over the brown leather decorative cushion. "But your ex..."

"As I mentioned in the bathroom, I felt guilty, as if I'd cheated. I'm not ready for intimacy, but I'm not giving up on us either." I bit my bottom lip. "Unless I've already scared you off."

"No, you haven't scared me off." He circled the sofa, grasped my arms and leaned his head against mine. "I won't lie, I desire you. But we can take things slow. You'll be amazed to learn how patient I can be." His long fingers tucked a strand of hair behind my ear, sending a shiver down my spine.

"Since our official date last night hadn't gone ahead." He leaned back and winked. "Care to try again?"

He had no idea how much I craved to hear those

words. "Yes."

In a show of relief, he closed his eyes, then gathered my hands. "Are you free tonight?"

The tournament! I bit my lip. "I can't tonight. I have plans with my son. How's next weekend sound?"

He leaned in and fused his lips to mine, his kiss soft and gentle, and my entire body relaxed.

"Sounds like a plan." He gave a playful wink. "We can sort out the finer details during the week, but let's avoid places with unsecured parking to prevent another trip to the ER."

I laughed while slipping out of his embrace. A repeat of last night? No thanks. For this next date, I'd let Hunter take the reins.

****

Once Carlo, Hunter's driver, dropped me off at home, I rushed into my apartment with an hour to shower and dress. Changed into a fresh pair of clothes, I grabbed my purse off the kitchen counter and rushed out the door to meet everyone at the stadium. Saturday traffic congested the roads, but I managed to arrive on time.

Inside the stadium, loud rock music blasted through the speakers. The echo of chants and cheers reverberated in the large space, and I blinked in awe at the crowd. Families, couples, teenagers, and grandparents filled the place. Sponsor logo banners draped the walls and railings. Below sat a massive skate bowl surrounded by several ramps and rails.

Butterflies danced in my stomach and my hands grew clammy.

"Mom, you made it."

I turned at the sound of my sweet boy's voice. "I

told you I wouldn't miss this."

He ran into my arms, and I secured him in a tight hug, running my fingers through his dark blond hair. "Are you nervous?" Helmet under one arm and wearing his protective gear, my blood pressure dropped a notch. At least he'd be safe out there.

He wore the widest grin, and a sparkle lit his pale blue-green eyes. "Not at all," he shouted over the noise.

I leaned in closer to his ear. "Okay, only me then."

He chuckled at my admission. "I'm super excited for my turn. Nine-year-olds get to go first, so they'll call me soon."

I straightened and fixed my bag strap over my shoulder. "I better go find your grandparents."

"Oh, they're over there." He pointed to the crowd.

Mom and Dad waved, seated among the throng of people.

"Zane Maxwell Hastings, please collect your pass and board at the information desk." The announcement resonated over the speakers.

He beamed and held out his palm for a high five. "Gotta go."

"Okay." I smacked his palm with my own and kissed the top of his head. "Have fun out there. I love you."

"Love you too, Mom," he hollered, racing off.

I clutched at my chest, rubbing the inner ache. Goodness, the birth of my son felt like yesterday. The wailing, wrapped bundle I took home from the hospital changed me from a teenager to a young mother overnight. Zane forced me to mature in ways I'd never imagined, and I'd bawled my eyes out in those first few weeks with my newborn, afraid I held, bathed, or fed him wrong. He'd grown so much since then...

My parents left the front porch light on, expecting me to return later than nine thirty. I opened the door and tiptoed into the house not to wake Zane or anyone else. As I made my way down the hall, banging emitted from the lit kitchen. I stepped farther into the room, taking in the flour-smeared countertop, small bowl of chocolate chips, and empty carton with eggshells. Those beautiful eyes gleamed at me, causing my heart to squeeze.

"Mommy, you're back."

"You're still awake?" I strolled over and draped my bag over the chairback. "It's late."

Mom wore her pink, fluffy robe tied around her waist, and the bags under her eyes confirmed she'd rather relax in bed than bake in the kitchen at this hour. "He couldn't sleep and asked to bake cookies."

I stopped her from spooning cookie dough onto a lined tray. "Ever consider trying a bedtime story? You went ahead with baking cookies?"

"Not any cookies." My four-year-old lifted the bowl and held the plastic under my nose. "Choc chip cookies."

"Don't get too close, darlin'," Mom warned with a raised finger. "You'll mess your dress."

I rolled my eyes, making my sweet boy chuckle. I cared zilch about messing this black number with cookie dough and flour.

Zane placed the spoon on the counter and dusted his hands. He grinned at me with a special twinkle in his eyes. "You look pretty, Mommy."

I cupped his face. He'd lost the chubby baby cheeks I used to love squeezing, his features morphing into an older, childlike face. "Thank you, baby. Let Grandma finish here and you come with me."

Michael and Jasmine moved in together the instant they graduated college and my parents remodeled Michael's old room for Zane since he'd outgrown his crib. A soft blue glow from the night-light lit the room, and I changed him into a clean pair of pajamas.

"I couldn't sleep," he admitted when I tucked him into bed, those round eyes unblinking, eyes a replica of his father's.

I parked myself on the edge of his bed and stroked his soft cheek. "Did you have a bad dream?"

He shook his head in response. "I was scared you weren't coming home."

No part of me fancied attending a downtown nightclub for my cousin's twenty-first birthday party. I would have rather stayed home and helped my son bake cookies, but my parents convinced me to make an appearance. With all of my evening classes, studying, and caring for my son, they said I deserved a night out. My throat tightened, and once again I leaned over and kissed his forehead. "I'll always come home to you. To be honest..." I kicked off my heels and scooted beside him. "I left the party early."

"Why?" He cuddled his teddy to his chest, giving me his full attention. "Wasn't the party fun?"

Nothing fun about evading the cheesy guy urging me to take shots and dance. Other than our age, I held nothing in common with the partygoers. "No."

His brows drew together. "Was there a bouncy castle?"

I snorted a soft laugh. "No, baby, no bouncy castle."

"Oh, no wonder you came home." His expression morphed into a serious scowl. "You can't have a party without a bouncy castle."

I tapped his little nose with the tip of my finger. "You're right, you can't, but I'll tell you the real reason I came home."

He blinked at me, awaiting an answer, and the ache in my chest intensified.

Max missed out on so many milestones every year, wonderful moments we'd never get back. Where are you, Max? *The frequent question plagued my mind. I guess I'd have to hold every memory and share all the details with him one day. At least I hoped I'd be able to. "Because there's nowhere in the world I'd rather be than right here with you."*

His grin widened, showing off his little white teeth. Leaning on his elbows, he kissed my cheek and settled back against his pillow. "I love you, Mommy."

I kissed his dark blond head. "I love you too, kiddo."

And now he competed in skateboarding competitions, for crying out loud. Squeezing my way through the crowd, I took a seat beside my parents.

"Hi, sweetie." Mom waved a triangular stick flag she'd embellished with Zane's name. Following in Max's family tradition, I'd given my boy his grandfather's name. At least this way, a part of him held his father's family custom.

"Roxanne." Mom dropped her flag into her lap and grinned my way. "I've called you all morning."

Funny, I never missed my high-chimed ringtone. I frowned, rifling inside my purse, rummaging through every pocket but found nothing. "Oh, no."

"What?" Mom gazed at the contents in my lap. "You lost your phone!"

I raised a palm. "It's either in my car, back at the apartment, or…" in Hunter's limo, or perhaps his hotel room.

Her dark eyebrows shot up in question. "Or where?"

I spared them both a reassuring smile. "It'll turn up. Let's not worry now. Zane's ready to enter the stage."

The announcer called Zane onto the platform, and heart in my throat, I gripped the rail. My son performed all sorts of tricks and stunts, sending the crowd wild. He'd skateboarded since age four, all thanks to my brother who bought him his first-ever board, and although Zane trained hard and excelled in skateboarding, all the skills in the world never eased my worries while watching him perform. He finished off with a final flip, and the crowd stood and applauded. Mom hooted the loudest, waving her little homemade flag. Dad chuckled as I clutched my chest and blew out a strong breath, standing with everyone else to clap at Zane's amazing performance.

Even though I encouraged my son to pursue his dreams, I wished he developed a passion for a safer pastime like playing guitar.

Zane found us in the crowd, and I gave him a big hug. "You were amazing, honey."

He peered at me with a sheepish grin. "Thanks, Mom."

We remained seated for the rest of the day, viewing other contestants. By late afternoon they announced the winners for each age group.

"And in first place with three hundred points we have…" The commentator paused into his microphone. I gripped my son's hand, holding my breath.

"Zane Hastings!"

We all jumped out of our seats, squealing with the crowd in cheers and hoots. I gave Zane one last hug, and he descended the stairs and ran onto the stage to receive his award.

So many people congratulated him on our way out.

Mom stopped outside the exit, and Dad handed Zane his overnight bag. "Why don't you come around for dinner tonight, and I'll cook a special meal for our little champion?"

I bit my lip, my smile apologetic. "I hoped to treat Zane out to dinner to celebrate."

"Oh." Zane bounced on his toes. "Can we try the Italian restaurant you mentioned?"

My favorite pasta? I'd never say no. "Of course, honey." I turned to my parents. "You guys are welcome to join. We can even call Michael and Jasmine too."

Mom hooked her arm with Dad's. "We'd love to, but I'd already defrosted chicken back at home."

"Besides," Dad threw in with a dismissive wave. "Jasmine and Michael have their hands full with the newborn and Dylan."

Yes, last I spoke with my sister-in-law she mentioned struggling to get into a routine with her two young children. The doctor gave Jasmine the all-clear to return to work at her last check-up, so after next week she'd no longer need me to take Dylan to daycare. A shame. I quite enjoyed the extra bonding time with my little nephew these last few months.

"You two have fun." Mom kissed my cheek.

"Roxanne, please call me once you find your phone."

With all the excitement I forgot I'd lost the device. "I will, and thank you again for watching Zane and meeting me here today."

"Our pleasure." My dad ruffled his grandson's head and hugged him goodbye. "We're proud of you, kid."

I bit my lip. The close relationship he shared with them filled me with gratitude. Without Michael and my dad, no other male role models existed in his life.

We stopped home first, and I let Zane shower and change as I searched for my phone with no luck, which meant I left the device at Hunter's. Should Zane and I stop by his hotel on the way to the restaurant? I tsked under my breath. No, my phone dilemma would have to wait until Monday. Bad idea for Zane's first meeting with my potential boyfriend to take place on Hunter's doorstep. At the appropriate time, I'd introduce Zane to Hunter over lunch at a nice location where I hoped the two of them would hit it off.

The waiter at Moretti's restaurant sat us at a window booth. Zane ordered his favorite, chicken parmigiana, and I requested potato gnocchi in creamy truffle sauce. Throughout dinner, Zane's smile from his earlier win remained glued on his face as he explained the technique and styles of each stunt he'd performed earlier.

Our desserts arrived and I dug into mine.

Zane, however, left his chocolate pudding untouched. How did this child go from cloud nine to slumping in his seat?

"Do you still look for him?"

The topic threw me off-guard. I discarded the fork,

neglecting my tiramisu. "Who?"

"My father." He sat unblinking, his words direct. "You told me once you search for him whenever you're out in public."

From a young age, Zane asked questions concerning Max. The older he grew, the more I told him the truth about how I treated his father. Better he learned the past from me than one day discover from another what happened. I expressed to Zane my immense remorse for the way I'd treated Max, even visiting local schools as part of an anti-bullying program a few years back. Zane commended my part in the program, but my good works never provided me those three little words I yearned to hear Max say—I forgive you. And could I blame him? I learned the hard way the consequences of hurting him. "It's become a habit of mine since high school. I've always kept my eyes peeled, hoping I'd run into him again one day."

He nudged at his dessert with his fork. "Even now you have a boyfriend?"

As if punched in the chest, I held my breath and forced the smile to remain on my face. "Who told you I have a boyfriend?"

"I overheard Grandma and Aunt Jasmine say you went on a date with your boss."

I bit the inside of my cheek. "Does my having a boyfriend upset you?"

He shrugged, the action giving him away.

"Zane." I placed my hand over his. "You can talk to me."

He frowned at the table, glancing back into my eyes. "I look out for him too."

I frowned. "Your father? But you've never met

him." We owned one picture of Max, the action shot from the rollercoaster I'd kept all these years in Zane's baby album, the side profile of Max from the speed of the captured shot not enough to distinguish his features.

"You said he and I share the same unique eyes. Whenever I meet new people, or whenever we leave the house, I'm always checking."

I caressed his hand, and my chin trembled. "Oh, Zane, buddy."

Over the years I'd run several internet searches and checked social media, including messaging every Maxwell Fields with a blank profile picture. Once I'd contemplated hiring a private investigator, but at the time lacked the funds.

Zane slipped his hands out of mine and reached inside his jacket pocket. "I thought I met him once when I ran into this stranger at the skate park."

I froze in my seat. "Explain to me why you're meeting strangers, young man?"

He scrunched his lips and shrugged. "It's okay, Mom. I had Big Zee with me." Zane withdrew a gift box from inside his jacket. "Here, I got this for you."

A gift? What? Why? "Zane, what's going on? It's not my birthday."

"Open it." He rubbed his hands together and grinned.

I opened the box and an expensive gold necklace with a heart locket sat encased inside. "Oh, my goodness, it's gorgeous." I leaned forward, and whispered, "How'd you afford this with your spending money? Please don't tell me your grandparents organized this?"

"I saved most of my spending money. When Big

Zee took me to the skate park, I defended a bullied kid. Anyway, a man there called me one brave dude. He too had been bullied in school."

"The stranger you mentioned. You assumed he was your father because he shared the same history as your dad?" Zane's desperate attempt to seek his father twisted my heart with guilt. I'd failed him as a mom. Perhaps we'd have Max back in our lives if I'd tried harder, searched further, and paid for an investigator.

He nodded, his lips puckered. "But this man had brown eyes, not my eyes." He took a sip of his water, gazing at me with all seriousness. "Now don't freak, but he also gave me two hundred dollars."

"Two hundred dollars," I whisper-shouted. He took money from a stranger, and I remained ignorant of the event until now!

"Big Zee refused, but the man insisted I deserved a reward." He grinned, his gaze falling on the gift in my hand. "I smashed open my piggy bank to collect all the money I'd saved, added to the amount the nice man gave me, and bought you a special present. By the way, you're lucky Big Zee took me to the jewelry store because Uncle Mikey suggested I buy new seat covers for your car."

Trust Michael to buy a car-related gift. Tears stung my eyes. "You're the best thing to ever happen in my life. I'm sorry for not doing all I'd promised."

"It's all right." He offered an undeserving bright grin. "The Grand Canyon isn't going anywhere. We'll visit one day."

Two hundred dollars. "I still can't believe you accepted money from a stranger."

His mouth quirked, mimicking his uncle Michael

which meant the cocky attitude stemmed from my side of the family. I clasped the necklace around my neck, eager to wear the beautiful locket.

"If it isn't my two favorite people." Darius approached our table, waving goodbye to a group of men and thanking them for taking him out to dinner.

Grabbing a napkin, I dabbed my mouth. I'd last seen Darius at his house, the day I canceled our date. He'd avoided my parents' Friday night dinners since, and although no one said anything, I blamed myself.

He returned my smile with a genuine one of his own.

"Darius!" Zane sprung from his seat, bouncing on his toes. "Guess what? I got first place in the skateboarding competition."

"Whoa, great job, little Zee." Darius raised his palm and gave him a high five. "Congratulations."

"Thanks." Zane's jaw dropped. "Mom, I see Jackson. Can I go over and tell him my news?"

Zane's classmate dined with his parents at one of the center tables. "Okay, sure, but be quick. They're eating dinner."

He dropped his napkin on his chair and hurried across the room, leaving me alone with Darius. My stomach hardened, and my face flushed with heat. Awkwardness stiffened my shoulders, a tension nonexistent weeks ago when we'd laughed and joked or made fun of Michael to stir him up.

Darius glanced over his shoulder, and I followed his gaze toward Zane in deep conversation with his friend. Taking Zane's free seat, he released a loud sigh and fixed his gaze on me. "I have to apologize—"

"Darius, don't." Our run-in took a turn for the

worse, broaching a topic I'd rather steer clear from. "You don't have to—"

"No, I do." He ran his fingers through his hair. "You were honest right from the beginning. Sorry I made things weird between us. You're an amazing woman, Roxanne, and you're going to make some lucky man happy one day."

"Thank you, Darius." My brother's best friend held a special place in our lives, and I prayed to one day see him happy with a woman he loved. "I wish the same for you too."

"We'll see what new beginnings bring me." He shrugged and crossed his arms over his chest. "I'm moving tomorrow."

"Moving?" Why hadn't Michael told me? Goodness, rejecting the man didn't mean I no longer cared. "Where to?"

"Florida."

I swallowed bile. My stomach coiled into knots. "Darius, I hope this isn't because—"

"I promise it's not. Work promoted me to manage the new head office. My team and I are moving there." He licked his bottom lip. "Although...I admit not seeing you will help matters. I'll miss you like crazy, but I'm excited to see where this opportunity leads me."

"We're going to miss you." A shot to further his career in another city. For that reason alone, I understood his temptation to leave. "How'd Michael take the news?"

"He's guilting me over leaving. I've reassured him I'll return for the holidays, and he, Jasmine, and the kids can visit anytime." He leaned over and poked my hand. "The invitation extends to you and Zane."

"Thank you." The familiar crinkle in his eyes set me at ease. Praise God no awkwardness lingered between us. "By the way, I don't blame him. The two of you have been inseparable since childhood."

"Michael will be fine." He rolled his eyes and stood from the chair. "He keeps making jabs about me moving, even telling Dylan to call me the naughty godfather, but I expected no less."

I chuckled low. Yeah, my brother acted no better than a whiny baby. Standing from my seat, I wrapped Darius in a hug. "Congratulations on the promotion."

He squeezed me tighter. A lump formed in my throat, and I gave him a gentle kiss on the cheek and peered into his eyes. "I do hope you find happiness."

"Same here." He rubbed his thumb across my cheek.

A light tickle danced down my front. My new necklace had somehow unclasped and dropped into the neckline of my top. "Oh, I mustn't have clipped it on properly."

"Here, allow me." Darius took the locket from my hands and motioned for me to turn around.

His gentle fingers grazed my neck as he clasped the necklace in place and keeping a smile on my face to not appear uncomfortable, I faced him again and gestured to Zane's empty seat. "Why don't you sit with me until Zane gets back from chatting with his friend? He'd never forgive himself if he missed the chance to say a proper goodbye."

Darius resettled in the seat and told me about his promotion. Our natural conversation grew lighter as we joked and laughed, retelling old stories from our childhood. When Zane returned to the table, and Darius broke the news, the pout on my son's face resonated deep in my heart. Zane had known Darius his whole life, so of course the news gutted him.

As we left the restaurant and got into the car, Zane gazed out the window.

"You're quiet."

He turned to me with a shake of his head. "It's sad Darius is leaving."

I gripped the steering wheel, controlling my emotions. "Life takes us in directions we don't expect."

He glanced at his lap for a moment. "Mom?"

We stopped at a red light. "Hmm?"

His head shot up and desperation welled in wide eyes. "Will I ever meet my father?"

Nothing but dust remained from the crushing force of my heart. "I don't know." No point in filling him with false hope and disappointing him later.

He nodded, his face twisting into a sad frown.

"I'm sorry, Zane. I pray to God you do meet him one day." The light turned green, and I continued down the road.

He gripped his knees and released a loud sigh. "About the boyfriend...I'm not mad at you. I do feel a tad weird, but I'm not angry."

What did I do to deserve such a beautiful, brave kid? "Thank you for your honesty. And whatever happens, nothing will change my love for you."

He turned his attention out the window again. "I love you, too, Mom."

Chapter 20

Max

I strummed my fingers over the solid table, phone to my ear as Jean-Phillipe detailed the next steps in our plan for the hotel. Roxanne pranced around in my mind since this morning, distracting me for most of the day. She'd imprinted her presence at my penthouse, and every time I sat on my couch I was reminded of our heated kiss, of her sad eyes reflecting back whenever I washed my hands in front of the bathroom mirror. And forget about lying in bed; her sweet perfume fragranced the sheets and teased me beyond belief.

"…I'll need those documents to sign."

I blinked, carried back to the conversation. "No problem, Jean. We'll meet on Monday and sort out the details. Talk soon." I hung up the phone and returned to working on my laptop. Rather than allow the images of last night to torment me, I headed to the office in hopes of providing myself a good distraction, but today the distraction proved futile. The sunset's pink and orange hues prompted me to spy the time on my watch. Georgina should arrive any minute now. In need of her advice, I'd called earlier asking her to meet me. What better person than my best friend to help me flesh out my predicament? I clicked open the files on my laptop and accessed all the information I'd gathered over the last ten years. Each person's little folder held their own documents from my private investigator. I opened the folder with Roxanne's name, and the report Bruce sent me months ago, the same report I never had the guts to read stared me in the face. Deleting the file, I breathed a sigh of relief as though erasing a heavy burden from my shoulders. Inside the same folder sat other files with Roxanne's images and a detailed list of all my schemes. Last night I deleted the copy on my personal laptop. Once I deleted these ones too, it'd all be over, and I'd erase all records of her from my computer. Gripping the mouse, I hovered the arrow over the delete button but stopped when a soft ding echoed from the elevator doors.

Georgina approached the foyer, holding a cardboard tray with two foam cups.

"Hey." She placed the tray on my desk and greeted me with a hug.

"Took you long enough." I returned the hug, taking in the familiar fragrance she'd used since college.

"Good coffee comes with patience, my friend." She eased out of the hug and handed me a cup. "It sounded urgent on the phone. What's going on?"

Warm liquid traveled the length of my throat, and the swirling steam rose to my face. "I'm quitting the plan."

Her bright green eyes widened. "You're at last throwing in the towel?" She set her cup on the desk, her face broke into a wide smile, and she breathed a relieved sigh. "Oh, thank God. Max, how fantastic." She shrugged, her gaze searching mine. "Why? What brought this on?"

A cynical laugh puffed from my nose. "You're

right. I've never gotten over her."

She placed one hand on her hip, her mouth twitching. "It took you ten years to realize you're not over her?"

I rolled my eyes. Trust her to throw her I-told-you-so attitude. "No…it's taken me ten years to admit the truth to myself."

Heat suffused my body, perhaps from the coffee, or the aircon on my floor malfunctioned, or the reason I set aside my coffee and stripped off my business jacket related to the insufferable stare Georgina shot my way. Her eyes blazed a clear message of humor and self-satisfaction. Then again, she always loved being right. I'd let her have this little moment of victory.

She chuckled, snatching her cup and taking another swig. "I'm happy for you, Max. You have a chance to forget the past and find happiness."

One problem though, my chance held hands with hopelessness. I calculated every step but never planned on pursuing the woman I sought revenge on. I tossed my folded jacket over the edge of the desk. With no idea how to forge ahead, I found myself stuck at a crossroads. "What should I do?" I pinched the bridge of my nose. "I mean, I can't confess everything."

Georgina cocked her head to one side, narrowing her stern eyes. "You can't continue deceiving her either. She's bound to find out your identity sooner or later."

I'd breathed these lies and schemes for the last decade, but to base my relationship on manipulation and deceit. The word *regret* never made the cut in my vocabulary, but now the meaning jolted through my entire being.

She cupped my shoulder, her smile sad but genuine. "Tell her the truth."

Months had passed since Roxanne first entered my office, the woven web too messy to disentangle now. "Telling her the truth will end the relationship. I'm Hunter Parker, a self-made man. She's not seeking a relationship with Max Fields."

"Oh, my goodness." Georgina gasped, leaning back to peer into my eyes. "You're going to keep playing Hunter Parker."

Why not? Work colleagues, associates, and tabloids used my pseudonym. Few people close to me called me Max. "It is my name."

She closed her eyes and puffed out a breath. "No, it's your middle name. Don't pretend Hunter Parker's not your disguise." She pointed an accusing finger. "Reveal yourself, show her you became the guy worthy of love."

I blinked and paced. "Oh, show her before or after she puts out a restraining order against me?"

"Stop being a baby. Tell her the truth; at least you won't have guilt eating at you." She straightened her spine and tilted her chin a tad. "If she can't understand and accept the truth, then she doesn't deserve you."

I stopped pacing. "But then I'll lose her all over again."

Georgina closed the space between us, one gentle hand caressing the side of my face. "But at least you'll have closure."

I closed my eyes. My nerves left me on edge. I'd never experienced this tension in my entire life. Exhaling a slow breath, I nodded. "Okay. You're right. I'll tell her. Tonight."

Georgina stood on her tiptoes and kissed my cheek. "I'm proud of you."

We placed our empty cups on Roxanne's desk, and I walked Georgina over to the elevator and hit the button.

"I'm meeting Aunt Esme for her dress fittings." She flicked her dark long hair over her shoulder. "Keep me updated on how everything turns out."

"I will. Thank you…for everything."

Once Georgina left, I strolled back into my office and dialed Roxanne…a few times. How unlike her to not answer my calls. I sank into my chair and swiveled around to peer out at the city view. Driving to her place might be an option, although she lived out of my way, and I harbored no reasonable excuse to show up at her doorstep. Truth be told, I hungered to see her again. Good grief, what a poor sap I turned into.

The ding from the elevator snapped me out of my daze, and I stood. "Georgina?"

My driver ducked his well-groomed white head of hair inside my office.

"Carlo?" I settled back into my seat.

"Sorry to disturb you, Hunter, but I found this in the back of the limo."

I recognized the pale blue cover when he handed me Roxanne's phone.

"Miss Hastings left her cell behind."

No wonder her phone rang unanswered. "It's fine, Carlo. I'll handle it."

He nodded and strolled away.

Placing Roxanne's phone in front of me on the desk, I grinned, now obtaining a reasonable excuse to visit her. What if surprising her backfired as me coming on too strong? A bitter laugh strained my throat. Once I spilled the truth, she'd kick me to the curb.

The phone buzzed on my desk, ringing out with a monotone song. A name flashed on the screen. Mom. Perhaps Roxanne used her mother's cell in hopes of locating her own? I answered without further delay. "Roxanne's phone."

"Oh...hello. My daughter misplaced her phone earlier today."

"Hello, Mrs. Hastings. I'm Hunter Parker, Roxanne's boss."

"Oh, thank goodness...It's all right, Roxanne's boss found her phone," she called out to whoever stood in the background. "I'm so relieved. I'll have to send her an email. I bet Roxanne will be thrilled you have it."

I leaned over my desk, my hand flattening over the smooth surface. "She left the device in my driver's limo. I can swing by if she's home?"

"She's out tonight with her special guy." She sang the words *special guy,* the cheer in her tone evident.

I froze. My throat constricted. "Special guy?"

"Oh, I'm sure Roxanne's told you all about him. Can you believe he won first place in the skateboard championship today? They've gone to her favorite Italian restaurant to celebrate."

No, in fact, she'd never mentioned a champion skateboarder. "At Moretti's?"

"Yes." She chuckled, the sound low and soft. "She keeps bragging they make the best pasta."

I forced a smile. "When you email her, let her know I'll leave her phone in her desk drawer."

"Thank you, Mr. Parker. I'll pass on the message."

"Have a nice evening." I ended the call.

Images of Roxanne on another date plagued my mind. I stormed out of my office, tossed Roxanne's phone in her drawer as promised, then threw on my jacket. Not bothering to shut off my computer or switch off the lights, I charged into the elevator.

Carlo sat parked in front of the building entrance, and I climbed into the back of the limo. "To Moretti's restaurant."

Carlo put on his flat cap, tilting the edge. "No problem, sir."

I kept my eyes peeled out the window. Please, let this all be one big misunderstanding and not mean what I feared most—Roxanne played me again.

The limo stopped at the curb. I mumbled thanks to Carlo and stepped outside. The restaurant's large floor-to-ceiling windows gave me a perfect view of each table from where I stood on the sidewalk. My throat dropped into my stomach. Roxanne. Inside, hugging another man. Roxanne eased out of the man's embrace and placed a soft kiss on his cheek, the moment intimate. They stared into each other's eyes, then a second later Roxanne turned with the brightest smile on her face as the man fastened a necklace around her delicate neck. Yeah, a special guy all right.

As they both resumed their seats, I clenched my fists and hopped back into the limo. "To Parker Hotel, Carlo." My voice boomed in the large space, but Carlo started the engine and drove away without asking questions.

Last night she acted traumatized from getting hot and heavy, and tonight she met with another guy. Could this man be the father of her child? Had our talk last night encouraged her to contact him and rekindle what they shared? But why feed me all her fluffy nonsense this morning? I gritted my teeth, punching the leather seat. Forget what I told Georgina earlier. No way I'd change my mind. I'd see this plan through to the end.

Chapter 21

Roxanne

The elevator doors parted, and I stepped into the bright foyer. Two foam coffee cups sat at my desk, and I strolled over and raised one. Empty. "Hunter?" He shouldn't be here. I received an email this morning on my laptop explaining he was meeting with Jean-Philippe. Even so, I ducked my head inside his office and headed over to his desk. Paperwork lay strewn across his desk and his computer sat open as though he'd left the building in a rush. Countless nights he'd stay late and spent most weekends working, but how unlike him to leave behind a mess, let alone not shut everything down. Hunter explained in his email he expected me at the office today, finalizing the latest report instead of attending this morning's meeting.

I threw the empty coffee cups in the trash can beside my desk, switched on the computer, and grabbed my phone from the drawer. My mother emailed yesterday, explaining Hunter called to say he'd left my cell on my desk.

An electronic tune rang out, and I clicked to answer the video conference call on my computer. Hunter's handsome face lit the screen, looking dapper in a pair of sunglasses. "Good morning."

"Morning." The vibration of the limo echoed

through the speakers. "Glad to see you found your phone?"

I waved the device in front of the screen. "It's dead, but there's a charger in my drawer. Are you on your way to meet Jean?"

"Carlo's driving me there now."

With the window down, I got a glimpse of traffic outside.

"Contact me by email until your phone's in use again."

"No problem." He made no mention of our date or us spending the night in each other's arms. Yesterday he'd acted normal, and yet this morning his professional tone sounded clinical, perhaps because he spoke with Carlo nearby, or the upcoming meeting with Jean-Phillipe distracted him. "I'll get started on those reports and have them ready by the time you arrive."

"Excellent." He nodded into the screen. "Nice necklace."

I stroked the heart locket resting against my chest. "Oh, gorgeous, right? A gift from my son."

His mouth scrunched. "Your *son*?"

"My father helped pick the necklace out of course, but yes."

He stilled, the way he tended to whenever the subject of my son arose. I entered into a relationship and had no idea about his views regarding children. In our short time together, he made his dislike crystal clear because whenever I mentioned my son he'd change the subject. Not to mention the time I brought Dylan to work, and Hunter's eyes bulged when holding him. That day Hunter expressed never envisioning himself as a father.

"I'll see you once I get back to the office." He uttered more unclear words and ended the call.

A weight slumped in my chest, and I worried my bottom lip. Sunday morning we'd parted ways with a kiss and a promise to plan another date. Now his cold demeanor toward my son's gift left me second-guessing if Hunter Parker held room in his heart for my little boy. Zane and I formed a package deal, but what if the fact was a deal-breaker? As much as I craved a relationship with this man, there was no way in hell I'd forsake my son.

No point in pondering such matters until I spoke to Hunter. I jumped straight into work and spent the next few hours finishing up the report. Due for my lunch break, I set the printed paperwork on Hunter's desk and headed to the exit, but as the elevator doors parted, the office phone rang, and I hurried back and leaned over my desk in an awkward attempt at snatching the phone.

"Hunter Parker's office." I held my breath to stop myself from huffing and puffing down the line.

"Hello, Roxanne."

"Jean-Philippe." I hobbled around and sank into the chair. "How nice to hear your voice. Are you still with Hunter?"

"No, he left. I forgot to hand Hunter a copy of the company list for the ballroom decorations and fittings. He seemed distracted throughout our meeting, and the document slipped our minds."

I straightened in my seat, a broad smile stretching my lips at his words. "The ballroom?"

"Yes, the extensive list ranges from chandeliers down to the last roll of carpet. Please print off a copy for Mr. Parker."

Goodness, this meant he liked my design enough to go ahead with my layout for the ballroom. "Oh, how exciting. I'm at my desk and opening your email now." I scrolled through the lists of contact numbers for several lighting companies, furniture, and drapes, until I scrolled to the bottom image with a scan of the floorplan. My smile withered.

"Not mine," I uttered, breathless. "This is *your* design."

"Well, of course, it's my design." He chuckled as though I made a joke. "Who else were you expecting?"

I sank back in my chair, my mind racing a mile a minute. "Hunter sent you my plans for the ballroom, right? He told me you'd go over them and see if we'd make my design happen."

Silence filled the line, then Jean-Philippe cleared his throat. "Hunter mentioned nothing of the sort. I had no idea you're skilled in designing."

I rubbed my fingertips over my temple, massaging away an oncoming headache. "He forgot to send you the floor plan." I reasoned more to myself than Jean-Philippe. "Or perhaps the email failed."

"Roxanne, when I met with him now, we discussed the plans for the ballroom…my original plans. He made no mention of changes, let alone a new design."

Heat scorched my cheeks. I prayed the ground opened and swallowed me whole.

"Roxanne, you there?"

"Um…" I struggled to get the words past the lump in my throat, but I feigned a smile and spoke unrushed to fake control. "I'm so sorry, Jean-Philippe, I must have misunderstood what Hunter said." I rubbed at the pulsating ache in my chest. "I'll leave a printed copy on

Hunter's desk."

"Thank you, Roxanne. *Au revoir.*"

"Goodbye." I returned the receiver as though made of fragile glass, and the phone clicked in its holder. A choked gasp escaped my throat. Why say he'd go ahead with my design for the ballroom? Because he liked me? A way to flatter me or get me into bed? Hands balled into fists, I stood from my desk, stalked inside my boss's office, and sat in the large armchair. Running the pad of my finger over his computer, the screen lit up. What the hell happened to the floor plan I sent to his email? As I shifted the cursor to the X symbol of the documents already opened, I froze at the name on the file. Alexander Braxton.

Why a file of the guy from my high school? Double-clicking the little yellow folder, several documents and images lay inside. I clicked the first picture. A scanned news article detailing how Alex's car accident left him incapable of partaking in professional fighting. Clicking next, I found other images of him too, out the front of a building, walking along a street alone, kissing a woman on the cheek at a bar. A private investigator no doubt captured these images since every image appeared snapped from a fair distance.

I backed out of Alex's file and toggled to the next opened document labeled Trevor Dallas. A shiver rocked my spine, flashbacks of the night in the diner parking lot shaking my equilibrium. Releasing a winded breath, I clicked through a trail of Trevor's images, again shot at a distance, until I stumbled on the last picture of a police officer arresting Trevor in front of a nightclub.

The next document. Brent Robinson. An image of a car business with a closed sign.

The next document. Olivia King. A picture of her on stage, pole dancing.

The last document. My heart dropped into my stomach and all the blood leached from my face. Roxanne Hastings. Images of me at work when this building belonged to Tower Hotel, another of me holding Dylan as I walked along the same street, taking him to his daycare. Bile rose in my throat, and I clicked an unlabeled document in my folder and stumbled upon a list. An agenda in point format.

Walking stick

Change hotel check-in

Pocket watch screensaver

TCQ Radio Station

Each point I read reintroduced the strange encounters I'd experienced since working for Hunter. Max's walking stick left on my car, the room mix-up when Hunter and I checked into the hotel while in Los Angeles, Max's pocket watch as a screensaver on my office desktop, and of course, the song request on TCQ Radio. The same station I called and confronted. These events happened for real, and for whatever reason, Hunter masterminded every single one…

Breath caught in my lungs as I pictured Hunter on our flight to LA when he had worked on his laptop, tongue poked out to one side. At the time I narrowed this to an action I'd seen him do in the office to explain away the sense of déjà vu, but now the same image merged with the memory of Max, sitting in class, nose in a book, and tongue poked out to the side in the same manner.

In our shared room in Los Angeles, I'd observed Hunter from a certain angle, struck by his minor likeness to the boy from my past.

And the other night when I'd surrendered to Hunter's passionate kisses…no wonder the familiar sensation triggered me. I'd kissed Max!

"This is so messed up." Gulping back deep breaths, I forced myself to remain calm. The drastic measure he'd taken to change his appearance, the thin teenage boy in my mind so different from the robust, bearded giant I'd worked for these last couple of months. Though the memory of Max faded over time, I'd never forgotten his dark blond hair and blue-green eyes since they replicated our son's.

I rubbed at my temples as my head pounded for answers. How else had Hunter attained these tiny details concerning our past? What reason to pursue Alex, Brent, Trevor, and Olivia? And what else lay in store for me? With shaky fingers, I dragged the mouse over another document, determined to search through each one and learn every last detail.

Chapter 22

Max

Carlo drove into the underground parking lot of the hotel building at four o'clock. My meeting with Jean-Philippe had finished hours ago, but I killed time at a local restaurant, fuming over the lie Roxanne fed me this morning when I video-called. She used the lamest coverup regarding her necklace, expecting me to believe her toddler gifted her such an expensive piece of jewelry when I witnessed with my own eyes her receiving the gift from her lover, the same man she embraced at Moretti's.

I exhaled a long breath as I punched the elevator button. Losing my patience solved nothing, nor led me closer to my goal of ending Roxanne. And to think I'd considered quitting and starting a real relationship with this woman. I let out a soft chuckle.

Roxanne once again showed me her true colors, reminding me of the type of person I dealt with. My feelings betrayed me a second time, but I no longer held any reservations. *You're going down, Roxy, like the rest of them.*

The elevator doors parted with a ding, and I stepped out into the hallway. Roxanne's purse and phone sat beside her lit computer screen. I crossed the threshold into my office and stopped short. Seated on the lounge near my desk, Roxanne held a yellow manila envelope in her lap. She peered up, the usual warmth absent from her eyes as she searched my gaze with great intent.

"Hello." She stood, rubbing one hand down her pale gray skirt. "You took longer than expected."

"I had to run a quick errand." I nodded to the envelope in her hand.

She glanced at said envelope in question, sauntering over and dropping the yellow manila on my desk. "A document for you to sign later."

Resuming her seat once again in the center of the sofa, she patted the empty spot beside her. "Come, sit. I haven't seen you all day."

With tension between my brows mimicking the force of repelling magnets, I strolled over and took a seat. She left me little room with her positioned in the center, but I crossed one leg over my knee and laid my arm on the metal armrest.

The tentative smile didn't meet her eyes. "You seem tense."

I puffed a laugh through my nose. "A bit of a rough day."

"I can help." Circling the sofa, she stood behind me. In the time I'd worked with Roxanne, she'd never displayed such candid behavior at work, even slapping me away when I'd tried sneaking in kisses last week. Now she'd grown comfortable and tested the waters of intimacy in the office. Her soft hands landed on my shoulders and kneaded.

"You are tense," she whispered above my head, her voice soft and coaxing.

My body relaxed as she worked the muscles along

my shoulders and I closed my eyes, resting my head against the lounge. "Like I said, rough day."

"I can imagine." Her cheek smoothed over my beard as she leaned close to my ear. "You've worked hard too."

"I have." No point denying facts. I released a soft moan as she massaged out a knot near the back of my neck.

"All this plotting and revenge must leave you exhausted, right?"

"Sure does." My eyes snapped open at my admission. A resounding clink echoed in the room, and the bite of cold metal wrapped my wrist. I blinked at the armrest. Roxanne handcuffed me to the one piece of furniture I detested in this office. "Roxanne?"

"Yes, Max?" Her poised tone hinted at sarcasm.

I swallowed hard. Yanking my hand, metal chimed against metal. Pain shot up my tender arm, and I stilled. No way I'd escape without the key.

She strolled around and stood in front of me, her face deadpan. Silence stretched between us.

Her small jaw flexed. "Take them off."

I frowned. "Take what off?"

"The contact lenses." She nodded. "Show me your eyes."

With my unrestrained hand, I removed the contact lenses and blinked a few times, raising my chin.

She produced a sad smile, the first real emotion she'd shown since saying my name. I held my breath, anticipating her next move. Without a word, she stomped over to my desk and settled in my office chair.

In my hurry Saturday night, I'd not shut off my laptop and left all those hidden folders open. I bit the inside of my cheek at my reckless behavior.

"Now, where…?" Her gaze darted back and forth over the screen. "Ah, here."

I grunted low in my throat. "Roxanne?"

"Shush." Brows pinched, she focused on typing into the laptop, not once glancing my way as she hit different keys.

"Roxy Hastings," she read aloud, her eyes meeting mine for a brief moment, and focused on the screen.

The basic document for when I brainstormed ideas and plotted my revenge was laid open for her to view. "Roxanne, don't."

"Hire Roxanne." Again she read aloud. Her slender fingers trembled as she typed. "Box ticked. Comments? Mission…complete."

Posture stiff, chin tilted, she carried an air of determination as her unflinching gaze focused on the screen. I squirmed against plush upholstery and doubted she listened to me anymore.

"Drive her mad with pranks." She snorted and tapping echoed in the room. "Accomplished…in…spades," she said as she typed. "I'm surprised this one didn't top the list since it's underlined."

Heat infused my cheeks, and the lump in my throat prevented me from speaking. The list ate me alive for weeks, and after our night together, I had been sure to erase the entire document. I'd been seconds away from deleting it when Georgina arrived yesterday.

Roxanne didn't understand vengeance kept me sane all these years. My insatiable drive for retribution on my high school bullies was the sole reason I sprung out of bed in the mornings. With the others, I experienced a euphoric rush when repaying them…but with her, my chest twisted in pain.

"Oh, this next one's my favorite."

Her glassy-eyed stare struck harder than any blow experienced in the ring.

"Break her heart. On the night of the opening, show her Jean-Philippe's ballroom, reveal your identity, then fire her on the spot." Her breath hitched and she bit her lower lip as though fighting the tears rimming her eyes. She typed a response, but this time refrained from reading aloud what she wrote. Not surprising if she typed an entire paragraph of expletives.

I yanked at the cuffs and cringed a second time. "Will you stop typing and release me!"

Tears fell, and each one streaking her face punched me straight in the gut.

"Roxanne…"

She swiped at the tears, then puffed out a harsh breath, her face pale, eyes wide. "Let's skip ahead to the end where you fire me." She jumped out of the seat, circled the desk, and within three strides stood opposite me. "After all, you set out to achieve this, right?"

No point in pretense. "Yes." I gritted my teeth. "Do I have to spell out why?"

Her rigid visage softened. "You're getting all of us back for hurting you years ago."

"Four years, four damn years I suffered at their hands…at your hands while you stood back and watched, or laughed, or passed condescending comments." I bared my teeth. "Why should I see them successful, you successful and living your best life when you and your friends destroyed mine?"

"Now you're left with me." She turned on her heels

and strode back to my desk. Leaning over, she grabbed the yellow manila and raised the envelope. "Inside contains my letter of termination, already signed. You need to do the same. I've also left the reason blank. I guess snooping in your office merits enough cause for dismissal."

Dizziness swept through me as the blood drained from my head. She...fired herself? "Why?"

Her head bowed for a nanosecond, and the silence stretched between us. "Because you won." She peered at the ceiling. "Hearing Jean-Philippe today say he'd never laid his eyes on my design..." She bit her trembling lip. "Wow, Max. You sure hit hard."

Her boyfriend securing the necklace around her neck flashed in my mind, and my chest rose and fell with my harsh breathing. "What do you expect from me, an apology?"

Roxanne licked her lips. She locked eyes with mine as she made her way over to the sofa and stood over me, hesitant. "Not an apology. You owe me nothing. But just know the news hurt like hell...so you've won. You got back at Roxanne Hastings." She leaned over and trailed her fingers through my beard, not breaking eye contact. "You're right. I remained silent. I stood back every time instead of defending you." Her small jaw tensed. "Not a day goes by I don't regret my actions." Her broken face smoothed over with a serious expression. "If this will heal you, having me fired, having my dreams crushed...then go right ahead." One shoulder raised in a shrug. "But if you think I've lived the high life, you're wrong. You have no idea what hardships I've gone through. At times I almost surrendered." She laughed, the sound mocking. "My first day here in this office, you asked me why I never sought a career in interior design. Because I made sacrifices. I abandoned a long-held dream since high school." A tear streaked her face. "And you, you handed me the same dream on a silver platter, an opportunity of a lifetime dangled in my face, then you snatched my lucky break away." She covered her face with her hands, dropping them by her sides and straightening. "Oh, how you must loathe me."

No denying Roxanne's talent. Her brilliant design blew my mind, the best ballroom I'd ever seen, and if not for the restaurant fiasco with her lover, I had every intention of showing her work to Jean-Philippe this morning and going ahead with her design.

She withdrew a small key from the pocket of her skirt. "You once told me you never wanted to see me again and to leave you alone. Now I'm echoing your words. Don't contact me, not now, not ever." She left the room and returned a moment later with her handbag over her shoulder. Placing the key beside me on the sofa, she glared. "Ten years, Max. You waited ten years to come back into my life and hurt me all over again." Shaking her head, she stormed out of the office without glancing back. The elevator doors dinged, signaling her exit.

She granted me my final wish. No euphoria. No peace. Numb, I forced myself to suck in a breath. Her final words, at last, registered in my brain. Hurt her again? Explain the first time I'd hurt her. "Roxanne!" Plunging the tiny key into the lock and uncuffing myself, I stumbled to my feet.

By the time the elevator descended to the underground floor, I spotted Roxanne's car leaving and retrieved my phone from my pocket, demanding Carlo bring the limo around. In minutes, he met me outside and headed toward the daycare center on the next street.

We stopped at the curb across from the building and I hopped out. Roxanne stood outside the daycare, talking to a woman holding Dylan.

"Roxanne!"

She spun around, face pale and eyes wide. "What are you doing here?" Outrage heightened her voice.

The woman holding Roxanne's child frowned, and I lowered to Roxanne's ear. "I won't keep you too long from your son, but can we please talk."

"Um no," the dark woman intervened. "I'm Dylan's—"

"Nanny," Roxanne cut in, her eyes boring into the other woman.

A strange tension circulated between the two.

"Uh, yes," the woman agreed, her smile wavering. "His nanny. Nanny Jasmine."

Roxanne hauled the diaper bag onto her shoulder. "I'm sorry for the mix-up, Jasmine. I'm here, so I'll take *my* son home, thank you."

The woman, Jasmine, gave a tentative smile and handed over the child. "Okay, Roxanne."

Roxanne clutched the toddler, who chuckled and played with the gold locket around her neck.

I swallowed and leaned in closer. "Please hand Dylan over to his nanny. We need to talk."

Those stunning eyes narrowed. "I've nothing to say to you."

"You said I hurt you all over again. Explain?" I demanded, no longer caring we had company.

She frowned at me as if I'd grown two heads. "Stay

away from me." She strolled off with her kid in her arms and the nanny keeping pace beside her.

My shoulders sagged, and in my silent defeat, I hopped back inside the limo and smacked the leather seat. None of the events of the last thirty minutes changed the fact she lied and another man resided in her life.

I ordered Carlo to drop me back at my office building. Every breath I drew failed in calming me. My heart weighed in my chest, and I wished to yank the pathetic organ out. I entered the elevator and hit the top floor. Once I stumbled into my office, I strolled past the handcuffs on the floor and over to the manila folder. I tore open the seal and poured out the contents. As promised, a termination of employment letter sat inside. Roxanne indeed signed the document. Scrunching the sheet of paper, I tossed the ball across the room and flopped into my chair. The page with my goals remained open, now checked off, and added with Roxanne's commentary.

Goals:

Hire Roxanne. (Check). Comments: Mission complete.

Pranks/Mind Games. (Check) Comments: Accomplished in spades.

Break her heart. (Check) Comments....

She had typed, "Completed. You broke my heart, the morning of..." The date read May fourteenth, dated ten years ago. The morning I'd dropped her off and told her I never wanted to see her again.

All this time I'd set up a plan to break her heart over her career dreams, but this related to us and our short-lived relationship. I read over the comments again, convinced I'd misread the first time. If Roxanne spoke true—the ache in my chest intensified and I yanked at my shirt, the action doing little to ease my discomfort—I hadn't lost her tonight, but ten years ago.

Chapter 23

Roxanne

I paced like a mad woman in front of my parents' home. Earlier when Hunter's limo drove away, Jasmine bombarded me with questions. I told her I'd explain everything once we arrived at my parents'.

Michael had taken Dylan into the backyard to watch Dad and Zane play catch. Baby Mia slept in her little Moses basket, and Mom busied herself in the kitchen, but I waved her toward the front, and she'd joined us outside. I spent the last thirty minutes explaining everything to the two women I trusted most in this world. Their faces shifted from shock to awe, then to anger and fear. The same emotions coursed through me not too long ago at the office when I sat at Max's desk and clicked through the distressing truth.

"Max? As in Max, Max?" Jasmine whispered, sitting on the porch step, her hands gripping the brick step for support. She shot a stare at both me and my mother. "Is this a sick joke?"

Mom dusted her flour-covered hands over the blue apron she wore. "So you never hallucinated these events. He played these games to mess with you. Goodness, Roxanne, this man sounds unstable."

I paused in my relentless stride to peer at the front door in case anyone overheard our conversation, including Zane. "I'm not angry." At least, not anymore. "Yes, I'm shocked by what I stumbled across on his computer, but how can I be angry?"

"How *can't* you be angry?" Jasmine clenched her fists. "He drove you insane...I feel like decking him in the face."

Good idea I left out the ballroom design. Otherwise they'd hunt him down if they found out he lied about an opportunity of a lifetime. "No, Jasmine. Don't you see? I deserve everything he's done."

Mom stood with her arms crossed and eyes narrowed. "Why do you say you deserve this?"

I sniffled, swallowing the lump in my throat. "I told you and Dad about how I treated Max in high school. Now he's gotten back at every single one of us. I'm no exception."

She frowned, her face ashen. Without a sound, she dropped her arms by her sides and rushed over to hug me. "Oh, Roxanne." She tucked a strand of hair behind my ear. "You confessed your wrongdoings to him even back then, and saying sorry counts too."

"My remorse means nothing to Max." My face flushed, and I lost the words to speak.

"But you still changed," she insisted, rubbing my arms. "He has a choice to forgive you and hasn't't."

"It doesn't matter. He rejected my friendship all those years ago and hasn't forgiven me." My mouth opened and closed, and I gulped back a deep breath as though a knife stabbed at my chest. "I hoped and prayed I'd see him again and have a second chance." I spent years waiting for his return, so we'd reconcile and start over, and all this time he'd searched for me too, but to hurt me, to pay me back. "He's never stopped hating me."

Jasmine approached, placing her hand over my shoulder in comfort.

I directed my next comment at Jasmine. "I jumped at the opportunity to pass off Dylan as mine."

She cocked one dark, shaped brow. "Nice move giving me the eye to stop me from spilling."

"Wait." Mom shook her head in disbelief. "So, he's hired a private investigator on you and yet has no information on Zane."

I clamped my lips together. "I haven't hidden the fact I have a son." Goodness, even the family picture I'd used as my computer backdrop contained Zane. "Other than a few images of me dropping off and collecting Dylan from the daycare center, there's nothing of Zane on his computer. Trust me. I triple-checked. He must assume Dylan's my kid. Hunter..." I sighed. "Max," I corrected. "If Max learned of Zane, I'm sure he'd have mentioned it by now."

Mom placed her fingers over her eyes. "So, what does this mean now? You're not going to tell him?"

"And ignore everything I learned today?" I dropped my head into my hands. "I can't." I sank onto the step Jasmine occupied moments ago. "What if I tell him, and he tries to take Zane from me as a form of revenge?"

"Would he?" Jasmine straightened, panic etched across her face.

Why not? Look at how far he'd gone, not just with me, but the others too. "I can't risk Hunter finding out. He has money for a convincing lawyer, Jasmine, and I don't."

"Roxanne." Mom raised her voice. "I mean what

will you tell Zane?"

My shoulders sagged. How to tell him the news? "I'm scared. I don't want to lie to him either. What should I do?"

"Mom, she needs time," Jasmine offered, clasping her hand together.

I nodded in agreement. "Jas's right. I will tell Zane the truth, but not yet. As for Max, I'll tell him one day, but not anytime soon. For now, I need to gather my bearings and start job hunting."

My mother raised her palm. "Not so fast."

I wiped the tears from my cheeks. "What, why?"

Mom clasped my hand in hers. "You and Zane should come with your father and me this weekend."

"Your lodge resort trip?" I sniffled, still overcome with emotion. "Mom, no. You and Dad deserve time away alone."

"Yes, and we go on vacation yearly." She cocked one dark brow. "Tell me the last time you took Zane on one?"

The reminder burned in my gut like acid. "Never," I whispered.

She tilted her head to the side. "You owe him this, Roxanne. Soon he'll be a teenager hanging out with his friends. Zane deserves to have at least one childhood memory of a fun trip." Mom raised a finger to halt my protest. "You've worked hard, but before you dive back into the deep end, take this time out. It's one weekend, and there's plenty of space; both upstairs and downstairs have bedrooms. You and Zane can rent bicycles, go hiking, or canoeing."

Time away from all this chaos sounded nice, but I had a resume to polish and jobs to hunt. "Thank you, the gesture means the world, but I plan on saving every penny until I find another job."

Mom waved her hand. "Your father and I will cover the expenses."

I mock-laughed at the preposterous idea. "I can't ask you to pay for our trip."

"Max has to pay you any outstanding entitlements," Jasmine threw in. "Come on, Roxy. Your mother's right. Enjoy time away with Zane."

For years I promised Zane we'd go on vacation, but never got around to booking one because of either work or study. I straightened my shoulders and sucked in a breath. "Okay. We'll go with you, but I'll pay for me and Zane."

"Oh, how exciting." She clapped her hands. "Come on. Let's go inside and tell the guys the news."

I blew out a breath, bracing myself. Max might have broken my spirit today, but he'd never destroy the bond with my loved ones. How sad for him, to have lived the last decade holding onto such hatred, to have revenge as his sole purpose.

This upcoming trip provided a great distraction, and even now my mind raced with a list of items to purchase. Buy Zane a suitcase, perhaps a new pair of sneakers, and whatever else we might need for the weekend away. Afterward, I'd reveal the truth to Zane. I didn't want anything to spoil our first trip away together. And I'd not deny my son's wishes to meet his father, but I prayed I wouldn't live to regret their inevitable meeting. Once I cleared my head at this little getaway, I'd decide what to do.

Chapter 24

Max

I waited for Roxanne to call or show up at work. Stupid of me. As if she'd resume her position. Since our head-to-head on Monday, I hadn't slept. Those dates she'd typed into my computer drove me mad. The workload piled high, and I lost my mind keeping on top of the duties Roxanne covered. Obvious solution—hire another assistant, but the idea of replacing Roxanne repulsed me.

So here I stood Friday morning in front of her apartment, determined to learn the truth regarding those dates, and the guy she met at the restaurant. I rapped the solid wood with my knuckles and waited.

"Just a second," her voice called out from inside. A peephole fashioned her front door. *Please, God, don't let her see me.* One peek through the glass lens and she'd ignore me. Heck, she might call the police.

Shoving my hands in my suit pants pockets, I relaxed my shoulders in hopes of betraying my body into feeling calmer than the nerves shaking my limbs.

"Are we ready to go?" The door flew open, a medium suitcase at her side. Her eyes widened and the smile on her face withered into a thin line. Could she be leaving with the man from the restaurant? The hairs on the back of my neck stood.

"I need to talk to you." I raised my hands in a show of surrender, my voice low and gruff.

She stepped out into the hallway with her luggage and shut the door.

"Going on a trip?" My question sounded like a snide retort.

"None of your business." She folded her arms over her chest. "Why are you here?"

I licked my lips and swallowed. "The comments you made on the file in my computer…were you joking?"

Those honey eyes narrowed. "Why do you care? You got your revenge." She clutched her luggage handle, and I jutted my foot in front of the baggage, stopping her.

"Because I do care, Roxanne. And I'm not done yet. I'm not even sure whether to believe you."

One shoulder bounced in a shrug. "I've no reason to lie."

"Don't deny facts," I insisted when her mouth parted to protest. "You told me we'd reschedule our date, and then the same night you met with another man."

Her brows pinched together. "What man?"

"Last Saturday night, you hugged a man at Moretti's restaurant."

Her gaze danced along the floor as though recalling the event. "Darius. You spied on me with Darius?" She shot me a stare. "Darius finished dinner with his work colleagues and ran into me. He's leaving town, and I wished him farewell. You witnessed a simple goodbye between two old friends."

My chin tilted as her words clicked in my mind.

"So he's not your boyfriend? But when your mother called in search of your phone, she mentioned you headed out on a date with your *special* guy."

Her nostrils flared, and she stared me dead in the eyes. "You're the one person I went on a romantic date with that weekend. No one else."

The conviction in her eyes and her tone shot right through me. "So, then who's this skateboard champion your mother mentioned?"

"A relative and, yes, I took him out celebrating his big win." She shrugged, her eyes boring into mine. "Again, why does any of this matter? You got your payback for all those years ago."

Euphoric relief swarmed my system, but I kept my spine rigid, not about to lower my guard. "Do you recall that morning ten years ago, I overheard you on the phone, spilling your plan to have me beaten up at the diner?"

"What?" she whispered. "You're insane. We shared an awesome day, why would I do such a thing?"

"You spoke on the phone to Alex or Brent, said you'd get me to a diner, and I'd regret ever touching you. You even mentioned how they'd spied on us. I can't believe you got them to spy on us on our day out and pretend to act as my friend to trick me."

She sank back against the wooden door, her eyes wide and tormented. "I spoke with my brother. Trevor, the moron, drove to my house hoping to take me to prom, and my brother covered for me saying I'd gone to visit my grandparents for the weekend. He called to tell me Trevor looked shocked, and he worried my missing prom ruined our plan to get back at the jerk for hurting me."

What the hell did the sicko do? "Get back at Trevor?"

"When I left you in the hospital, he chased me in his car and threatened me. The pocket watch Olivia stole from you—he planned on using the money for drugs and got pretty mad because I no longer had it. My brother and his friends swore to pay him back for hurting me but asked me to play along by luring him to the diner."

I swallowed hard, my heart pounding in my chest at a furious pace. "Hurt you how?"

Her shoulders sagged in defeat. "He left some pretty disturbing bruises on my neck, enough for my brother to see red."

Trevor, the bloody scum. Heat scorched my throat at the image of Trevor laying a hand on Roxanne. Thank God Roxanne's brother cornered the dirtbag. But if Roxanne targeted Trevor and not me...then the night we shared... "I had no idea your feelings were real."

"Max, we spent the night together." She held out her palms, the gesture beseeching. "We were each other's firsts."

"Can you blame me after overhearing your conversation?" I raked my hands through my hair. "You should've told me your plan to get back at Trevor, then I wouldn't have assumed your conversation involved me."

"Oh, I'm sorry, should I have shouted from a rooftop I liked you?" She sneered, stepping into my space. "You mistook me coming onto you as a form of revenge...as if I used my body in some master plan to destroy you. I mean, come on?"

Heat wrapped my neck, and I tugged at my collar

with a jerky hand. "Okay, yeah, when put that way I sound crazy. I had no experience with girls, or anyone my own age. I was the worst person to read into a situation, considering I had good reason—"

"Mom!"

Our attention whipped toward the boy skateboarding up the hallway.

The child skated to a halt in front of Roxanne, who all of a sudden gazed at me like a deer in headlights.

"Grandma and Big Zee are in the car." He arrested the board with one foot. "What's taking you so long?"

The kid called her Mom! No, I'd seen her toddler with my own eyes. This older kid averaged at least nine or ten years old.

Ten years?

A replica of my pale blue-green eyes smacked me in the chest. I'd seen this kid not too long ago. No. Impossible. No way.

"Hey, skate-park guy." The kid recognized me as well. "What are you doing here?"

Roxanne glanced from me to the child. "You've met?"

The child grinned at his mother. His mother! "Yeah, this man rewarded me for helping out the bullied kid."

Roxanne placed her fingers over her necklace, and her mouth quivered.

The boy shook his head, gazing between the two of us. "What's he doing here, Mom?"

Roxanne lowered to his level. "Sweetie, he's my boss."

"Your boss?" Panic crossed his young face. "But you said you're not working there anymore. We're still going away for the weekend, right? You promised."

"What's going on?" A woman entering the hallway called out, an older man by her side, the same man I spoke with at the skate park.

Roxanne rubbed the child's shoulders. "Hey, listen. We're going on this trip."

The boy paid little attention to what she said and like the first time at the skate park, stared at me with intent. "Mom?" He turned to Roxanne. "His eyes," he whispered. "They're—"

"I know." She cut him off in a firm tone. "I need you to go with your grandparents. Right now." She stood and faced the older couple. "Mom, Dad, please take Zane downstairs. I'll meet you guys in the car. I need a minute with Mr. Parker."

Roxanne's mom eyed me, the surprise on her face telling me she discerned the situation. "Don't be too long, Roxanne. We have a flight to catch."

Roxanne nodded without saying a word.

"Come on, Little Zee." The older man grabbed hold of Roxanne's suitcase and headed back down the hall. "Let's go downstairs, and you can show me your new stunt."

The boy held his skateboard under his arm and followed his grandparents. He turned to glance back. The sight struck me with instant déjà vu of the time Roxanne peered back after her friends had finished forcing me to kiss their shoes, but this time my own features stared back at me, like seeing the future through the past. A cold shiver trailed my spine.

They vanished around the corner, but I continued staring down the empty hallway. A thousand questions pounded through my mind, causing my head to ache.

"Max?" Roxanne's gentle and cautious voice coaxed the roaring in my head.

"How old is he?" I demanded, my fists clenched by my sides.

She mashed her lips together, her chin trembling.

"Answer me, how old?"

She hugged her arms around herself. "He's almost ten."

The confirmation in her eyes pummeled my chest, and I staggered back, my spine hitting the wall. "You didn't tell me," I whispered.

Her pinched face eased. "I've tried for years to find you and tell you. You'd blocked my number. And when I visited your house, I found out you'd sold it."

I rubbed the back of my tensed neck. "Impossible...at the time you said you were on the pill."

She shrugged. "It failed."

"You didn't tell me." Clarity rang in my tone.

She held out her hands. "I explained why."

"No." I raised a pointed finger. "Not back then, the other day when you confronted me in my office. You insinuated the child you collected in front of the daycare belonged to you. So, Dylan's your baby also?"

She stared at the wall, not meeting my eyes. "No, he's my nephew."

"Your nephew?" I scoffed. She'd lied to my face on purpose. "You pretended he was yours."

"I learned the father of my child hates me and plotted against me. As if I'd drop the bomb about Zane then and there."

"Your father's name, right? We've worked together for months and every time I overheard you mention the name Zane I assumed you spoke of your dad, not a ten-year-old."

"Every time I mentioned my son, you'd give this strange look, so I figured you disliked kids, and I avoided the topic to not make you uncomfortable."

Because in my warped mind, another man fathered her son, not *me*. "When were you going to tell me—"

She threw her hands in the air. "Stop. I can't do this right now. They're waiting."

I grabbed her wrist. "Let them wait," I gritted through my teeth. "I need answers."

She yanked her hand out of mine. "No. I've left my son waiting too long. You've no idea how hard raising him all on my own has been. I've missed out because of night courses at college and working to keep a roof over our heads. School recitals, summer breaks, skateboarding competitions. I've never taken him on vacation! I'm pretty sure I'd never have a chance if not for my parents, who insisted we go on this trip with them." She pointed her finger down the hallway. "I made my son a promise, and I'm going to keep it. He's waited too long for this, and I'm not going to disappoint him."

The same circumstance pained me growing up. My mother worked hard, and in turn, we never traveled anywhere until Richard entered our lives. The boy's face had crumpled when he assumed they'd no longer go wherever they'd planned on going.

My nostrils flared, but I lowered my hands by my sides. "Then when, because we need to talk."

She squared her shoulders, revealing bravery I'd never seen...not even in high school. "I'll call you on Monday when we get back. We can arrange to meet then."

I nodded, and she gave me one last glance as she stalked away. Once she turned the corner, my hands clutched my hair, and I sank to the floor. My mind raced with the explosive information. Everything in the last ten years that held meaning came crashing down around me in ten seconds. How my world changed in an instant. I'd fathered a son! A nine-year-old. Impossible for a detail like this to slip under the radar with the best private investigator hired for the job.

Digging inside my suit jacket, I whipped out my phone and speed-dialed Bruce. He answered on the third ring.

"Hello, Mr. Parker."

"Why didn't you tell me Roxanne Hastings had a nine-year-old son? You told me she had a toddler."

"Yes, when I first started investigating her, I assumed the baby belonged to her, but further digging led to the discovery of the older child. Every time the conversation of her child arose, your temper got the best of you. Have you forgotten you threw me out of your office? Or the fact you refused to let me share anything on Miss Hastings unless prompted by yourself? Other than her marital status, occupation, and address, you asked no further questions regarding the woman."

I cringed. My consuming jealous rage stopped me from uncovering greater than surface-level information on Roxanne. The fact I begrudged her sharing a child with another man and all this time I'd envied myself, jealous of myself.

"Mr. Parker. I did my job well. Although you refused to let me speak or share with you what I learned, I'd left all the details in the final email document I sent. I'm surprised you've taken this long to read through it."

I clenched my jaw. The answers sat right under my nose all along, but I lacked the guts to open and read them. Too late now since I deleted the report file over a week ago when I decided I no longer wanted to hurt Roxanne. I released a long sigh. "I'm sorry for disturbing you, Bruce." I ended the call, the phone slipping from my fingers and bouncing on the floor. No point in blaming Bruce since my stupid reluctance placed me in this current predicament. Once again, I assumed without researching the situation. As I'd done all those years ago when I assumed Roxanne plotted to hurt me. Roxanne never should have made my list of enemies. Ten years! I'd lost ten years with her because of my own stupid beliefs. I'd lost ten years raising my child. How the hell would I recompense her, both of them? And a bigger question, considering everything I'd done, would she allow me into my son's life? The ache in my chest intensified. No chance in hell.

Chapter 25

Roxanne

Zane and I helped each other drag our hired kayaks to the lake. We arrived at the lodge yesterday late afternoon, settled into our rooms, and headed downstairs to help my parents prepare dinner. I took the time to appreciate the magnificent location my parents chose. The two-story cabin decorated in plush fur rugs, leather upholstery, and oak-wood furniture oozed comfort and tranquility. The floor-to-ceiling window beside the stone fireplace in the living area bestowed breathtaking views of rocky mountains and the glistening lake. A balcony wrapped around the entire upper floor with an outdoor jacuzzi which I promised myself I'd enjoy along with a nice white wine. I organized a lot of activities for Zane and myself. Kayaking, bike riding, hiking the mountain trail. However, my usual, chirpy son disappeared and no matter what adventures I threw at him, he responded with a half-hearted smile.

Our little entertainer loved sharing jokes and riddles over dinner, but last night he'd kept quiet. Instead, he'd perched his elbow on the table, resting his cheek on one fist, and nudged at his peas with a fork.

The encounter with Max yesterday bothered him. To not kill the mood, I pretended nothing happened when I hopped into the car, and we drove to the airport. Once Zane fell asleep last night, I explained to my parents what transpired between Max and me. Max had discovered the truth now. What he planned next with said truth, I had no idea, but a courtroom in a battle for my child sent a frightful shiver down my spine. There'd be hell to pay if he dared take my child from me. I doubted not even Max held the capacity to be so cruel. Then again, I lacked the best judge of character concerning this man. My parents suggested I enjoy my time here with Zane and not worry until we arrive home. I agreed, not about to let stress ruin my son's first-ever vacation.

We both hopped into our kayaks and rowed down the peaceful lake. Birds chirped, flying toward the majestic scenery of mountains and hills. Flowing water and dancing butterflies guided us through an arcade of tall trees. Sweet pine filled my nose, the sharp scent refreshing. Not a cloud marred the sky. The sun beat on our heads, and my muscles relaxed as I soaked the warmth and cherished this beautiful day. But the grandeur was all in vain. Zane oohed at the sights and sounds, but like last night he'd said little since waking this morning.

I had to discover the reason for his silence if we hoped to enjoy ourselves. I steered my kayak closer to his path and used the gentlest voice. "Are you okay, buddy?"

He peered at me, eyes blank as he nodded.

Nice try, kiddo. No fooling this momma. "What's troubling you?"

Again, nothing but the lapping of our paddles passed between us.

He then released a long sigh. "I'm waiting for you to tell me what happened yesterday. You got into the car and started talking to Grandma and Big Zee about our trip. But I'm not stupid, Mom. You looked sad."

Goodness, how I wished for a further minute to pull myself together yesterday. I'd have caked on makeup and covered my distress if we hadn't already been running late. "Zane, there's a great deal we need to discuss, but let's not ruin our trip." How ironic since the events from yesterday already ruined this getaway. My sole purpose for accepting Mom's offer to join them was to share wonderful, lifetime memories. And yet, Zane would relive this vacation, but for all the wrong reasons.

His small jaw clenched, uncannily similar to Hunter. The many times I'd seen the same reaction in Hunter and missed the similarities between father and son. A hollow ache burrowed in my chest.

Zane paddled slower now, his shoulders sagging. "I can't enjoy myself until you tell me the truth."

There goes waiting until we returned. "Where to start?"

He squared his jaw and shot me a serious stare. "Your boss? Is he my father?"

I swallowed. The next words out of my mouth would change his life forever. "Yes, Zane. He's your father."

He glanced at his knees. "Last time his eyes looked different, but yesterday his eyes matched mine." He muttered the words as though to himself. Then his sharp gaze snapped to mine again. "So, you've worked for him all this time and not once told me."

The anger in his voice tore me to shreds. "No,

sweetie. It's complicated."

He shrugged, his face scrunched. "Then explain so I understand."

No point in beating around the bush. "He disguised himself. I learned the truth a few days ago."

Zane frowned, the confusion on his face deepening. "Why?"

No way I'd tell him the real reason and tarnish whatever image my son built of his father. Zane's learning of the schemes and tricks might do further damage. "Because he waited to reveal himself." Not a lie. At least the reason saved me from spilling the entire truth.

Zane blinked, his gaze widened. "Like, he tested to see if you'd changed into a better person since high school?"

He bought my cover story, hook, line, and sinker. "Yes."

His little nose twitched as his eyes reflected the lake water. "Did you tell him about me?"

My bold and brazen boy lacked his usual confidence, somehow appearing younger than his age. I craved to hug him and wished we'd parked our kayaks. "Yes, he found out yesterday at the apartment."

Zane grew quiet again, then his small hands gripped the paddle handles and maneuvered to the edge.

I frowned as he rowed to the shoreline and followed. "Zane, where are you going?"

He hopped out, yanking his kayak on the sand and stomping over to plunk himself on the plush grass. I dragged out my own kayak, parking the lightweight paddle boat beside his. Afraid to frighten him off, I took careful steps as I made my way over.

He wrapped his arms around his knees, and the pout he wore broke my heart. "He doesn't like me, does he?"

"What?" I sank into the grass beside him, bowing my head to meet his gaze. "How can you say he doesn't like you?"

His brows puckered as he dug his toes into the grass. "Did you see the way he looked at me? Like I'm a monster."

My heart shriveled. Yes, Max gazed at him like he'd seen a ghost, but my son took his father's reaction to heart. "He laid eyes on you for the first time in his life. He learned you existed when you skated up the hallway. He has a right to be a little shocked."

"I guess." His voice remained low, unconvinced. He gripped fistfuls of grass and ripped the blades out, tossing them aside. "I waited for him to follow you downstairs, hoping to meet him."

Ever since discovering the truth, I feared what Max meeting Zane meant. I feared the revelation inspired greater acts of revenge. Now, however, I prayed Max wouldn't disappoint our son. "I don't doubt for a second he's anxious to meet you."

Those unsure eyes met mine. "How can you be so sure?"

Because of how he reacted. Max's face filled with hurt and regret. "I already told him I'd contact him once we return from our trip. He has a lot of questions about you. Remember, this is all new to him too."

He released a sigh, leaning back on his elbows and peering at the trees. "I want to meet him. But only if he wants to. I can't force him to be friends with me."

Oh, my poor, sweet boy. To have these emotions

plague his mind. No wonder he failed to enjoy himself here. A soft smile graced my lips. "Let me speak with him on Monday, but in the meantime can we at least try and have fun?"

He absorbed the sun by the lake a moment longer, then straightened and gave me a slight grin. "Under one condition."

I tilted my chin, having no doubt he'd bribe me into letting him stay awake past bedtime or consume an entire block of chocolate. "Which is?"

He sprang to his feet, sprinting off mid-sentence. "Race me to our kayaks."

Laughing aloud, I chased him to the shore.

Chapter 26

Max

I slammed my laptop, ceasing my futile attempt at getting any work done, and massaged the bridge of my nose between my fingers, blowing out a long, winded breath. I considered myself well-organized and focused, but today I struggled to do simple tasks such as pouring a cup of coffee without spilling the contents. No point in working when Roxanne's text asking me to meet at her apartment in the afternoon occupied my mind.

A knock sounded at the door, and I opened it to find my mother staring at me, one brow cocked.

"Why are you ignoring my calls?" Without waiting for me to invite her inside, she barged past.

I followed behind her, collecting discarded items of clothing and shoes along the way. "I've been busy."

She waved a dismissive hand, oblivious to the messy state of my penthouse. A surprise, since growing up, I'd receive a scolding for setting a single muddy foot on her pristine floors.

"Oh, please. Have you forgotten my husband is covering for you? Now, for my son to put aside his workaholic ways, there must be a woman in his life. Who is she?"

I followed her into the living room where she sat on my lounge and folded her arms, her expression stern.

No way she'd leave until she got answers. "Now isn't the best time to talk."

"Max, there's never a good time." She patted the spot next to her. "Will you sit and spill?"

I sighed and took a seat. "Where do I start?"

She parked her designer purse on the floor by her feet. "Try from the beginning."

Though I'd sworn I'd take my secret to the grave, I revealed all my past troubles in high school, relaying every gruesome and embarrassing detail. I portrayed Roxanne the way I remembered, even delineating the times she showed me kindness and how she'd apologized to me in the end.

Mom's face morphed from shock to sadness, then she cried over the revelation of the horrific treatment I received at the hands of my bullies. Her trembling mouth fell open as I explained my ten-year-long plan and how I made each enemy pay.

"Max." She twisted her fingers together in her lap. "All this time...oh my goodness." Her face collapsed into her hands as she sobbed. "Your drastic change, your interest in fighting sports. Here I assumed you'd grown this new confidence following your operation, but no, you disguised yourself this whole time." She laughed without humor, puffing out a breath. "I wish you told me. I wish I'd been there for you. Richard will be heartbroken."

My stepfather showed me nothing but support over the years, but I'd come this far in confessing the truth to my mother and refused to quit now. "Richard's known all along."

Her face paled. "No," she whispered. "He wouldn't lie."

"I made him promise not to tell you. He hated keeping secrets from you, but don't blame him. He hasn't betrayed your trust."

Those last words snapped a dangerous glint in her eyes. "No, you betrayed my trust." She swiped at her wet cheeks. "Why didn't you tell me?"

"And break your heart? Stress you out?" My voice rose in my defense. "Or worse, have my school problems come between your relationship with Richard and be the reason you lost your chance at happiness?" I gripped my knees, giving my emotions a beat to calm. "You sacrificed everything for me, and in my silence, I hoped to do the same for you."

I squirmed when she bit her bottom lip and wrapped her in a hug. "Please don't be mad at Richard or let my secrets come between the two of you."

She patted my back and kissed my forehead. "I'm not mad, honey. In fact, I'm relieved you at least confided in Richard over the years since you consider him a father, but I wish you'd approached me." She leaned back to stare into my eyes. "I'm not going to sit here and pretend I'm not spooked over the fact you trailed these people for the last ten years."

I avoided her eyes as my throat closed. "I'm sorry I'm a disappointment."

She cupped my hands. "You could never disappoint me, Maxwell. Never."

I squeezed her hands in mine. "There's more."

Her weary eyes regarded me, and she squared her shoulders, bracing herself.

What a mistake to have kept this from her for so long and to now unload every secret all at once. I underestimated my mother's strength and ability to help me carry my burdens. "The girl I mentioned, the one who befriended me."

"Roxanne? You hired her as your assistant, right?"

"Yes." I rolled my eyes, tilting my head. "At least until a few days ago."

"Why seek revenge on her if she treated you with kindness in the end? You said she apologized to you in the hospital and returned your pocket watch." Mom shrugged, confusion scrunching her face. "Why target her then?"

Shame from my actions forced my eyes shut. "I used revenge as an excuse to scheme my way back into her life because I've never forgotten her." I inhaled a sharp breath. "The other day I discovered she has a child. A boy who's nine years old."

My mother's eyes narrowed.

"Mom, he's mine." I gave her fingers a gentle squeeze. "The boy's mine."

She yanked her hands from my grasp, and her round eyes burned holes into my head. "What do you mean he's yours?" She stood from the lounge and paced. "Max, are you kidding me?" Stopping dead in her tracks, she smacked her hands on her hips. "You never went anywhere but school, work, and home. You never once invited a friend over, let alone a girlfriend!"

"One night, weeks following my recovery, you and Richard took a trip out of town. Remember? Roxanne planned an outing for us, doing activities normal teenagers do."

"Normal teenagers," she repeated in a mock tone.

I rolled my eyes. "She spent the night at our house, and the next morning I acted so cold toward her. I misheard her phone conversation and assumed she'd hung out with me to lure me to her friends. But I learned in the last few days, the conversation hadn't involved me." A smile toyed at my mouth. "Her feelings were real." Then my heart twisted. "And I crushed her. I dumped her the next morning. She contacted me several times, but I ignored her calls until I changed my number. I didn't see her again until years later when she set foot into my office a couple of months ago."

Mom dropped her head into her hands. "Good grief. Have you met this boy yet?"

"I've seen him." I swallowed, my gut twisting. "He's perfect, Mom. He has my eyes and my hair…he's a spitting image of my childhood photos."

"Oh." She smiled, covering her mouth with trembling hands. "And…what of his feet because clubfoot is hereditary?"

The same question plagued my mind too. "From what I've seen he's fine. He's athletic; he loves skateboarding."

"Skateboarding?" A shimmer brimmed in her eyes. She stared at the ceiling, blinking back the tears. "Oh wow, Max. My son has a son."

I breathed a soft laugh. Mom took the shocking news better than expected.

"So when will you meet him?" She flurried over, taking the spot beside me.

I flicked my wrist to view the time. "I'm meeting Roxanne in thirty minutes to talk."

My mother stood and grabbed her purse. "Go on, then." She leaned over and hugged me. "Please, Max, no more secrets."

I returned her embrace. "I promise. I'll call you

later tonight and tell you what happened with Roxanne."

"Please do." She fastened her handbag over her shoulder and glanced at me as she always did, with affection pouring from her eyes. "Love you."

"I love you too, Mom."

****

Once again I stood in front of Roxanne's apartment. Crazy, how a few days ago I arrived here seeking answers, resulting in my world flipping upside down. And now I was back for those same if not more answers. I tapped on the door, and within seconds the thick wood swung open, the beautiful sight of Roxanne greeting me. She wore a simple navy dress adorned with tiny white flowers. Feet bare, her toenails polished in a deep red, and her hair piled at the top of her head with a few strands loose around the nape.

She stepped aside, gesturing with her hand for me to come inside. "Hello."

I stepped into a tidy yet small apartment, finding myself already in the living room and kitchen. A pile of ironed and folded clothes sat in a basket atop an ironing board. The reality of her life hit me. Roxanne had worked long hours at my company, and no doubt rushed home to cook, raise a child, and perform these mundane duties. She played mother and provider for ten years, and yet she'd come into work every morning, refreshed and cheery, ready to start her day.

"Can I get you anything?" She thumbed over her shoulder. "I'm not big on soda drinks, but we have chilled water."

The way my fingers shook, I feared accidentally breaking any glass she handed me. "I'm fine, thank you."

She sauntered over to the lounge and took a seat. I followed her, taking note of the picture frames on the wall. A few of Zane at different ages and stages in his young life and others of the two of them hugging for the camera. A pang erupted in my chest. I missed out.

"Zane's at his grandparents' house, but he'll be here soon." She licked her bottom lip. "I told him over the weekend." She smiled. "He figured it out. He's a smart kid. He's worried you'd refuse to meet him."

Worried I'd refuse? Here I panicked about how the child would receive me, but he too feared the same. "Of course, I want to meet him."

Roxanne breathed out a long breath, sounding too much like relief. "Good." Her jaw clenched. "One problem I need to be sure of first."

Unflinching, I regarded her leveled stare. "What?"

"Are you done seeking revenge on me? Because if you try to take our son away from me as payback, I will fight you with everything I have. Hate me all you want, but Zane's innocent in all of this."

"Roxanne." My startled voice rang in my ears. "I don't hate you. And I would never take him from you. Ever." My cheeks heated. Did she consider me a freak? "You think I'm unstable, don't you?"

She swallowed again, meeting my gaze. "The Max from high school would never—

"The Max from high school had no backbone." A threat of tears stung my eyes, but I held them back. "He does not exist anymore, Roxanne."

Her nostrils flared, and a flash of sadness swept across her face. "But that's the Max I've been looking for all these years." She smiled, staring off into the distance. "The same Max who I've told my son about."

I flinched. Who would Zane meet tonight, Max Fields, the unassertive weakling, or Hunter Parker, the ruthless businessman? "You must have freaked when you learned you were pregnant. I wish—" I inhaled a breath. "I wish I could turn back time. I missed out because I let my anger fester and put all my energy into seeking revenge." A framed picture on the wall displayed a portrait of Zane as a toddler, seated on the carpet and holding alphabet blocks. "I should've supported you both, and helped you raise him."

Roxanne followed my gaze. "Hold on a sec."

She rose and left the room, returning moments later with a pale blue album. She took the seat beside me and placed the album in my lap. I opened the first page and met the face haunting my dreams. A picture of Roxanne sitting on a sofa, her beautiful, youthful face staring into the camera with an unsure smile. She wore a white hoodie I'd seen her wear a thousand times at school, but this time the garment stretched with her full-grown tummy carrying our child. Staring at her photo, I pictured her unsure smile extended in full-blown joy with my teenage self, sitting beside her. The fake imagination teased me with how different our lives could have been.

Next to the picture sat a black-and-white ultrasound. As I turned the page to an image of a baby boy bundled and lying in a hospital crib, his mouth shaped in a perfect O with the little yawn the camera captured. I smiled. In the picture a birth card sat above the crib, *Zane Maxwell Hastings. Weight: 6lb 7oz. Height: 19.5 inches.*

"You gave him my name?"

"I also followed your mom's tradition by naming him after my father too."

The fact she included me in many ways... A warm, foreign sensation consumed my insides. "Big Zee and Little Zee." I chuckled, recalling the day I met Zane at the skate park. "The nicknames make sense now." I turned to her with all seriousness. "Does he suffer the same condition as me?"

Roxanne shook her head. "No. At the time they said the chances of developing clubfoot were fifty-fifty. However, I got the all-clear during my final scan."

I closed my eyes in relief.

She placed her hand over mine, her eyes filled with tears. "I loved him the second I learned of my pregnancy. Having the same condition as you would've changed nothing."

Her words flooded me with relief. My biological dad wanted me aborted when my parents learned I had clubfoot, but my mother refused. I'd never shared my father's request with anyone but buried the pain deep inside. One deformed foot wrote me off as unwanted to the man who fathered me.

As I turned the pages, Roxanne commented on each photo captured. Zane's first steps. A four-year-old Zane on his first skateboard his uncle Michael bought. His first day at school. His toothless grin when he first lost his tooth. I studied each stage of his life, soaking in the details. Breath ceased in my lungs when I flipped to the last page, not an image of my son, but of Roxanne and me on the rollercoaster at the theme park. I lifted the book closer to inspect the photo.

"Trevor's brother worked at the theme park. Trevor planned on using this photo of us to blackmail me into becoming his girlfriend."

I shot her a quizzical stare.

She gave one slow, deliberate blink. "Over my dead body."

I ran a finger over the picture in my lap, over the exact scenario greeting my dreams each night. Years passed, but I relived the day we shared every night in my sleep.

She stared at the picture with such fondness, then raised her chin and gave me a soft smile. Guilt consumed me like a living entity, and losing all control over my emotions, I leaned over and clasped her hands in my palms. "I'm sorry, Roxanne. For everything. For not giving you the benefit of the doubt, for abandoning you all these years, and I'm sorry for the last few months."

The tear trailing her cheek tore me inside.

"Revenge empowered me. The feeling became addictive, and every person I targeted renewed my satisfaction. But I experienced no such satisfaction with you. Every trick and scheme left me disgusted with myself. My mind demanded retribution, but when I acted out on you, I never received the same victorious feeling. I deleted the remainder of my schemes on my laptop the night of the mugging." I squeezed her hands. "I do not hate you. And I'm sorry. I should've never included you in my hit list for revenge." Although she should have never made my list, I admit if I hadn't added her, I'd have never sought her out. I'd have never seen her again or shared the moments I shared with her in the last few months, and I wouldn't have discovered the child we shared.

I dug into my jacket pocket and handed over an

envelope. "Open it."

She frowned and withdrew the printed paperwork. Those honey-colored orbs widened to the point of strain.

"Everything's paid for. You and Zane will enjoy the comfort of my private jet."

"Max," she whispered, dropping the paper into her lap. "A trip to Hawaii? We can't accept this."

"Yes, you can. You've spent ten years taking care of our son and like you said, you've missed out."

She tilted her head, and her features softened. "But I don't expect anything from you."

"I grew up in a single household where my mom worked hard to provide. I can't give you back ten whole years, but this I can do. Please, say you'll go. Let me do this for you, for him? I'm begging you, Roxanne."

Her throat bobbed and she swiped at the tears with the back of her hand. "Okay," she breathed out. "Okay, we'll go. Thank you."

A knock sounded, and my entire body tensed.

Roxanne glanced from me to the entrance. "Are you ready?"

I nodded, ready as I'd ever be. Roxanne strolled over and unfastened the security chain. She conversed with her father, thanking him for collecting Zane from his school vacation program. I rose from the sofa, staring at the ajar wood blocking my view. At last, he passed the threshold, and his curious gaze roamed the house. I swallowed hard as Zane's gaze stilled on me for a long time, and I contemplated who'd speak first. As the door clicked shut, I snapped out of the trance I fell into.

"Hello, Zane." My voice constricted with emotion.

The boy smiled and strolled around the sofa to face me. "Hello, nice to meet you."

"You too," I said, meaning every word.

Roxanne neared us, smiling at our son with pure adoration in her eyes.

"Do you want to play a game of chess with me?" Zane announced as he tossed his backpack on the lounge.

I met Roxanne's soft grin.

She crossed her arms with a proud tilt of her head. "I taught him how to play."

Bending to Zane's level, I peered into the mirror-image of my eyes. "Yes, I'd love to play chess with you."

Zane grinned, but Roxanne stopped his chance to dash away. "Backpack in your room, please. Don't leave your mess around."

"Yes, Mom." He snatched his backpack and ran down the hallway.

Zane returned with a large box and set the board and game pieces on their small round dining table.

"Max?" Roxanne stood to the side, not coming too close to our table.

"Hmm?" I regarded her over my shoulder.

She fastened an apron around her small waist, not breaking eye contact with me the entire time. "Would you like to stay for dinner?"

Our first meal together, just the three of us? I nodded. "Sounds nice."

She thumbed over her shoulder toward the kitchen. "I'll start cooking and let you boys get back to your game."

As Roxanne prepared dinner, I turned to our son.

"So, how do you like school?" The starting question opened the door to a full-blown conversation. Zane shared the excitement of his school life, and I soaked in every piece of information. His best friends, Tommy, Kane, and Hector, skateboarded with him most weekends. His favorite teacher, Mr. Stimmel, rocked a guitar and always gave him awards. A grade-A student too, thriving in topics I too excelled in at his age. He boasted of his love for skateboarding and pointed at the bookshelf exhibiting the many trophies he'd won since competing.

We conversed as we engaged in our game, shocked I played against such a talented player. The fact Roxanne played all these years, even teaching our son, proved she included me in his life.

Zane also asked many personal questions regarding my parents, and if I indulged in hobbies or played sports. I found myself sharing with him the ins and outs of my life. He surprised me with his question of whether or not I'd been married or had other kids. And as we ran out of topics for one another, he hit me with, "Would you rather eat pizza or ice cream for the rest of your life?"

I tilted my chin, pretending to ponder. "Pizza."

Two dimples indented his cheeks with his smile. "Good answer."

"Checkmate," Zane called out, fist-pumping the air.

I chuckled at his enthused reaction. No words described this new emotion sprouting within me. Satisfaction involved getting back at my enemies, but this escalated into a feeling far greater. Pursuing a lifetime of negativity and destruction, I now embraced a positive goal, a purpose good and pure.

Chapter 27

Roxanne

My phone vibrated in my purse. Holding the items to my chest with one hand, I dug for the device. *Hunter* flashed on my screen, a name I had to edit considering I'd called him Max since learning the truth.

—Finishing up here at work. See you in one hour. Hope you're both packed and ready.—

I stepped forward in the queue at my local retailer, carrying several nice dress shirts for Zane for the nights we planned on eating out. I also grabbed myself a new tankini, sarong, and neck cushion to take on the private jet. So, no, not quite packed and ready. Four people stood in front of me in the queue, and I sent up a silent prayer for the cashier to hurry. Tonight, Zane and I would leave for Hawaii, the trip Max surprised us with three weeks ago.

I'd have done this shopping trip earlier if not for the entire day of online job searching. Praise God I had one job interview lined up once we returned from our trip. But in case the opportunity flopped, then at least I made a head start applying for others.

Crazy, how life changed in a matter of weeks. Since meeting our son, Max returned every night and shared a meal, the both of them conversing about their day while enjoying a game of chess. They formed a strong bond in such a short span and grew fonder of one another with each new day.

For the first time in my life, I avoided stressing over a nine-to-five routine and enjoyed taking Zane to the skate park and movies, then returning home and waiting for Max to join us for dinner. We'd become an instant family, partaking in a normal routine like any other household. As for myself and Max, I had no idea what to make of us, and we'd found no real opportunity to talk with Zane around either.

During his visits, he'd not once initiated his intentions regarding our relationship. My heart constricted. Sure, he pretended to like me when I had no idea of his identity for the sake of his scheme, but despite his actions and manipulations, I still cared. I still wanted Max, and the realization he might not feel the same way frightened me to death.

I waited next in line, my gaze dancing over the magazine stand. The stack of *Ladies Weekly* stiffened my spine. A picture of Max, *my Max*, stamped on the front cover, dressed in a handsome tux and smiling for the cameras. The beautiful woman on his arm, none other than Georgina Belmont—in a lilac chiffon gown no doubt costing beyond anything I'd ever owned in my lifetime—gazed at him with utmost adoration. The issue date stamped on the top corner of the magazine revealed yesterday's date. A recent release. My heart ricocheted to my throat at the main cover line: *GEORGINA NEXT TO TIE THE KNOT? Exclusive insight into the billionaire heiress and her relationship with Hotel CEO Hunter Parker.*

A tap on my shoulder startled me, and I turned to a frowning customer. "You're up, honey. What are you waiting for?"

"S-s-sorry." I snatched the magazine and dumped all the contents at the register. My hands shook, and a cold sweat broke out along my neck. Paying for my items, I rushed out of the store, speed walking the entire time to my car. Once seated behind the driver's seat, I inhaled a deep breath to steady my ragged breathing.

Max visited us every day except...the last two weekends. I assumed he'd resorted to his workaholic lifestyle and spent the weekend at the office, but he'd made time for Georgina and whatever fancy gig they attended. I rounded the corner to my street, my arms stiff as poles as I gripped the steering wheel. Parking the car in the underground area of my apartment, I charged upstairs to my floor.

Inside my apartment, Mom and Zane sat at the kitchen counter drinking chocolate milk.

"Here she is." Mom turned in my direction and her smile wavered.

I slung my purse strap over the back of the breakfast stool. "Are you all packed?"

Zane nodded, shoving the last cookie into his mouth and taking his empty cup to the sink. "Yep." The word muffled between bites.

I dug into the shopping bag and handed him the shirts. "Add these to your bag and be quick. Max will arrive soon."

His grin stretched from ear to ear. "Okay. I can't wait to see Hawaii." He bolted down the hallway and into his room.

"What happened?" Mom carried the empty plate and glass over to the sink as well. "You look like you've seen a ghost."

In no mood to get into this with her, not when I tried processing what I'd learned, I waved a dismissive hand. "I'm flustered. I still have packing to do."

Mom grabbed her car keys and phone off the counter. "Let me get out of your hair." She kissed my cheek and peered into my eyes. "Don't stress. You're meant to be going on a fun vacation. Go on and pack. I'll see myself out."

I forced a smile. "Thanks for watching Zane. I'll call you as soon as we land."

"Please do. Have a wonderful time." She waved goodbye and shut the door.

Grabbing the shopping bag, I stormed down the hallway and into my room, locking myself in. The contents bounced on my mattress when I emptied the bag, and I snatched up the magazine. Flicking through the pages, I found the article littered with images of Max and Georgina. They celebrated Esme Belmont's fifth marriage. Few pictures displayed the happy bride and groom, but Max and Georgina covered the majority of the page. One of them dancing, another of Max whispering in a grinning Georgina's ear, another of them laughing, and of Georgina fixing his tie as they stared into each other's eyes. A picture said a thousand words, and this one spoke volumes concerning the intimate couple. I read the entire article...twice. Sources explained how the inseparable couple couldn't keep their hands off each other at the lavish wedding reception, and how a doting Mr. Parker stayed glued to Georgina's side. A close friend guaranteed the next event of the year would involve the couple's own nuptials.

My stomach churned as I paced. Stopping opposite

my dresser, I dropped the magazine, placed my hands flat on the smooth table, and stared into my reflection.

Break her heart. Those words on Max's computer flashed in my memory.

No secret he exacted revenge to hurt me. So no way he harbored real feelings. He lied about not having a woman in his life because of his ploy at the time. With the truth all out in the open, he no longer pretended nor hid his feelings for the beautiful Georgina Belmont. Nothing stood in his way of chasing the woman he loved. "You fool." I gritted my teeth. "You stupid, stupid fool." I leaned my forehead against the cool glass and squeezed my eyes shut. Dragging my knuckles to my chest, I beat at my heart, begging the ache gone, pleading with my heart to give up on this infatuation with love.

I rushed into the ensuite and splashed cold water on my face. Every time I closed my eyes, the magazine images taunted and mocked me. I cringed, dampening my face with a towel. No time to dwell on how pathetic I was. I had to finish packing and get my emotions in check prior to Max arriving.

A knock sounded at the door.

"I'll answer it," Zane shouted, his footfalls thumping down the hallway.

I opened the drawer, grabbed a bottle of cover-up, and dabbed my puffy eyes and reddened nose. I rushed out of the ensuite and shoved the new items I purchased into the open suitcase by my bed. Muffled voices sounded in the distance outside my door.

Preparing myself to see Max, I clenched my jaw, forcing away the tickle in my nose preluding to tears. Without dwelling on the matter a second longer, I strolled from my room.

"—my second time on a plane. I hope I get the window seat again," Zane told Max as I entered the living room.

"On this plane, you'll have your own hostess, and you can order anything from chocolate milk to a bowl of candy."

Zane's mouth formed a perfect O.

"Not so fast." My declaration burst my son's happy bubble. "I won't have you spoiling your appetite on junk and sugar."

Max peered at me with an apologetic smile. "Oops."

I glanced at Zane, unable to face Max for long. "You can have one treat."

He rolled his eyes. "Okay, Mom."

Max helped us with our luggage, and we made our way to his car. I took the backseat with Zane, pretending to read emails on my phone, but listening in on their conversation. Max's parents wanted to meet Zane, and Max planned to arrange a lunch visit with them soon.

"If it's all right with you, Roxanne?" Max peered at me through the rearview mirror.

I kept my focus on the lit screen, nodding in acknowledgement. "Sure, no problem."

He failed to mention whether or not I'd join them. Then again, why would he? No need for me to meet his parents since he held no romantic feelings for me. Perhaps Georgina would accompany them. My heart clenched in my chest. The fact this woman would be part of my son's life, whether I liked the idea or not, tore me to pieces. Every time I imagined Zane reuniting with his father, a stepmom never entered the picture.

We arrived at the private airport and drove right beside the jet. The staff loaded our bags and checked our passports. Max stood to the side speaking with the pilot, while Zane frowned at the aircraft. This marked his first time on a private jet, and although he had no fear of heights, he might be feeling nervous over this longer trip. I knelt at his level. "Hey, are you okay?"

He pointed to the aircraft staff. "Those people loaded our luggage onto the plane, but where's Max's bags?"

My entire body froze at the statement. What gave him the impression Max joined us? I made clear Max gifted us with this trip, but not once promised he'd tag along too.

"What's going on?" Max stood above us.

Zane shot him a perplexed stare. "You're coming with us, right?"

Now Max wore the same startled expression. He too knelt at Zane's level. "No. You're going on this trip with your mother."

Zane's furrow deepened. "I won't see you for a whole eight days. Don't you want to spend time with us?"

Max gave him a genuine smile. "I'd love nothing more than to come with you."

"Then come with us," Zane insisted, stomping his little foot.

I stood to my full height and wrapped a comforting arm around Zane's shoulder. My heart heaved at the level of determination he portrayed.

Max peered at me, his eyes filled with question and uncertainty. "Are you okay with this?"

If I said yes, then I'd be stuck facing the sole reason for my heartbreak. And if I said no, I'd disappoint my son. Talk about trapped between a rock and a hard place. Both decisions tormented me, but I'd go through hell and back for Zane's happiness. "Yes. What a great idea," I lied, keeping the smile on my face for good measure.

Max grinned at Zane. "Okay, I'll join you."

Zane jumped into Max's arms and hugged him. The act alone threw my rattled emotions into overdrive.

"Yes! Thank you. We're going to have so much fun."

I bit my bottom lip as the two of them embraced.

Eyes glassy, and a small smile brightening Max's face, he returned the hug. A beautiful sight with me left out. I stamped the negative emotion and beamed to appear as excited as Zane.

The three of us strolled over to the tarmac and ascended the stairs, greeted by a cheerful hostess inside. Zane asked to use the bathroom and the hostess took him to the back. I turned to Max. "What about clothing?"

He nodded toward the back of the jet. "It's fine, I always keep a packed suitcase on the plane in case of last-minute business trips. But as for the hotel, I'll call them and see if I can get a suite close to yours. Then again, I booked you two in the largest suite in the hotel containing several bedrooms. I can stay in the same suite if it's okay with you."

He spelled out what I dreaded. Bad enough Max joined us on this trip, but now I'd find a way to handle him sharing the same room too. I inclined my head, hoping to appear casual. "Why not."

His brows furrowed together as he studied me. "It's settled then. I'll take the guest bedroom." He sat back in his seat. "Are you all right with this?"

I pretended to be focused on the task of buckling up, avoiding his gaze. "Of course, why wouldn't I be?"

"I'd hate to make you uncomfortable, and this feels like I'm trespassing."

The long pause after his comment gave me an inkling he waited for me to meet his stare, but I refused. "You're not trespassing. Zane wants you here."

"But do you?"

I swallowed, unable to respond.

Zane rushed back and saved me from answering. "The hostess said I'm allowed to check out the cockpit. Can you come with me?"

"Sure." Max nodded, rising from his seat and heading with Zane to the front of the plane.

Staring after them, I turned to the hostess. "I'll take a glass of red wine, thank you."

The hostess nodded and sauntered over to the bar to fetch my drink. I needed a distraction, my already flustered state combined with the nervous energy of flying once again too heavy to bear. The first time on a plane, Max helped me through the experience. No wonder he'd displayed such considerate attentiveness since his ultimate goal involved taking me down. No time better than the present to slip into my big-girl panties because no knight in shining armor dared rescue me now.

Chapter 28

Max

We'd arrived in Hawaii three days ago and the words *unwanted guest* rang alarm bells in my mind. The other night on the tarmac, Roxanne agreed to me coming along because of Zane, in spite of the discomfort stamped across her stiffened face.

Could I blame her, considering all the hell I'd put her through? We both shared the same goal, not to disappoint our son.

The last few days, we'd ventured out sightseeing and partaking in various activities, and although Roxanne participated, she kept quiet and reserved. She'd smile at Zane and chuckle at the right moments as if pretending to enjoy herself for our child's sake, but I bet she'd be more relaxed and carefree without me present. Leaving would better allow them to spend quality time together. I could always make the excuse work required me, not an excuse at all since I had plenty to do leading up to the opening night of Parker De Luxe Hotel.

Roxanne's cold-shoulder treatment shaped our new reality. I'd broken her trust, and in turn, she spurned the idea of us together, from a romantic point as well as a platonic one. Her rejection tallied my price to pay, and yet, a part of me refused to admit defeat. I made the biggest mistake ten years ago when I assumed I knew Roxanne's feelings, and no way was I about to repeat history. With Zane around, I lacked a chance to get Roxanne alone and talk. But as soon as the opportunity presented itself, I planned on asking her where I stood in her life. She'd have to tell me to my face she didn't want me.

Zane threw me the Frisbee, and I sprinted along the beach to catch it. Roxanne had joined us for the first two rounds but then perched on the sand in the sun. Her silky hair sat above her shoulders, and the sun lit her golden head like a halo as she read the book she'd purchased at a used book stall from our trip to the flea market this morning.

I'd lost those last two games all thanks to her blue tankini and figure-hugging white sarong setting my libido aflame. Although her modest swimsuit revealed little, the blue piece distracted me the moment she slipped out of her summer dress. I avoided staring at her all afternoon for the sake of not seeming inappropriate.

Zane jogged over to me, huffing and puffing with his hands on his knees. "I'm hungry."

I chuckled at this kid's insatiable appetite. "Should we head back and get ready for dinner?"

He handed over the Frisbee we'd purchased at another stall from this morning's shopping trip. "I'll go tell Mom." He ran over to Roxanne, and she peered up for the first time since opening her book. I headed over as she stood from the sand and folded our beach towels, placing them into the tote bag.

"Any place in mind for dinner?"

Roxanne avoided eye contact but continued

packing the beach bag. "I hoped we could order room service. I'm not in the mood to head out to a fancy restaurant."

Fancy restaurant or fast-food chain, neither establishment shook her out of the sour mood she seemed hell-bent on remaining in. "Fine with me."

I held out my hand for the packed bag. "Here, let me help you."

"I got it." She brushed past me, heading back toward the hotel.

I expelled the sigh emanating from my throat. Roxanne remained ahead of us on our walk back, while Zane skipped alongside me, suggesting all the activities we'd do tomorrow. I listened and responded to my son but kept my gaze on the woman ahead. Her coldness frightened me to death because unlike several weeks ago, this overwhelming sense of loss hit.

Once back in the hotel suite, Zane headed in for a shower, and I found Roxanne on the balcony lounge chair, once again her head stuck in her book.

I leaned against the doorframe, blocking the sheer curtains from billowing out with the breeze. "A romance?"

"A thriller." She flicked the next page, not bothering to glance up. "More realistic than romance novels."

I clenched my jaw, unable to stand another second of this behavior. "What's going on with you?"

"What do you mean?" At last, she paused from her reading and regarded me.

Still, her features gave nothing away other than a bothersome expression as though I buzzed around her like some annoying insect. She grew determined to make me work harder for a decent answer. "Ever since the airport you've been so...distant."

She raised her arms, flippant. "Give me a break. I'm enjoying myself, relaxing."

She called ignoring me enjoying herself? I stepped closer and knelt at her level. "Roxanne, I worked with you for months and can tell you're not having fun here. I arranged this trip for you to enjoy time with Zane, and I feel like I'm getting in the way." I ran a hand through my hair. "Should I leave?"

"No, don't." She straightened, and the first real show of emotion in days widened her eyes. "Zane expects the both of us here."

The fact this woman put our son first filled my heart with gratitude, and any other time I'd condone her, but not in this instance when she grew determined to alienate me. "Yes, but I'm considering you too."

"Why?" She scoffed, rubbing at her arms from either nerves or the breeze picking up. "Why concern yourself with how I feel?"

What a royal mess I'd made. No matter how much I apologized or what measures I took in making amends, the trust Roxanne once held for me vanished, along with her feelings toward me. "Because I care about you."

"Do you?" she spat, her small jaw ticking.

Panic suffocated every breath I took, but on the outside, I appeared as cool as a cucumber in hopes to coax her into trusting every word I spoke. "Roxanne, you're the mother of my child. Of course, I care."

She nodded. Her gaze flittered to the floor for a moment. "The mother of your child," she uttered. Her chin lifted and I met a pair of hard-set eyes. "Thank you for respecting me, Max. I appreciate it." She folded her arms over her chest. "But you don't need to worry about me. I don't expect anything from you. So, let's try and have fun for Zane's sake and get through this trip together, okay."

She strolled past me and back into the suite, leaving her book behind on the chair.

At dinner we sat around the dining table, eating our orders from room service. The lapping calm of the ocean made for an enjoyable atmosphere but did nothing to ease the current tension. Zane yawned several times, deciding he'd rather go to sleep after all than stay up late and rent a movie.

"Brush your teeth and get into bed," Roxanne instructed him once he finished his meal. "We have another big day planned tomorrow."

A pale red smear across his nose confirmed sunburn, and his bloodshot eyes revealed his tiredness. He ran around and hugged me, the embrace taking me by surprise once again. On several occasions throughout our trip, Zane's show of affection tugged at my chest. He'd hugged me goodnight every evening and had even taken hold of my hand as we'd shopped in the flea market. To onlookers, we'd resembled any other mundane father and son, but I cherished each minute by his side, collecting these special moments into my memory.

"Goodnight, Dad." He yawned aloud.

Dad? I froze in place. Did he call me Dad due to absent-minded exhaustion or a deliberate attempt to forge us closer? "Goodnight, son." I swallowed away the raspiness of my voice as I stroked his head. Instead of overanalyzing, I decided to enjoy another endearing moment. My gaze drifted over to Roxanne with her deer-in-the-headlights stare. Zane then jogged over to his mother, hugged her goodnight, and departed to his room.

The smile on my face remained glued in place. One simple word prompted such a powerful impact, and I doubted I'd get much sleep tonight without replaying the wonderful sound in my head. Standing from my seat, I collected our empty plates and set them on the cart to leave outside our door for room service to collect. Roxanne also stood from her seat to help, and I took hold of the dish in her hands. "Go relax. I can handle this."

She let go with reluctance and wiped her palms down the front of her pants. "What are your plans for the rest of the night?"

The first time she initiated a conversation with me since arriving here. "Shower, then make a few calls and complete some work on my laptop."

Her lips clamped together, offering me a soft smile. "Well, goodnight."

On instinct, I grabbed her wrist. Her gaze danced from my grip, returning to my eyes. "I hate this between us." I sighed, releasing her wrist and stepping around to stand in front of her. "You wouldn't be wary around me if I hadn't betrayed your trust. I wish you'd look at me the same as before."

She rolled her eyes, not condescending but rather a show of defeat. "You mean when I fell for your charming tricks?"

"Help me, Roxanne. How do I fix this?" My fingers twitched by my sides, eager to take her into my arms and not let go.

She glanced to the side as if gathering the strength to meet my gaze. "What do you want from me, Max?"

I stepped into her personal space, my chest brushing against hers. "I want the girl who danced like a crazy person on the arcade game, who squealed in sheer horror on the rollercoaster but calmed once taking my hand, who overcame her fears on the Ferris wheel and kissed me, the girl who smashed me in her first game of chess, who TP'd my horrible neighbor's house." I cupped her hands, resting my forehead against hers. "I want the woman who challenged me at another game of bowling after losing, who danced with me at the banquet in LA and made me the envy of every man in the room, who took care of my stubborn butt when stabbed by a mugger, who gazed at me with open trust."

Her eyes fluttered closed, pain crinkling her face. "What are you saying? You don't really want me. I'm nothing more than a means to an end who happened to have your child."

I cupped her face, forcing her to stare into my eyes. "Yes, I set out to crush you, to drive you mad with my mind games. I won't deny the schemes, but I never planned to fall for you in return. Like the first time ten years ago, I fell for you hard, Roxanne. In fact, I'd never stopped." I tucked a strand of hair behind her ear. "It's always been you, Roxanne. Always."

Her mouth parted and she gazed into my eyes as though trying to read the depths of my soul. "If you're playing another game—"

"Another game?" My voice rose in sheer desperation. "Roxanne, no. I'm not up to my old tricks."

"Because I saw—" She blinked and blew out a

breath. "—the tabloid magazine of you and Georgina at her aunt's wedding. You love her." Her jaw clenched. "So please, for all our sakes, stop with the schemes and go be with Georgina."

Georgina? All this time Roxanne's cold treatment stemmed from what the stupid press printed. "Roxanne, she's my best friend and invited me to her aunt's wedding months ago. We danced and had a fun time at the party, end of story."

Her jaw and puckered lips worked. "The pictures look rather convincing."

I desired to kiss that stubborn look right off her face. "Of course they do. We're no strangers to the fake press and their exaggerated stories. We even laugh over the fabricated mess."

Her brows pinched together as she stared at the column of my throat. "Just friends, you say?"

"Yes." I squeezed her shoulders. "And I can prove so, too."

She cocked a brow in silent acceptance of my challenge.

I stroked my thumb across her soft cheek. "The night you brought me home from the hospital…you said you hadn't slept with anyone since the father of your son."

She glanced at my chest, a pink hue staining her cheeks. "Even when I attempted to move on with you as Hunter, I had never let go of Max."

"I've never let go either." My tone softened with the force of emotion erupting from deep inside. "Not once in the last ten years."

"What do you mean?" She laid her hands on my chest, and her gaze searched mine, eager for truth.

"Clarissa told me Georgina's your ex. You obviously found a way to move on."

"And we dated for an entire year." I cupped her face once more and shrugged, hiding nothing. "She's a wonderful person and a great friend, but we were never intimate."

Her eyes bulged. "Never? In the entire year you dated?"

Now Roxanne understood the power she wielded over me. "I could go no further than kiss her, until even kissing felt off."

Roxanne secured the wrists of my hands holding her face. "Are you saying all these years you've avoided relationships too?"

Not just avoided, but also averse to the idea of entering a romantic relationship. No matter how much I fought with myself, I lost the battle Roxanne held over my body and soul. "A few years ago, I grew determined to get over you. I'd go home with the first girl who caught my eye at a bar, but the idea of touching another woman, or having them touch me the same way you... I couldn't stand it. I sent them back in the taxi, never having stepped foot in my building. The mere idea of sleeping with another repulsed me and tarnishing or replacing my one memory of you made me sick. Every touch, every caress, every all-consuming sensation had your name stamped on me. The night we spent together you left a mark on me. I'm yours, Roxanne. I always have been."

"Mom," Zane called out from the bedroom. "Could you please get me a glass of water?"

Roxanne blinked and stepped back as though struck by an electric wire, avoiding my gaze as she headed for the kitchen. "I think I've heard enough for one night. Goodnight, Max."

Heard enough? I poured out my heart, admitted how I struggled to live life without her for the last decade, and still the truth did nothing against the barrier she'd raised between us. Hanging my head, I made my way into my bedroom. The sound of Roxanne tinkering in the kitchen echoed behind me.

Once showered and dressed in a pair of briefs, I hopped into bed. Emails filled my inbox and important missed calls saturated my phone, but I checked on the process of the hotel first as I'd done every night. Richard sent me pictures and updates and I received a lengthy email from him every morning.

From my peripheral vision, the bedroom door swung open. Roxanne stood at the threshold, the sight of her dressed in navy silk pajama shorts and a matching camisole took my breath away. The time on my laptop showed past midnight. My spine straightened, and I threw back the bedcovers, swinging my legs over the side. "Everything all right? Zane?"

"Everything's fine." She raised her hand in reassurance.

My shoulders relaxed. No emergency, so why enter my room? "Did you need something?"

"Yes." She stormed toward me, her arms wrapping around my neck and her lips clinging to mine in a ravenous kiss.

My hands gripped her silk-encased waist as the hunger building exploded into overdrive. I hauled her hard against my body, too damn selfish to stop whatever had gotten into her.

Roxanne broke the kiss first, gazing into my eyes.

"What you said in the dining room…"

"I meant every word."

She smiled and kissed me again. "It's always been you for me too." She kissed my neck and jaw, working her way to my mouth.

I gripped her shoulders, distancing her to peer into her eyes. "Are you sure you're ready for this?"

"No more waiting." Her gentle fingertips brushed back my hair from my forehead. "I've always loved you, Max."

I cupped the back of her neck. "And I love you."

Chapter 29

Roxanne

We sat in the back of the limo, passing the lights of the city. Zane stuck his nose against the glass window, gazing out at the traffic and scenery. He'd traveled here several times since we returned from Hawaii three weeks ago and obsessed over the luxurious car.

Since our first night together in Hawaii we hadn't slept alone, and soon Max settled into my small apartment. We'd fallen into a functional routine. Most nights Max helped Zane with his homework before the two of them plunged into a game of chess. Other times the three of us headed to the skate park for Zane to practice. On a few occasions, Max stayed back at work and returned to my apartment in the late hours of the night but spent time with Zane by taking him to school the next morning. He'd broken away from his usual workaholic ways and transformed into the ultimate family man.

"Zane, I have a present for you." Max grinned at our son who dragged his gaze away from the window.

Max dug inside his jacket and withdrew the pocket watch, the same one from all those years ago in high school.

"What's that?" Zane gathered the gold timepiece out of his palm with gentle precision.

"My old pocket watch. It belonged to Grandpa Richard and his father, and his father's father before him. I'm going to tell you the same thing he told me. It's not a good luck charm, but a comforting keepsake passed down to the Parker men."

The sentiment filled our son's eyes with pure excitement. "This is so cool. Thanks, Dad."

Max turned to me, losing his smile. "Do you mind if we stop by the hotel for a moment? I won't take long."

The last time I'd stepped inside the hotel I'd discovered the truth. I never shied away from asking Max about his day at work, and he always kept his answers vague without any real insight. But I missed working with him, missed seeing the process of Parker De Luxe, and yet my stomach twisted into knots at the idea of setting foot in the place. Max told me the three of us would be heading to a business dinner. This marked the third business event we attended as a family. My heart warmed at the fact Max included Zane at these dinners rather than have him babysat. He loved showing off our son to members of the board and business associates. So, for the sake of time, I trusted him when he said he wouldn't take long and was happy to wait in the limo for him to return. "Sure, no problem."

Ten minutes later we stopped at the front entrance instead of descending into the underground parking level. Max fixed his bow tie and leaned over to open the door.

Zane beamed and shuffled closer to Max and the exit. "Can we come with you?"

I prayed my smile appeared firm and unwavering.

"He won't be long, Zane. We can sit here and wait for him to come back."

"Oh, please, Mom." He'd used the same pout since his toddler years, and somehow over time perfected the expression. "I haven't seen where Dad works."

Max winked, nudging my side. He'd trimmed his beard in the last day, and my breath caught at the sight of his handsome, structured face.

"Come on, Roxanne, a quick tour won't hurt."

Left little choice, we stepped out of the car and I adjusted the spaghetti straps of my blush-pink off-shoulder evening dress before heading inside Hotel De Luxe. The foyer had undergone its final finishes, and the large, exquisite painting I inspected on our day out at the gallery hung in the seating area.

Zane listened as Max explained what he'd replaced and refurbished. We headed straight for the ballroom, and I froze outside the large oak doors to the last room I dreaded seeing. "I'll wait out here while you show Zane inside."

Max paused in front of the door and strolled over to me. Taking my hand, he peered into my eyes. "Please, Roxanne. Will you come inside?"

Refusing to show him how this affected me, I squeezed his hold and followed him into the ballroom. As we stepped inside, the dimmed lights brightened.

"Surprise!"

I stumbled back at the sight of my and Max's families standing in the distance. A surprise? What for? My eyes adjusted to the room with its soft, romantic lighting, from the burgundy chandeliers to the drapes, to the tableware, down to the floorboards and carpeting. Breath ceased in my lungs. I covered my trembling mouth with a shaky hand and turned to Max. "My design. When? How'd you do this?"

"I had help." He nodded in the direction of Jean-Philippe who winked. "What do you think?"

"It's incredible." I sobbed, sucking in a breath. "It's a dream come true."

I ran over and hugged him, kissing his cheek. "Thank you. Thank you, thank you, thank you. A thousand times, thank you."

Max laughed at my passionate gratitude and stared deep into my eyes. "Now I've made your greatest wish come true, can you make mine come true too?"

He eased me to my feet and took hold of both my hands.

"You once told me a family is what makes a home." Max then knelt on one knee, staring up at me the entire time. "Be my home, Roxanne. Marry me."

Here I stood in my ballroom, believing the design a dream come true, but Max's proposal was my real dream come true. "Yes, I'll marry you." I kissed him full on the mouth and he scooped me into his arms, holding me as our loved ones cheered and hooted around us. Easing out of the kiss, I laughed at the happiness overwhelming me.

Zane ran to us, wrapping his arms around us both, and we hugged him in return. The room full of delighted faces increased the joy emanating within me, and I couldn't wait to spend the rest of my life with the man I loved.

Epilogue

Max

One Year Later

I drove into the parking bay of Dr. Hefferman's building, secured a spot, and released a long, anxious sigh.

Roxanne leaned over the console and kissed my cheek. "Don't stress. Let's get through this together like we promised."

Soft mewling echoed in the backseat, and with one last peck on the cheek, Roxanne got out of the car and opened the back door to retrieve our three-week-old daughter, Claire.

Discovering the news at Roxanne's sonogram appointment where—I'd hoped against hope for a healthy child from head to toe—the doctors pointed out my worst fears, our baby had clubfoot. The idea of my daughter facing the same hardship and pain I suffered almost broke me. If not for Roxanne reassuring me we'd win this together, I'd have fallen apart.

"We'll get through this, Max, because she has you as a father. We'll support her and encourage her every step of the way. Don't be sad. She's a blessing; she's our little blessing."

I smiled at my wife. "I want what every parent wants, the best for their child."

A tear escaped her eye. "I haven't walked this road, but you have, and with you by her side, she can do anything."

Roxanne spoke true. I'd traveled this path, and I'd support my daughter every literal step of the way.

I hopped out of the car and hit the lock button. A pink blanket wrapped a not-so-happy Claire with her face scrunched up into a grimace. Roxanne hushed her and kissed the baby's blonde tuft of hair. My lungs expanded at the sight of my beautiful wife and daughter, calming my shaken nerves.

With our baby girl snuggled against her mother, I wrapped my arm around Roxanne's shoulder, and we headed into the clinic.

We had a long journey ahead of us, but we had overcome so much already, and no matter what struggles awaited as long as we had each other, nothing stood in our way.

A word about the author...

As a full-time housewife and mother, Marianne Willis daydreams in her spare time and turns those dreams into novels. Happily married, she lives in Sydney, Australia, and can't imagine living anyplace else.

Aside from writing, she enjoys spending time with family and friends and is a lover of lychee martinis and cheese platters.

Thank you for purchasing
this publication of The Wild Rose Press, Inc.

For questions or more information
contact us at
info@thewildrosepress.com.

The Wild Rose Press, Inc.
www.thewildrosepress.com